"WHAT?" OMAHA EXCLAIMED. "You're going to *Venice*, with *Drusie DeSoto*?" And no sooner had she spoken those words when, unbeknownst to her, the layer of ice surrounding her heart slowly and barely perceptibly began to show signs of cracking.

And our man Blue, like a wild beast in the forest smelling blood at last, replied soothingly, "Only for four nights, that's all."

Other Books by Norma Howe

God, the Universe, and Hot Fudge Sundaes

In with the Out Crowd

The Adventures of Blue Avenger

norma Howe

BLUE AVENGER CRACKS THE CODE

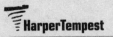

HarperTempest

An Imprint of HarperCollins*Publishers*

Grateful acknowledgment is given for permission
to use the following:

To Everett Howe, Hendrik Lenstra, and David Moulton
for permission to quote their limerick *My Butter, Garçon*;

For *Shakespeare Made Easy: Hamlet*, edited and
rendered into modern English by Alan Durband,
Barron's Educational Series, Inc.;

For *Horse Latitudes*, by The Doors.
Copyright © 1967 Doors Music Co. Copyright renewed.
All rights reserved. Used by permission.

Library of Congress Cataloging-in-Publication Data
Howe, Norma.
  Blue Avenger cracks the code / Norma Howe.
    p.   cm.
  Sequel to: The adventures of Blue Avenger.
  Summary: In his new identity as Blue Avenger, sixteen-year-old David
visits Venice, Italy, and continues to pursue various crusades, including
trying to solve the mystery of who really wrote Shakespeare's works.
  ISBN 0-06-447372-4 (pbk.)
  1. Shakespeare, William, 1564–1616—Authorship—Juvenile fiction. [1.
Shakespeare, William, 1564–1616—Authorship—Fiction. 2. High
schools—Fiction. 3. Schools—Fiction. 4. Venice (Italy)—Fiction. 5.
Italy—Fiction.] 1. Title.
PZ7.H829 Bl 2002   2001051749
Fic—dc21   CIP
                                                                 AC

Typography by Henrietta Stern
❖
First Harper Tempest edition, 2002

Visit us on the World Wide Web!
www.harperteen.com

author's note

The future does not bode well for Blue Avenger. After a series of spectacular achievements, the tide is about to turn. So let us leave our hero for a moment as he dangles in limbo before plunging headlong into a temporary state of melancholy and ennui, and follow the incoming tide away from the sea and back into the estuaries whence it flowed, fighting our way upstream in the murky river of time, back through the droughts and the floods, now and again catching snapshot glimpses of generations long gone, one moment a mother and her babe in front of a cozy fire and in the next a street beggar with her brood wincing in anguish as they live out their miserable days in filth and despair, but now dead, all dead, while we continue to forge back up the river of time for four hundred years until we reach the England of Queen Elizabeth I and the man we know only as William Shakespeare, the greatest poet of all the ages, and then, reaching our destination at last, we gaze down from our vantage point of the past with knowledge of the future, watching the events to come unfolding one upon another, spreading like the creeping tendrils of some vast cosmic weed, until at last they reach the present, where they will touch and engulf our Blue Avenger, drawing him willingly into the greatest mystery in the history of literature!

Whew! You have just survived a sentence of 220 words! So you made it through okay, did you? Good. So, now that we've weeded out the slackers and the faint-hearted, those who don't know the meaning of "ennui" and are too bored to look it up, those who can't comprehend the inevitability of coincidences and would only whine and complain and insist that this or that could *never* happen, or who can't seem to understand that a hero possessing Blue Avenger's unique and disarming charms most certainly *could* run around San Pablo High wearing his deceased father's blue fishing vest with a blue towel wrapped around his head à la Lawrence of Arabia without being harassed by his fellow students—now that we've smoked out the bubble heads and goof-offs who think the highest praise they can give a book is *I finished it in one day!*—now that we understand each other, we can get on with the adventures at hand.

Oh, and yes—thanks again to you, Randall the Third (wherever you are) and members of your so-called clan, for allowing access to your many studies and surveys, some of which have yet to be mentioned in these works.

BLUE avenger cracks THE code

Major Characters

Blue Avenger, born David Schumacher

Joshua "Josh" Schumacher, Blue's younger brother

Sally Schumacher, Blue's widowed mother

Grammy, Blue and Josh's grandmother, mother of Sally Schumacher

Vixen, Grammy's Shih Tzu

Byron, Grammy's new husband

Uncle Ralphy Schumacher, Blue's uncle, brother of David's deceased father

Wayne's Samwich Wagon, Blue's vehicle, gift from Uncle Ralphy

Omaha Nebraska Brown, the girl Blue loves, now and forever

Margie, Omaha's single mother

Mr. Johnny Brown, Omaha's dad, whom she hasn't seen since she was eleven years old

Travis, Omaha's half-brother (referred to only)

Louie DeSoto, friend to Blue and twin to Drusie

Drusie DeSoto, twin to Louie and friend to Blue

Tuesday Thomas, friend to Blue, Louie, and Drusie

Wylie Seratt, schoolmate to Blue

Jackson Seratt, owner of computer-game company (referred to only)

Miss Wooliscroft, English teacher at San Pablo High School

Dr. James Wood, English teacher at San Pablo High School

Ahmed, hotel clerk in Venice

Angela, an Italian girl

Mr. Agostino, a shady character

Tina, Mr. Agostino's girlfriend

Minor Poets

Pearl Lee Washikimas

Ariel Melissa Pekhaw

Pia Marie Skelleshaw

Sheree Siam Kapwilla

Sparkie Leah Wilseam

Elias Walker Peshami

Sam E. "Killer" Haaswipe

one

It is after midnight.

Blue, having made a trip to the bathroom and taken a drink, is at this moment climbing back into bed. He is sleepy now, really too tired to read any more. So why does he reach for the book? What am I doing? he says to himself. Why don't I switch off the light?

Oh, no, his lips finally mutter the words. Is it time for that game again? Am I going to close my eyes when I choose, or am I merely part of some plan? Am I not the captain of my ship, am I not completely in control? So here we go testing, just one more time. I'll count to five and put the book down, snap off the light, and close my eyes. (Or will I?) One, two, three—

Blue paused for a moment and drew in a quick, shallow breath before mouthing the final numbers—*four, five!* Blue did not shut off his light. Instead, he found himself picking up the book he had been reading moments before, a well-worn volume called *A Complete Travel Guide to Rome*. Ordinarily, Blue would not have chosen to read a travel book about Rome at this stage in his life. He was doing so only because of a private vow he had made three years before, in the wake of his father's death. The idea had come to him quite suddenly one evening as he was sitting in his father's favorite chair. There, on the left, was his dad's bookcase, ignored and untouched since the day of his death. Blue walked over to it and ran the back of his hand across the rows, lightly grazing every volume. What better way to honor his father than to read his favorite books?

Blue was particularly pleased that his new girlfriend, Omaha Nebraska Brown, thought this idea was one of the loveliest tributes she had ever heard. (But is it completely accurate for Blue to think of Omaha as his *new girlfriend*? For one thing, the word "new" implies that there was an *old* girlfriend, which is not true. Omaha is the first. And what about the word "girlfriend" itself? Although he had been attracted to her from the very first moment he saw her in his English class at the beginning of the term last September, they hadn't begun to really get to know each other on a more meaningful level until a little over a month ago, on the eleventh of January— Blue's sixteenth birthday, to be exact—the day he changed his name from David Schumacher to Blue Avenger and found the courage to blurt out that he loved her. And although he's now sure that the feeling is mutual, there has yet been no firm commitment, no formal declaration that they are, indeed, a *couple*. Blue is planning to do something about this situation very soon.)

After he finishes *A Complete Travel Guide to Rome*, Blue will have read 88 out of the 115 books on his father's shelves, leaving only 27 more to go before his vow will be fulfilled. The final book in the collection (located on the right-hand corner of the bottom shelf) is *The Complete Works of William Shakespeare*. Blue has already thumbed through its 1,337 pages with feelings of trepidation and misgivings, but a bargain is a bargain, if only with oneself, and he is committed to completing the task he had set for himself no matter how painful, and regardless of his suspicion that perhaps his father didn't make it all the way through the *Complete Works* himself.

But now Blue has found the place where he had left off in the travel book. He notices the photo of the statue on page 23, and because of a recent conversation with Omaha, he immediately recognizes the name of Giordano Bruno. With growing interest he reads the text:

In the center of the *Campo dei Fiori* (meaning "field of flowers") there stands a haunting, brooding statue of Giordano Bruno, a sixteenth-century philosopher and heretic, who was burned at the stake on this very spot by the Inquisition on 17 February 1600 because he refused to recant his belief that the sun is the center of our planetary system and that the universe is infinite. Credited with inspiring the European liberal movements of the nineteenth century, particularly the Italian movement for national political unity, Bruno is also regarded by many as a martyr for the cause of intellectual freedom.

The faithful still gather at the foot of his statue on the seventeenth of February each year to solemnly commemorate the date of his death.

Blue suddenly bolts upright and swings his legs over the edge of the bed. What did that say? He ducks his head closer to the page and quickly rereads the final sentence. *The faithful still gather at the foot of his statue on the seventeenth of February each year to solemnly commemorate the date of his death.*

Holy Moses! he breathes, using one of Omaha's favorite expressions. That's it! That explains why Omaha's father—the man who walked out on Omaha and her mother five years ago, a man obsessed with the life and times of Giordano Bruno—travels to Italy each year! He wants to be among the faithful commemorating the date of Bruno's death! And if Omaha really wants to see Mr. Johnny Brown again after all these years, all she has to do is show up at the Campo dei Fiori in Rome on the seventeenth of February and pick him out of the crowd. Amazing. Simply amazing. Should I call her now and tell her this wonderful news? No, a telephone call this late at night would surely upset her mother. But just think of it! The reuniting of a father and daughter, hinging merely on my reluctance to switch off my light!

(But who can say how many other amazing incidents throughout the years were set in motion because of a reluctance to extinguish a light! Take, for instance, that much-publicized event of 1897, when a little girl named Virginia O'Hanlon didn't blow out her candle, but instead wrote a letter to the editor of a New York newspaper called the *Sun* and asked if there really *was* a Santa Claus. The answer was supplied by Mr. Francis Church in an editorial which appeared on 21 September 1897. "Yes, Virginia. There Is a Santa Claus," he wrote in this amazing document, which also included another incredible statement: "Not believe in Santa Claus! You might as well not believe in fairies!" The immediate and lasting influence of that one editorial may help explain the climate of daffiness and gullibility that pervades the American landscape even to this day. Just to set the record straight, it must be stated bluntly: *Sorry, Virginia. Listen carefully. There is no Santa Claus.*)

Blue called Omaha as soon as he got up the following morning.

"Hello?" a female voice answered softly after the first ring.

"Omaha?" The last time he called, he had mistaken her mother's voice for hers and whispered *Omaha, my sweet!* in answer to the *Hello* he heard, so this time he double-checked.

"Oh, Blue! Did you see where you got your name in the paper again, sort of?"

Even though Blue had news of his own—thrilling, exciting news—he was intrigued enough to put it on hold for just a second and ask, "Sort of? What's *sort of*?"

"Well, actually, they got it a little wrong. They called you The Blue Revenger. Other than that, it's a pretty nice article—first page of the Metro section. The headline says, *City council votes to ban bullets,* and then the article goes on to tell what happened last night at—"

But Blue simply could not wait a moment longer. He had to interrupt her. "Listen, Omaha, thanks. I'll read it later. But now you'd better sit down and hang on to your socks, because I've got some news for *you*. Remember on the way home from Travis's wedding you told me that when you were a little kid your father used to go to Rome every year to see Giordano Bruno, but you could never figure out how he could do that because Bruno died four hundred years ago? Remember you told me that? Well, late last night I discovered the reason! I read about it in a book called *A Complete Travel Guide to Rome*. It seems that every year—listen to this, now—*every year,* on the seventeenth of February, there's a gathering of Bruno buffs for a little ceremony around his statue in this Roman square called the Campo dei Fiori. So, if you want to see your father, all you have to do is be there!"

Blue gripped the receiver and waited. He could hear her radio playing softly in the background—the weather report, *Light fog along the coast expected to burn off by mid-morning*—"Omaha? Did you hear me? I said—"

"I heard you," she answered, finally. Her voice sounded so far off he could barely hear it. "I'm just trying to—I mean, I can't *believe*—"

"I know, I *know*! It *is* hard to believe! But it makes sense, doesn't it? It explains—"

"Oh, God! My heart's beating so fast!" Omaha caught her breath in short little gasps. "But did you say the seventeenth? Is that when they meet? What's the date today? When's the seventeenth? I can't think!"

"Today is the fourteenth. It's Tuesday, remember?" he added, not mentioning the valentine she would find in her mailbox that day. "The seventeenth is Friday. If you leave tomorrow, you'll be there by Thursday. And then the next day will be Friday, the big day. So, you just catch a plane tomorrow, and—"

"Catch a plane! What are you talking about! That's, well, that's impossible—" Omaha paused a moment, then added softly, with her mouth up close to the phone, "But—holy Moses!—wouldn't it be *so great*! I wonder what he'd *do* if he saw me! Do you think he'd recognize me? Would I recognize *him*? Oh, Blue! I *wish*—" She broke off suddenly. It sounded like she might be crying.

"Listen! We have to make some plans. We don't have much time." Blue paused. "Omaha? Are you okay? Hey, you're not crying, are you?"

"I'm not crying. I'm just shaking all over."

"Well, quit shaking, and listen. You're going to need a passport in a hurry, but I'm pretty sure I can handle that. And I can get you the airplane ticket—"

"Airplane ticket? Passport? Are you *serious*?" Omaha's voice became a whisper. "I don't have that kind of money, and my mother would never agree to buy—"

"Ah, but you're forgetting something, my sweet," Blue interrupted, thinking, of course, of the check for two thousand dollars sent to him just weeks before by a retired high-school principal living in a nursing home just outside of Austin, Texas. (And whose checkbook was subsequently confiscated by her horrified children, but that is another story.)

"Forgetting?" Omaha asked. "What am I forgetting?"

"My admirer from Austin, Texas, and the check for two thousand smackers that she sent to me?"

"Oh, no, Blue! I could never use that!"

"Of course you can! Hey, *you* were the one who advised me not to send it back! *You* were the one who said I could use it for Blue Avenger business! And what else could this be but genuine, one-hundred-percent Blue Avenger business!"

"No. I can't—"

Blue sighed loudly. Maybe threatening to return the check would change her mind. "Okay," he said. "Here's the deal. If you *don't* use that money to go meet up with your father, I'm just going to send it back to that Mrs.— whatever her name is!"

Omaha cleared her throat and reached for a tissue, for she actually had been crying, just a little. "Her name is Mrs. Laverne Livingstone."

"I'm just going to send it straight back to Mrs. Laverne Livingstone. I mean it, Omaha!" And when she didn't answer right away, he added, "Just look at what we have here, sweetie! Remember when we were talking about how circumstances are always being *presented* to us, and then it's up to us to make choices? Well, look at these circumstances! You know where your father's going to be, and there's money for your plane ticket and hotel. What other circumstances do you need? Either you're going to consciously *choose* to go, or your brain has already made the choice and just hasn't bothered to tell you yet. But—hey!—either way, *I* know you're going!"

Omaha was twisting the phone cord around her fingers and smiling one of her rare smiles. She liked the way he always called her sweetie. "I'm so mixed up now I don't know what you're talking about. I can't worry about why or who or what's making the choice right now, but all I know is that I really *want* to go."

"Okay, so that's settled!"

"Oh, Blue, if this really works out, I'll never, *ever* be able to thank you! Enough, I mean—"

Blue held his breath, savoring the euphoria that engulfed him, feeling it swell up in his chest like a great bubble of indescribable joy. Surely this moment must be the pinnacle of all his Blue Avenger feats!

Finally, when he had reached the apex and was forced

to exhale, he was prepared to come face to face with hard reality. "Uh-oh," he said. "I just thought of something. What if your mother won't let you go? The *last* thing I want to do is cause more trouble between you two. I mean, I know she still blames me for taking you to Travis's wedding—"

"Oh, God! My mother! Of course she won't *want* me to go! She's practically made a *career* out of keeping me and my father from finding each other. That's why it's just so *amazing* that you were able to—you know—like solve the Giordano Bruno mystery! But, anyway, she *has* to let me go! I can't talk to her now, though. She's been working the P.M. shift at the hospital this week, so she'd kill me if I woke her up now—especially with news like this!"

"Okay, time to get practical," Blue said, taking complete charge of the situation and loving every moment. "I'm almost positive Dr. Blankenship can help you get a passport on such short notice, since he *is* a city-council member and this *is* an emergency. After I see about that, I'll go get your plane ticket."

"What about school? You're going to miss school."

"Hey, we've got business to attend to! What's missing a few classes! But you'd better go talk to Mr. Frazier, since you're going to miss the rest of the week."

"Yeah, you're right. Especially since the semester finals are this Thursday and Friday. So I'll go talk to him—" She broke off suddenly. "Is this really happening? I can't believe it!"

"Believe it!"

Omaha laughed. "Right! So after I see Mr. Frazier I'll come back home and tell my mother, and then I'll start packing." She paused. "Listen, my mom leaves for work about three-thirty, so, if you come over after then, you won't have to face her."

"I'm not afraid to face her."

"Yeah. I know." Omaha paused. "Blue, you're really something, you know that?"

The first thing Blue did after hanging up the phone was to explain the situation to his mother and get her permission to miss a couple of hours of school that day, even though it would be an unexcused absence. Then he called his friend Dr. Milton P. Blankenship (malaria expert and member of the Oakland City Council), who had promised him on a previous occasion that Blue only had to "say the word" if he ever needed assistance of any kind. So, in answer to Blue's question this morning, Dr. Blankenship was happy to assure him that he could facilitate the procurement of an "urgent request" passport for Omaha that very day and set a time and place to meet them both late that afternoon. Furthermore, he offered to have his secretary arrange for Omaha to be transported from the airport in Rome to a reserved room in a hotel just steps away from the Campo dei Fiori.

Blue called Omaha again and told her about their date with Dr. Blankenship. As soon as the bank opened he withdrew the two thousand dollars and phoned a travel agent on Broadway. Then he drove to her office in Wayne's Samwich Wagon and purchased a plane ticket for a flight to Rome leaving early the following morning. He got back to school just in time for his fifth-period class.

Although Omaha's mother tried not to think about it anymore, she would never get over the bitterness she felt for Mr. Johnny Brown, and after he walked out, she figured that the best way to handle the situation—both for herself and Omaha—was to cut off all contact with him. Oh, sure, Margie and Johnny had been happy enough at the beginning. With all those Chinese take-outs and sleep-overs, who wouldn't be? But once Margie became preggers and started to put more and more pressure on him, everything began to change. That's when she finally began to fear the worst, that Johnny Brown was not *ever* going to muster up the courage to wed. And she was right, for Johnny was the sort of person who considered his mind and body as a complete entity, perfect and whole, and he wasn't about to destroy it by piecemealing it out, least of all to a wife.

If the situation presented in this little scenario were to be given as a writing assignment in an English-composition class, a bright and overly imaginative student might compare Margie's love to a poor scrawny rosebush withering away just beyond the reach of the hose. And if Margie were the rose, then Johnny was surely the hose—but with only a ten-year guarantee, for when it expired didn't he simply crack and split? But where in this original conceit could Omaha be placed? The faucet, perhaps? Or a bag of fertilizer in a leaky sack, too small to be of any use? (Oh, heavens, no! That would be totally inappropriate, and would surely merit whatever disparaging remark the teacher could muster up!) Ah! The gardener! That's it—the gardener, who loved both the rose and the hose but didn't have the power to save them.

In any event, when Omaha approached her mother out of the blue this morning with her amazing plan, Margie was both dismayed and incredulous. "He's going to be *where*, and you want to do *what*?" she exclaimed.

"*Why?* Why would you want to see him? Don't you remember? He just walked out on us!"

"Well, wasn't that what *you* wanted, too?" Omaha responded. "Listen, Mom. I was only eleven, but I remember how weird you guys started acting just before he left. You guys were just so ultra-*polite* to each other I knew *something* was going on!" Omaha took a deep breath. She really didn't want to go back to all that. "And anyway, you did just like he predicted you would! He said, 'Sure as shootin' she's going to move away with you and never leave a forwarding address.' And that's exactly what you did!"

Margie was speechless. She hadn't heard *sure as shootin'* for years.

"Anyway," Omaha was saying, "I just want to see my father. Is that asking too much?"

"And this Blue of yours is *giving* you the money?" Margie asked for the third time, her voice growing shriller at every question. "How does that compute?"

Omaha turned away from her mother. *How does that compute!* Oh, God! She still says that! She drives me crazy! How can I reason with her? I should just walk away.

"And anyway, how do you know he'll really *be* there, at that place in Rome?"

"I told you, it says in the guidebook that the faithful

gather around that statue every year. Blue showed me—"

"Blue again! First he drives you all the way to Walla Walla for Travis's wedding, and now this! Can't that kid ever mind his own business?"

That did it. Omaha stood up. "And he's driving me to the airport tomorrow morning." She paused. "Do you want to come?"

Margie knew when she was beaten. Margie was a single mom. She didn't have the luxury of saying, Wait until your father gets home! Anyway, Omaha wasn't proposing robbing a bank or dealing drugs. It was, after all, just a little trip across the ocean and back again.

"No," Margie said finally. "I don't want to come." She turned away. She couldn't believe that three years after quitting cold-turkey she was suddenly desperate for a cigarette. She turned back to Omaha. "And I don't want Blue driving you to the airport, either," she heard herself saying. "So I'll take you."

Omaha touched her mother's shoulder. "I know it's hard for you, and I'm sorry," she said, in a wonderful demonstration of the fact that committed determinists can be the most forgiving of all humans—as long as the little chemical factories in their own brains are able to produce a sufficient amount of the calming elements needed to allow their actions to coincide with their philosophy.

"Me, too," said Margie. "I'm sorry, too."

Their hug was cold and brief. Even so, it was better than no hug at all.

"Well, we did it," Blue said, keeping the engine idling in Wayne's Samwich Wagon as they sat in front of Omaha's house late that afternoon.

"Thanks to you. And without Dr. Blankenship I could never have gotten through all that red tape." She held up the envelope containing her airplane ticket. "And for this, too. Thanks." She leaned over and gave him a quick, impulsive kiss.

"That's all I get?" he teased.

"The neighbors are watching our every move," she whispered, pretending to be under surveillance at that very moment. "Especially Mrs. Caruso, across the street." Omaha's voice hardened a bit. "Actually, she really *is* watching! It's partly because of *her* that my mother made that new rule about not having you in the house when she's not home unless someone else is there, too. But you know what the *real* reason is? It's because she's afraid I might make the same mistakes *she* made!"

Blue didn't know how to respond to that.

Omaha reached for the door handle. "Look at my hand shake! I'm so nervous and excited I can hardly stand it! Are you sure you can pick me up when I get back Saturday night? My mother wanted to, except she has to work."

"Well, I guess it's up to me, then," Blue said. "What a pain." He reached over for one last kiss, and she kissed him back, in spite of Mrs. Caruso's prying eyes. "I'll be thinking of you the whole time," he whispered in her ear. "And I miss you already."

(A recent study by the famous child psychologist specializing in adolescent development, Dr. Richard Ayers of Picayune University in Arizona, suggests that the great majority of parents who have been judged as being "very strict" by their offspring have genuine firsthand experience of the perils likely to be encountered in a dating situation, whereas those parents judged "easy" were often among the best-behaved during their own adolescent years. Dr. Ayers points out that this is an excellent example of a "generation-skipping" trait. He also cautions that children of "very strict" parents would be wise not to confront their elders with these findings.)

A well-known national tabloid recently considered using a "person's opinion of the eucalyptus tree as an indicator of personality" in its popular and long-running "What

Kind of Person Are YOU?" series. According to the theory, eucalyptus lovers (who think the trees are beautiful and aromatic) are usually well-adjusted and even-tempered individuals, whereas eucalyptus haters (who call the trees ugly and smelly nuisances) are just the opposite. The column never made it into print, however, because the eucalyptus tree—a native of Australia and a member of the myrtle family—is rarely seen in the United States beyond the Pacific Coast region, so that Midwesterners and Easterners would be in no position to judge. The "What Kind of Person Are YOU?" editor couldn't see what neverminds that would make, but he was soon overruled by clearer heads.

Blue Avenger was a eucalyptus lover, and he especially loved the huge one in the Lawsons' front yard, directly across the street from his house. He was awakened that night by the sounds of an approaching storm, and in the morning, when he stepped outside to pick up the paper, he noticed how beautiful the tree was, with its leaves and branches being buffeted about by the wind and rain.

Blue rarely drove the Wagon to school, since it's only about a fifteen-minute walk and parking is a real problem. He did consider driving that morning, however, but just as he was about to leave, the storm suddenly abated and he decided to walk after all.

The largest limb of the eucalyptus tree crashed down on Wayne's Samwich Wagon at three-fifteen that afternoon. Luckily, no one was hurt, but Blue's beloved vehicle was totaled. When Blue returned home from school that afternoon, he gazed upon the wreckage with a heavy heart, and as he looked up at the tempestuous sky, he shuddered to see that the storm had barely begun.

The rain was pounding hard when Mrs. Blankenship called Blue that evening to tell him that she was very sorry but she and Dr. Blankenship had decided to hire a live-in nanny and, regretfully, would no longer be needing his services as a kid-sitter for their boys. Oh, sure, she made a point of explaining how sorry she was and how impressed they were with him, even relating how Lance and Vance had lobbied valiantly to retain him. Nevertheless, obtaining a full-time person was really the best solution for them at this time.

In the space of a few hours Blue had lost both his car and his only source of income, and the long-range weather forecast warned of an even larger storm front approaching from the west, which was due to hit the Bay Area over the coming weekend.

Blue had a lot of studying to do for the winter-semester finals on Thursday and Friday, but still his thoughts kept centering on Omaha and the joy and happiness she would experience at finally being reunited with her long-lost father.

When Friday evening came around, Blue was particularly relieved to have his finals over and done with, and when his mother requested—as she occasionally did—that he stop by the mall and rent a movie, he was happy to oblige. She preferred the old classics—movies like *Lawrence of Arabia* or *The Maltese Falcon*—and on this particular Friday she suggested one of her all-time favorites, a movie made in the early sixties called *Whistle Down the Wind*. Both Blue and Josh enjoyed watching these films from what they jokingly referred to as the olden days, and they felt a certain sense of self-satisfaction and pride whenever they happened to recognize allusions to them in modern-day contexts. But on this particular Friday, the evening before Omaha's return, Blue took a little longer than usual at the mall, stopping at Macy's after he had rented the movie and picking out a special pair of earrings just for her.

When the phone rang late Saturday morning, Blue rushed to answer it, hoping it might be Omaha calling from New York. He figured she should be there about now, waiting for her connecting flight home. He was disappointed that she hadn't called him from Rome, yet he knew that if there had been any serious problem her mother surely would have contacted him.

But the phone call was not from Omaha. It was from a reporter for the Oakland *Star*.

"Hello? Is this the residence of—uh, let's see here—The Blue Revenger?"

"No. I'm afraid there's no one here by that name," Blue answered with obvious annoyance. But then his curiosity got the better of him. "However, there does happen to be a personage here known as *Blue Avenger*. Could that be the party you're look—"

"Oh, yeah," the voice cut in. "Sorry. Is this you, Blue?"

Blue didn't answer straightaway, hoping to imply by his hesitation that he was insulted by the lack of formality manifested by this complete stranger. The last thing he wanted was to be treated as if he were some kind of a celebrity—public property, so to speak. "Yes," he said finally, in his most formal tone. "This is he. May I ask who's calling, please?"

"This is Margaret Jennings, staff reporter for the *Star*, and I just wanted to ask you a few questions, okay? Have you heard the latest rumors on the status of that ban-the-bullets motion you presented to the city council last Monday?"

"No—"

"Well, it's being bandied about that Councilman Pinkerton may have joined forces with the local chapter of the Save Our Guns League and they may intend to run this through the courts before proceeding any further. So we're just checking some possible sources, you know. Uh, so I take it you haven't heard anything about that?"

Blue was absolutely devastated at this unexpected turn of events, but he decided to play it cool with Ms. Jennings. "Well, what gives you the idea I'd know anything about it? Why don't you ask Councilman Pinkerton? He'd be the logical—"

"Well, we have, of course. But so far he continues to deny it. However, in the meantime I'd like to recheck some of this background material we have on you, if you don't mind. Let's see, now—on your sixteenth birthday you decided to change your name from David Schumacher to The Blue Revenger—"

"No!" Blue exclaimed, starting to lose his temper. "It's Blue Avenger! *Not* The Blue Revenger! Is that so difficult? Jeez!"

"Well! Excuse me for *living*!" Margaret replied sarcastically, since this kid was starting to get on her nerves and she never did care for assignments involving high-school students in the first place. "Anyway, you changed your name to match this cartoon character you used to draw.

That part's right, isn't it?"

Blue was getting edgy. She'd better not ask *why* he started drawing his cartoon character. He was not about to talk of his father's death in *this* conversation. "Yeah," he said flatly. "That part's right."

"Okay. So after you changed your name but before your ban-the-bullets suggestion to the city council you saved your principal from killer bees by jumping into the swimming pool with her—for which you received national publicity—and you also came up with that Weepless Wonder Lemon Meringue Pie recipe that got printed in the 'Ask Auntie Annie' column. Why did you do that?"

Blue was confused. "Do what?"

"Change your name! Why did you change your name?" Was this kid dense, or was he dense!

"You know," Blue answered, deciding to see if he could irritate Ms. Jennings as much as she was irritating him, "I'm still not quite sure why I did that. Maybe it was a decision I made of my own free will because of certain events that happened in my life previous to that decision and because of the particular state of mind I was in the morning I made the decision. Then again, looking at it another way, it could have been fate—an event that was predetermined from the very dawn of time. And that's a powerful argument, too. But at this point, there's just no way of knowing, is there?"

There was a long pause at the other end of the line. "I guess not. But tell me this: Are you going to miss running around school with that blue towel around your head and wearing that crazy blue fishing vest—or whatever it is—now that school uniforms are being phased in?"

Ah. Now she had touched a *really* sore point. "Well, in the first place, I don't wear my Blue Avenger outfit *every* day, you know! And besides, I don't see what that has to do with—"

"Well, weren't you in that getup the day the president of the school board happened to be visiting San Pablo High?"

"Well, I don't know," he replied, although he suddenly remembered that the last time he wore his vest and cape to school was that Monday morning in January when he spoke to the staff of the school newspaper regarding the condom flap. The president of the school board was there that day? Just my luck!

"The way I heard it," Margaret Jennings was saying, "was that she reported to the school board at their regular meeting that very evening that she was shocked and appalled at the way *some* of you kids—meaning you,

Blue—were attired. And I believe your unusual head-dress was singled out as being particularly offensive. Her report was enough to sway the two members of the board who were still on the fence regarding the uniform proposal, so I would be inclined to say that your appearance that day was responsible for the final adoption of the policy." Ms. Jennings paused to breathe. "Wouldn't you agree?"

"No, I wouldn't! It wasn't just *that*, you know. It was those gang shootings in—"

"Uh-oh. My other line is ringing. Thanks for the info. Bye."

Blue slammed down the phone and threw himself on the rug. Lying on his back, he raised both hands to his head and ran his fingers through his hair so ferociously that loops of his tight red curls actually discharged bursts of static electricity which would have made a startling sight to behold in a darkened room. The loss of his car and his job were bad enough, but now these rumors about the possible delay in the courts of his unique plan for the elimination of deadly bullets from the city of Oakland were almost too much to take.

But wait! This was still Saturday! Blue checked the time. In just seven hours and thirteen minutes, he would hop into his mother's car and drive to the airport and watch for Omaha to appear at her arrival gate. Should he kiss her, right there at the airport? Why not? Oh, it's true, she's not the exhibitionist type—far from it—and neither is he, but this is the *airport*, for God's sake. Everybody's kissing someone at the airport. Now he fingered the tiny black box tied up with the silver ribbon in his left pants pocket. Where could he take her afterwards to give her his little gift? Starbucks? No. Much too generic. But what about that espresso place at the Fairhaven Mall where they went on their very first coffee date, the day he received the check from Mrs. Livingstone? The Café Metropolitan. It would still be open. Maybe they could get their same table, the one in the corner next to the potted ficus tree. That would be the perfect place to present his lady with a pair of delicate earrings—earrings in the shape of his initials—a B for her right ear and an A for her left, the latest in a long line of "Initial Encounter" gift ideas from Macy's, made and advertised expressly for high-school couples in love.

Meanwhile, a recently hired meteorologist at a television station across the bay was wondering if she had time before the five o'clock news to duck out and buy that spiffy new outfit she had her eye on, because she was quite certain the camera would linger on her and her isobars and isohyets a little longer than usual this evening. That massive new front rapidly approaching from the Pacific was really going to be a doozy, possibly ushering in the longest rainy season since the floods of '82.

two

In an ancient square near the center of Rome on the seventeenth of February at two-forty-five in the afternoon, Omaha Nebraska Brown finally spotted her father. He was standing among a group of men who were gazing up reverently at the brooding, hooded statue of Giordano Bruno, the countenance of which was forever destined to fix its accusatory stare directly toward the Vatican. The days of the Inquisition have long since vanished, but for Giordano Bruno and countless others, to be burned alive at the stake was a terrible way to die.

"Daddy! Daddy!" Omaha shouted, waving both hands in the air. But he was too far away and didn't hear her cry. The day was windy and cold, and the members of the Giordano Bruno Society—along with a goodly showing of unaffiliated Bruno aficionados and curious tourists—were bunched together, hunched over in their heavy overcoats, those without gloves rubbing their hands and blowing on them with steamy puffs of air.

Making her way through the crowd, Omaha pushed forward and soon found herself standing at her father's side.

"Daddy!" she said, touching his arm. "Look, Daddy! It's me!"

Johnny Brown, appearing much older now, with his beard more bushy and his hair hidden under a dark, knitted cap, turned to look at the misty-eyed teenager standing beside him. Prolonged dwelling on the unfortunate fate of his hero had already transported Johnny to a heightened emotional pitch, and the unexpected shock of hearing the word Daddy and seeing Omaha standing there, looking and sounding so much like her mother when first they met, filled him with a strange mixture of cautious pleasure and genuine alarm.

"Omaha!" he exclaimed, moving to embrace her but at the same time nervously scanning the faces around her. "What are you doing here! Oh, look how you've grown! And your mother—is your mother here with you?"

"No, Daddy! It's just me! I came here all alone! I've missed you so much and I wanted to see you so bad!"

Those persons standing nearby, most of them not comprehending the words but still sensing that they were witnessing an occasion of some singularity, instinctively backed off and gave the pair some space. And what a moving sight it was, too—a father and daughter, obviously, who had probably not seen each other for quite some time. It was so touching, in fact, that several of the more softhearted and observant bystanders were almost moved to tears.

It cannot be denied that there *was* a fleeting moment of pure joy in their reunion, like the sudden sharp burst of thunder before the diminishing crackling of the moving storm, or that first hair-raising rush as the roller coaster finally reaches the top of its long climb and hurtles downward at breathtaking speed, only to lose its momentum all too soon and come to a dissonant and sluggish stop.

So why, after that initial thrill of discovery, was Johnny Brown suddenly beginning to feel so morose? Could the answer lie hidden in the next words he spoke? "Oh, Omaha," he moaned. "What has happened to you? Where oh *where* is that little girl I left behind!"

And as for Omaha, why did her arms suddenly grow weak around his neck as she heard those words? Why did the first sickening wave of disappointment begin to encircle her heart? "Well, I guess I grew up, Daddy," she finally managed to say. She took a good look at him then, seeing him for the first time on his own level, her eyes just a few inches below his own. "You look different, too, you know. Like, I don't have to look *up* to you anymore."

She laughed nervously as her words seemed to hang in the air. "It *has* been five years, you know," she added quickly, hoping to divert his attention from the double meaning of her previous statement, even though it wouldn't be long before she herself would fully realize the truth of that observation tossed off so carelessly within moments of their meeting.

"Five years!" Johnny repeated. "*Five years!* That can't be possible!"

"Yeah, I know! But did you—I mean, did you ever *try* to find me, like check with Mom's friends at the hospital in Tulsa, or—"

Johnny Brown stiffened. Being introspective and acutely self-aware by nature, he understood his aversion to those who would impinge upon his freedom in any way, even though he could not explain its origin. (Sympathetic and generous-hearted people can forgive him for this trait, knowing that it can be explained most simply by the phrase "That's just the way he is." But, then, using that same argument, sympathetic and generous-hearted people themselves shouldn't be praised for their own kindly feelings, because that's just the way *they* are.)

Now Johnny gripped Omaha's shoulders and held her for a moment at arm's length. Who *was* this person? Could this be his own darling little girl, his sweet and compliant little girl of old, now all grown up and asking for an accounting? So what would she ask for next? Just as his brain was beginning to formulate that question and the psychological forces within him were alerted and already starting to form their usual protective shell, his thoughts were suddenly interrupted by the appearance of two uniformed police officers heading toward the center of the crowd and motioning for the people to move to one side.

"Uh-oh! We have to get out of the way here," Johnny said, abruptly and purposefully changing the mood. "They're clearing a path for the dignitaries and getting ready to start the ceremony. Look, Omaha! See that woman there, with the banner across her chest? She's a member of the Italian Parliament! And that man with the red necktie—that's my friend Paolo. He's the president of the GBS—the Giordano Bruno Society. He's been a big help to me, gathering information for my book, and he's the one who'll do the Italian translation. Do you remember my Giordano Bruno book, or were you too young at the time? Well, anyway, it's all but finished now. In fact, I have an appointment later this afternoon with—" He stopped short, exclaiming, "Oh, look there! The Italian Color Guard is bringing up the flag! We wait *all year* for this, Omaha. It's how we pay our respects to

Giordano, that great martyr for the cause of intellectual freedom, and the man who—"

"Shhh!"

Omaha turned and looked behind her. A woman holding a long-stemmed red rose in her hand was shushing Johnny Brown.

The ceremony was entirely in Italian and lasted for more than twenty minutes. Omaha, still overwrought from lack of sleep and disoriented from her long journey, listened in a daze. What was she *doing* here, standing in this Roman square alongside this man who couldn't seem to realize she was no longer a little girl?

When the tribute had finally ended and the crowd slowly began to disperse, Johnny pointed toward an outdoor *pizzeria* in one corner of the square. "Come on," he said. "If we hurry, we can get a table over there." He quickly looked at his watch. "We can talk for a while before I have to go."

He took her cold hand in his and quickly led her to a place out of the wind and motioned for her to sit down. A waiter seemed to appear from nowhere and clasped his hands behind his back. *"Birra?"* he asked Johnny, adding in English, "As usual?"

"Sì, Ricardo, per favore."

"The waiter knows you?" Omaha asked with raised

brows. "And isn't it too cold for beer?"

Johnny Brown unbuttoned his jacket and pulled off his knitted cap, somewhat defiantly. God Almighty! She not only sounded and looked like her mother, she acted like her, too! "I've been here in Rome for a couple of days," he said, ignoring her comment about the temperature. "So—what do you drink? Are you hungry? I have time for a pizza, if you want one. Do you still like pepperoni?"

Omaha nodded. Actually, she now preferred vegetarian. "Pizza would be good," she said. "And I'd really like some coffee, too, please."

"Coffee? Whatever happened to cocoa?" Johnny asked with a sad little smile. "Do you still have that little bear mug I gave you?"

Omaha shrugged and didn't try to hide her annoyed sigh. What was wrong with him, anyway? Couldn't he realize the past was over and done with? Couldn't he at least *try* to relate to her *now*?

Two hours later, Johnny Brown looked at his watch and told his daughter that he was truly sorry but he had to leave her now. His friend Paolo from the GBS had set up a very important meeting with an Italian publisher for that afternoon, and he barely had time to hail a cab if he wished to arrive at the appointment on time. And, oh, darn! He couldn't see her off in the morning, either, since he was a guest in Paolo's home and Paolo's wife was going to prepare a special breakfast just for him.

Then, just as he stood up to leave, he impulsively tore off a corner of the paper place mat under his empty dish. "Listen," he said, handing her the pen the waiter had left on the table. "Write down your phone number here, will you? After all the trouble you took to locate me, I'd hate to lose contact with you again."

Omaha didn't take the pen. Instead, she put her elbows on the table and brought her hands to her forehead, staring down at the little bits of pizza crust on the edges of her plate and blinking back her tears. Her mother wouldn't like that at all, after all the pains she had taken to keep her whereabouts unknown to Johnny.

"Don't worry," Johnny was saying, now tearing off another corner of the place mat and writing his own phone number on it. "I know your mother doesn't want anything to do with me. She made that *very* clear, and I respect that. So I promise—I won't be bothering her at all. But I do want your number." Johnny placed his own scrap of paper next to her elbow and checked his watch again. "Here's my number in D.C., although I'll probably be spending more time here in Italy."

Omaha didn't raise her head until Johnny nudged her elbow. "Please?" he said.

Omaha sighed and scribbled her number on the paper. "Okay, but if my mother answers, hang up," she said, really meaning it, even though it sounded like a bitter, ill-conceived joke.

Johnny took her head between his hands. Then he kissed her on the forehead. "I have to go now, baby," he said. "This has been truly wonderful, and this time we'll keep in touch." The next second he was gone.

I have to go now, baby—the exact same words he had uttered five years before. *And this time we'll keep in touch.* Omaha was determined not to cry. She was strong, and she was independent, and she didn't need him anymore. *This time we'll keep in touch!* Oh, right! Who did he think he was kidding? She pushed her plate to one side and put her head in her hands. She would take a moment to pull herself together and then she would get up and leave.

A sympathetic tourist from Tallahassee, Florida, noticed her there and bent over to speak to her. "Was he bothering you, honey?" she asked. "Are you all right?"

Omaha looked up, surprised to hear someone speaking with a Southern accent in Rome, oblivious of the fact that she herself still had traces of Tulsa in her own speech.

"Oh, yes," she said, blowing her nose on a tissue.

"Thank you. I'm all right." And then she got up from the wobbly table and, in spite of her shattered hopes and unsteady bearing, walked resolutely back to her hotel.

But, of course, she wasn't completely all right. She was upset and shaken and disillusioned and embarrassed by her own vulnerability, but most of all she was resolved. And by the time she stepped off the elevator and entered her room, she knew that never, ever again was she going to depend on others for making her dreams come true. She was never going to allow herself to be hurt by the callousness of others, especially by a self-centered man who was utterly ignorant of the traditional duties and responsibilities of fatherhood. And, like her mother, who was waiting for her back home, she never wanted to see Johnny Brown again.

Now she threw herself on the bed and let the tears come. What was that crazy stuff he was trying to tell her? Something about how he hoped she had received all the love and good wishes he had sent her *telepathically*, because he *did* think of her often, and he *did* really love her and miss her.

But not enough to even try to find me, Omaha thought, recalling the words he spoke just as the waiter brought the pizza: *I'm just so happy you've found me! I've been so concerned about you, but now that you're all grown*

*up I can still treasure the memory of that little girl you were,
but without the worry!* Omaha Nebraska Brown would
never again touch a pepperoni pizza.

After a while she got up from her bed and looked out
her window at the cobblestone street below. She could
smell dinner cooking in the hotel restaurant, but she
couldn't stand the thought of eating. She began to
wonder if she would ever be able to forgive the man
named Johnny Brown. Would she be able to stick to her
theory that, after all is said and done, Johnny Brown was
no different from anyone else? He just had to do what he
had to do. Oh, but in this case, absolving him from all
guilt was not going to be easy. In fact, it very well might
be the ultimate test of her deterministic philosophy.

It wasn't until late in the night, as she lay still sleepless
in bed, that she began to see the problem of forgiveness
in another light. If it turned out that she could not bring
herself to forgive him, who could say that she herself
actually had a choice in that decision? Perhaps, in not
forgiving him, she would merely be following the path of
her own predetermined destiny.

Omaha started getting a terrible headache shortly after
her connecting flight took off from La Guardia Airport in
New York City. And the pounding in her head was

certainly not helped by the growing realization that, instead of looking forward to seeing Blue, she was actually beginning to dread it. Of course he'd ask what happened in Rome, but she didn't even want to *think* about it, let alone discuss it! Oh, how she wished now that he had never solved the mystery of Giordano Bruno! She was so much happier before this trip. At least she had the *hope* of someday— Oh, no! What's wrong with me? she thought. It's not fair to blame Blue for that! But now I've got to decide what to do about him—what do I do when Blue wants to talk about *us*, because I know he does. After all, when you come right down to it, he *is* just a kid in high school. What did that article say—the one I read in that magazine at the dentist's office? Teenage boys are notorious, that's what it said. They're notoriously fickle. Everyone knows that. Girls are looking for love, boys are looking for sex. They find it and the next minute they're gone, looking for it somewhere else. Oh, God. I wish I had an aspirin. Anyway, that's it. I'm not going to take another chance. I watched my father walk away from me twice and I survived, didn't I? I don't need anyone. But, then, Blue is different. He really is. He's so sweet, and so funny. Ah! Stop it right there, you fool! Remember, *I have to go now, baby*—that's what they say!

Eventually, that's what they all say. So I'll just go it alone. I'll be friends with Blue, because I do love him. But without any strings. That's the safest. That's the best.

Blue couldn't decide on the best place to stand. First he stationed himself leaning up against the pole directly in front of the arrival ramp, but later he chose to move closer to the gate itself, even though he had to remain in back of the restraining rope. He kept smiling to himself and fingering the little black box with the earrings, fidgeting with it, taking it out of his pants pocket and transferring it to his jacket, and then putting it back in his pants. But after briefly rehearsing how he would present it to her, he realized it would be more graceful to produce it from his jacket rather than from his pants, so that's where it ended up.

Some fifteen minutes later, his heart took its first dip as he caught sight of her trudging down the ramp toward the waiting throng. He knew immediately that things had not gone well. Even so, he rushed up to meet her and awkwardly attempted to relieve her of her small carry-on suitcase.

"Hello, Blue," she said. "That's okay. I have it."

He gently pulled her to one side, out of the flow of

traffic, and tried to give her both a hug and a welcome-home kiss, but the suitcase was in the way and a woman pushing a stroller bumped into them, so his kiss landed somewhere between her left ear and her nose.

Blue couldn't decide whether to risk asking how it went, so he just settled on the simple question "Well, was he there?"

Omaha immediately started to cry—not a noticeable, sobbing kind of cry, but just a gentle show of tears accompanied by an embarrassed shake of the head. "He was there," she said. "But if you don't mind, I really can't talk about it."

Blue suddenly felt ill. The swing from happy anticipation to grave disappointment was just too much to handle, and the effect was like a sudden, unexpected loss of altitude in an unpressurized plane. "That bad, huh?" was all he could manage to say.

They didn't speak again until they were on the third level of the busy airport parking lot, weaving their way down between the rows of automobiles, lost in a sea of blinking red taillights and the roaring echo of engines and slamming doors.

"I'll probably never see him again," she said, looking down at the pavement. "I never *want* to see him again."

She took a deep breath and dug around in her shoulder bag. "Oh, God. I'm out of tissues—"

"Here," Blue said, pulling his handkerchief out of his jacket pocket. "Use this."

She took the handkerchief from his hand. "Thanks—"

After what seemed like half the night, they were finally out of the airport and on the freeway. It was raining quite hard by now, and Blue switched the wipers onto high. "I thought maybe we could go have a cup of coffee at that place in the mall," he suggested lamely. "What do you think?"

"Jeez, I don't think so. I've got a really splitting headache, and I think I'm probably catching something. You should have heard all those people coughing on the plane. I just want to go home and go to bed."

Blue nodded. Maybe that would be best, after all. This didn't exactly feel like the most ideal time to ask her—well, in effect, to ask her to make it official—to wear his initials on her ears for all to see.

"You'll probably want to sleep late tomorrow," Blue said, as he pulled up in front of her house. "But I'll call you in the afternoon—"

Omaha avoided his eyes. "Well, actually—I mean, let's wait a while, okay? I've had a really bad experience,

and I need a couple of days to—you know—to think."
She attempted a smile. "Besides, I wouldn't be very
good company—"

Blue shrugged. "Sure," he said.

Once they had arrived at her house, Blue waited until
she was inside before driving off, but after just a few
blocks he had to pull over and stop because he thought
he was going to throw up. He was wondering why the
misery he felt seemed vaguely familiar. And then he
remembered. It sort of reminded him of when his father
died. After several minutes the wave of nausea subsided,
and before starting up the engine again he reached in his
jacket pocket for his handkerchief. Oh, yeah. He gave it
to Omaha. But wait. What happened to the box with the
earrings? He felt again in his pocket. Then he felt around
in the other one. Oh, God! It must have fallen out in the
parking lot. He reached behind the passenger seat, where
he knew his mother kept a box of tissues, and grabbed a
handful. Well, what did it matter? The way Omaha was
acting, he didn't even know if he still had a girlfriend at
all, let alone a steady one.

The final blow arrived on Sunday morning, when Blue
happened to see the blaring headline over the lead story
in the Metro section in the *Star*:

"Ban-the-Bullets" Could Be Shot Down in Courts

Backlash Triggered by Councilman Pinkerton

By Margaret Jennings, Staff Reporter

It can now be stated with certainty that the ban-the-bullets motion presented at the last meeting of the Oakland City Council is headed for the courts, according to Councilman Dwight "Dwighty" Pinkerton.

Pinkerton, reached by this reporter at the popular Back Alley Bar and Grill late yesterday afternoon, finally confirmed persistent rumors that he has switched his allegiance to join forces with the leaders of the Save Our Guns League to fight the proposal. "I'm confident this duck will never fly," Pinkerton said. "It's all but dead in the water now."

However, Councilwoman Peters, who was also on the scene, was quick to disagree. "Quack quack!" she said loudly, to the amusement of the bartender and several bystanders.

The bullet-ban idea was the brainchild of an unlikely high-school hero known as The Blue Revenger, who, according to SOGL member Percival "Ace" Blodgett, "looks like just another one of those silly-assed kids who run around wearing towels on their heads."

Utilizing a new form of tranquilizing darts called Winger Stingers, the proposed ban would still allow for gun possession, but mandate the exchange of lead bullets for the non-lethal darts. While the idea sparked wide initial interest, veteran observers of the political scene (See BULLETS, page M-9)

Well, that was it. The final straw. Blue left the paper on the table in disarray and dragged himself to his room. *What happened?* he thought, flopping onto his bed. One minute on top of the world, and the next—zero. *The Blue Revenger!* My God! They couldn't even get the name right! Blue suddenly recalled his school counselor's words last month when he had first approached him requesting the name change. "Why the *#%! do you want to change your name, David?" Mr. Frazier had asked. "Two weeks from now you'll just want to change it back again."

Blue reached up to the calendar hanging on his wall by the side of his bed and flipped back the page. Actually, it has already been five and a half weeks, and I haven't wanted to change it back yet. So what does he know!

Blue closed his eyes and was alarmed to discover he was actually shuddering in his misery. However, although he had no way of knowing it, perhaps he had finally reached the lowest of the low. If he could just get by for the next few moments—if he could manage to survive even while the collage of recent events swirled around in his mind—Wayne's Samwich Wagon being towed off to the wrecking yard, no more regular income, Omaha acting like a stranger, and the specter of continued carnage caused by cone-shaped missiles of lead—if he could just open his eyes and gaze once again at the calendar on the wall, he would sink no lower.

Blue did, indeed, open his eyes, and he did look once again at his calendar. It was the one he had made himself by printing up the days and dates on the computer and then attaching some copies of his favorite Blue Avenger comic strips on the spaces above. The strip he used for the month of February was his very first—the one that featured Blue Avenger ripping off Death Incarnate's black cape, revealing underneath a sniveling little coward begging for mercy in his filthy underwear.

Blue got up from his bed and went directly to his desk. He opened the drawer and pulled out his pencils and drawing paper and immediately set to work, sketching four identical panels of his comic-strip hero, dressed for action but merely looking out the window at the pouring rain. Blue knew it might take weeks or even months, but he was willing to bide his time. With patience and determination, Blue Avenger would rise again!

A short filler news item datelined Venice, Italy, was printed in the "Our World" section of the *Star* that same Sunday, but Blue never got around to reading it:

VENICE, ITALY — Another cache of centuries-old papers and books has been found by work crews demolishing a condemned building in the Castello district, just steps away from the Church of Santa Maria Formosa in the Campo of the same name.

This is the second time in recent months that the wrecker's ball has struck gold, and several factions are already battling over who owns these valuable relics of the past, some dating as far back as the mid-16th century.

According to reliable sources, three small bundles have already disappeared from the latest find and two workmen have been detained for questioning.

"Centuries of dampness and actual flooding have taken their toll on this material," said Ennio Fazio, demolition superintendent, adding that he knows nothing whatsoever about the rumored missing bundles.

A growing problem for the authorities is the sudden influx of forged documents falsely reported to be those unearthed during previous work projects in the area.

THREE

The following Monday morning marked the beginning of the new semester at San Pablo High. Though Blue was disappointed to find that he and Omaha were not in any classes together this term, he was surprised and pleased to see his old friend Louie DeSoto walk into his junior honors math class. Blue had first met Louie—along with his twin sister, Drusie—in the second grade at Martin Luther Elementary School. However, since high school, their friendship had become somewhat distanced by fate, manifested by the school district's main computer's failure to assign them to any of the same classes.

As Blue and Louie were shooting the breeze before the bell rang, who should rush in but Tuesday Thomas, another old friend from the second grade!

"Hey, Tuesday!" Blue said, reaching over and high-fiving her.

"Just like old times!" Louie said, adding with a grin, "You're a sight for sore eyes!"

Tuesday laughed. "Yeah," she said. "How you guys doing? And, hey, David, what's with this Blue Avenger thing? Are you going to keep that name forever, or what?"

"Yes, I plan to. I'm kind of in a low place at the moment, but it shouldn't last forever—"

Tuesday extended her lower lip and shrugged sympathetically. Then she quickly scanned the room. "But where's Drusie?" she asked, looking around for Louie's twin sister. "Isn't she in this class?"

Louie shook his head. "Nah," he said, "she couldn't cut the mustard for honors, at least in math." Then he added with a little half-smile, "But future movie actresses don't need to know math. That's what accountants are for."

"Well, it's too bad she's not here," Tuesday said. "It would have been a real trip down memory lane." She stared at Louie. "Louie, you look different." And a second later she tapped herself on the forehead and said, "Oh, I see what it is. You got contacts!" She laughed. "You used to wear the thickest glasses I've ever seen. Hey, do you guys remember Mrs. Reuben's class and the Famous Four?"

Blue and Louie feigned blank looks.

"Famous Four? What's that? The Beatles?"

Tuesday laughed. She was about to remind them of

the Famous Four's Super-Duper Puppet Show, but just then the bell rang, and Mr. Compton told everyone to pipe down and take a seat.

Of course Blue remembered the Famous Four—Louie and Drusie, Tuesday and himself. Who can ever forget their second-grade pals? Blue often wondered if Tuesday had ever revealed to anyone the special secret that he had confided to her way back then. (No, he decided, she would never do that.) It was about his "private bins," as he called them. He remembered how he and Tuesday were sitting on the bench outside of Mrs. Reuben's room at recess when Brian Goody walked up to them. First he made a crude and racist remark about Tuesday and her dreadlocks, and he followed that by knocking off David's baseball cap for no reason at all. "Well, why don't you pick it up, *Da*vid?" he taunted. "Are you too *smart* to pick it up?" After he sauntered off, David looked at Tuesday and said, "Never mind him. I like your hair like that." Tuesday only grinned and reached for a handful of his red curls, but David ducked just in time. "Well, there goes Brian," he said a minute later. "Right into the bin marked Garbage." And then he explained how, sooner or later, everyone he knew landed in a particular bin in his brain. "So what bin am I in?" Tuesday had asked, pretending that she wasn't going to like the answer but knowing that she probably would. But he sure surprised *her*. "Well, you're in a bin marked Too Tall Tuesday," he said, coining the nickname on the spot, since he wasn't about to tell her that she was at the top of the heap in his Best Friends bin. "Too Tall Tuesday, huh!" she yelled. And she immediately began to chase him around the blacktop and over to the grassy play area—both of them screaming and laughing all the way—where she knocked him down and sat on him, for she was a good six inches taller than he was and just as strong. However, Tuesday Thomas was proud of her height and wasted no time proclaiming herself as Too Tall Tuesday to everyone in class. Not surprisingly, the nickname has stuck even to this day, more often than not in school newspaper headlines filling her with justifiable pride:

TOO TALL TUESDAY HIGH SCORER AGAIN AS SPH GIRLS WIN HARD FOUGHT FINAL GAME AGAINST BULLDOGS

And, after the school elections last year:

TTT NEW JUNIOR CLASS PREZ!

Even though Blue remembered the Famous Four, he had all but forgotten about the Famous Four's Super-Duper Puppet Show, which the four friends had presented to their fellow second-graders on the sixth of March in honor of Mrs. Reuben's birthday. The Super-Duper Puppet Show featured the Famous Four's crudely made puppet quadruplets named Omo, Bomo, Nomo, and Egads—the latter of which was Blue's own creation.

After the show, Louie—who never saves anything—tossed the little puppets into the garbage can beside Mrs. Reuben's desk. So why weren't they there when the custodian came around after school to empty the trash? Whatever became of those cute little buggers?

After being reunited in honors math, Blue and Louie again became as thick as thieves—as Louie would say, since he got a big kick out of using clichés whenever the spirit moved him. Naturally, Blue noticed his friend's newfound penchant for these sometimes trite but handy linguistic shortcuts, and soon he, too, fell under their spell. Sometimes it almost became a battle of wits between them, which was probably not the best idea in the world from the standpoint of original thinking, but, still, it was more fun than a barrel of monkeys.

Mostly, though, Blue was intrigued by his friend's vast knowledge and involvement with computers, and Louie was pleased and gratified at the chance to share his expertise with such an intelligent and willing pupil. After the new semester got underway, Blue began stopping by the DeSotos' on his way home from school and spending an hour or two just fooling around on the computer and talking with Louie. Of course, that kooky Drusie was usually there, too, flitting about, practicing her tap-dancing in the family room or experimenting with wild makeup and wigs. Blue thought it was funny, the way she looked at him the first afternoon he stopped over and said imploringly, in a wonderful comic takeoff on Ingrid Bergman, "Please, Victor, do not go to the underground meeting tonight!" Of course, Blue recognized the line from *Casablanca*, the old Bogart movie containing one of *his* favorite quotes. "Okay, I won't go," he said to her with a grin, "if you'll round up the usual suspects."

In just a few days Blue's visits with the DeSotos became the high point of his otherwise humdrum existence. He soon realized how much he had come to depend on them, because it was obvious that Omaha had not yet snapped back to her usual self. Oh, sure, she was worried about school, since she still hadn't made up all her final exams from last semester and had to take an incomplete in several of her classes, but it was more than that. The last time Blue talked with her she told him in so many words that she still had a lot on her mind and just wasn't ready to deal with him yet—whatever *that* meant.

■ ■ ■

Sunday morning, just two weeks after he had resumed drawing his comic strip, Blue received a call from Louie. "I got news," said Louie.

"Really? I got milk," Blue answered.

"Well, just wipe off your mouth and listen. You know Mr. Forni, my boss at EduGamesInc—"

"No. Never had the pleasure—"

"I don't mean do you *know* him, you fool. I mean do you know *of* him!"

"Oh, know *of* him! Sure, I've heard you talk about him enough." Actually, Blue was quite impressed with what he knew about Louie and his Mr. Forni—how Louie's vast knowledge and ability with computer programming landed him a job in Mr. Forni's company, and how he was soon assigned the task of designing little kids' games about famous cities in the world, using a bit of map-reading and elementary math instruction in the process. So far he had done the cities of Boston and San Francisco and was waiting for his next assignment.

"Did I tell you he wants me to work on a Venice game next?"

"No, really?" Blue asked, quickly adding a follow-up comment in the somewhat sarcastic vein they liked to employ when conversing with each other. "Sounds like that poor guy is perpetually pixilated."

Louie laughed. "Very sly," he said, in a rare, honest compliment. "But see how this grabs you. Forni just called and asked if I'd like to actually *go* to Venice! He wanted to know when our spring break was, and when I told him it was early this year and that we'll be off the week of March 20, he said that was just perfect, and he told me about this special airline promotional deal going on, inaugurating some kind of new service to Venice— they call it Four-for-Three-for-Two—which means that three people can fly to Venice for four days for the price of two." Louie stopped for a breath and then continued right on. "So here's where you come in. He offered to let me invite a friend along! EduGamesInc will pay for our airfare and hotel, but not for our meals or other expenses. We'd leave on a Monday, two weeks from tomorrow. Want to go?"

Blue hesitated a moment before answering. "Oh, I sup*pose*," he said. "If I *have* to." Then he added, "Of course, I'll have to check with my mom, but I don't see any problem there—"

"Great! You made my day! So I'll e-mail the details to you right now."

After Blue hung up the phone he got on-line, picked up Louie's mail, and printed out two copies. He found his mother folding clothes on the back porch and, waving Louie's e-mail in the air, asked, "What would you say if I told you that I just got an invitation from Louie—well, actually from Mr. Forni, Louie's boss at EduGamesInc—to go to Venice for four nights—plane fare and hotel included?"

"What? Let me see that!"

Blue stood there smiling while she read Louie's message.

"Well, this is wonderful!" she exclaimed. "So Mr. Forni will pick you up here at five-thirty in the morning on the twentieth of March and take you to the airport, and the three of you will arrive in Venice on Tuesday afternoon. You'll all be staying at the Hotel Bartolomeo—you and Louie sharing a room—and leave there four days later—let's see here—on Saturday the twenty-fifth. Uh-oh," she added. "I see your meals are not included." Then she laughed and handed the sheet of paper back to him. "But he says there are several McDonald's and other reasonable places to eat in Venice. I guess our budget can handle that."

"You mean I can't dine at the Hôtel des Bains?" Blue asked with an exaggerated pout, referring to the five-star hotel on the Lido where most of the action of *Death in Venice* took place. "Oh, darn! But, hey, did you see that part about the used-book store that rents computers?" Blue scanned the letter. "Here it is. It's called Agostino's. Mr. Forni made arrangements for us to use a computer there whenever we want, so I can send you e-mail from Venice. Pretty cool, huh?"

"Very cool! But you know, Blue, I just can't get over this! Here I am, a forty-two-year-old matron, wanting to visit Venice for as long as I can remember, and what happens? An opportunity of a lifetime just falls into your lap—plop, like that!" Then she laughed and gave him a quick hug—not too tight or too long, but just right to fit the occasion.

The prospect of a free trip to Venice, which would have so delighted his mother, was not enough to rescue Blue from the horse latitudes, even though he was prepared to endure the boredom and stagnation for as long as it took. But aside from the ongoing problem with Omaha, the main reason for his malaise seemed to be that he was just coasting along, with no new and great challenges in sight to test his courage or his intellect. As a knight needs a dragon and a sheriff needs a rustler, Blue needed a cause.

He knew he'd better get on the ball and do *something* to rouse himself from the dumps. So out came the pencil and drawing paper, and before he knew it, he had drawn the first panel in his usual four-panel strip format—Blue Avenger, writing a letter to God. Now, anyone can write a letter to God, but it takes a superhero like Blue to get an answer! The first panel shows Blue sitting down writing the letter. The second panel shows the letter: *Dear God: If smoking is bad for your people, why did you create ashtrays?* The third panel shows the hand of God writing a reply: *Dear Blue: Those thingamabobs were never meant for butts and ashes! They're for myrrh!* And the last panel shows a close-up of Blue Avenger's puzzled face looking sideways at the viewer and asking, *Myrrh?*

Blue laughed. It felt good to lighten up a bit for a change. Maybe he could think of a second strip, building on the word "myrrh." An entire myrrh series! In the meantime, his own comic-strip creation gave him an even better idea: Until a real challenge came along, Blue Avenger would start writing actual letters himself—but these would be hard-hitting, no-holds-barred letters laced with sarcasm and intended to correct some of the more annoying grievances and injustices he saw about him every day. And he would start off with something that *really* bugged him—encoded expiration dates on jars of salsa. In fact, it had bothered him so much that, some months before, he had spent several hours breaking the code and then outlining the method he had used.

Now he didn't waste a second. Right then and there he went to the cupboard and took down one of the jars in question—a jar labeled LA CASA DE VEGGIE SALSA SAUCE. The company had a website, so Blue immediately checked it out. Unfortunately, they didn't have an e-mail address, but they did give the names of the company's corporate officers. Blue addressed his letter to Mr. Herbert L. Reese, Chairman of the Board of La Casa de Veggie Foods, Inc., at the corporate headquarters in San Diego.

Dear Mr. Reese:

I have noticed for some months now that the expiration dates stamped on the bottom of your La Casa de Veggie Salsa Sauce bottles are encoded and are thereby rendered indecipherable for the very persons who would benefit by this information.

Therefore, I am formally requesting herein that you henceforth print the dates in regular military style, i.e., day, month, year (example: 4 July 1776)

on all your company's products as soon
as possible.

Sincerely,
Blue Avenger

P.S. By the way, Mr. Reese, you may be
interested to know that I have broken
your code (see attachment) and was
alarmed to find that seven expired bottles
of your products are presently on the
shelves at three different stores in my
neighborhood alone. I shudder at the
thought of how many more are scattered
throughout the land. I would hate to
have to report this situation to the
authorities, so please let me know when
the revision of your dating procedures
will take place.

After Blue finished writing the letter, he skimmed it
with some measure of satisfaction and then stapled it to
the attachment he had prepared before, the one outlining the method he used to decode La Casa de Veggie's
dating system. Then he addressed the envelope, sealed

and stamped it, and put it in the basket with his mother's outgoing mail.

It was good to at least be doing *something* again. Oh, and yes—he really should stop procrastinating and write to Mr. Chase R. Wanner, president of the Wanner Cornstarch Company, and ask whatever happened to that lifetime supply of cornstarch he was supposed to receive in appreciation of his Weepless Wonder Lemon Meringue Pie recipe. After all, a promise is a promise, even if it only involves cornstarch.

Blue really meant to start on his English assignment then, but, somehow, just the idea of reading "An Introduction to William Shakespeare" left him cold. Besides, he would get around to studying the material before the next test, so he could just coast along during the class discussion and let the class talkers carry the ball.

In place of Shakespeare, Blue much preferred to reread a fascinating book called *Fermat's Enigma*, which is an accounting of how, in 1994, a young mathematician named Andrew Wiles came to solve the most famous problem in the history of mathematics— Fermat's Last Theorem.

Like Andrew Wiles, Blue first became aware of Fermat's Last Theorem while in elementary school. David (as he was called back then) happened upon a children's book in the school library that explained the problem clearly. He was immediately intrigued by the circumstances surrounding the Last Theorem—how, in around the year 1637, a Frenchman named Pierre de Fermat had professed to have discovered a "marvelous" solution to the problem and had written in the margin of the math book he was reading, "I have a truly marvelous demonstration of this proposition which this margin is too narrow to contain."

What made the problem itself so attractive to David was that on the surface it seemed so simple, since it was based on the equation $(x^2 + y^2 = z^2)$ that appears in the easily understood Pythagorean theorem, which he had mastered in the second grade. Little David studied the library book and read the Fermat theorem over to himself several times: *There are no whole number solutions for the equation* $x^n + y^n = z^n$, *if* n *is greater than 2.* Then he gave it a try. He wrote $2^3 + 2^3 = 3^3$ and figured out the equation: $8 + 8 = 27$. Well, that didn't work, but he didn't expect to solve it right off the bat. This was his first truly grown-up challenge, and in his naiveté he sincerely believed he might have a chance at cracking it. He changed the first number in his equation to 3^3, so then it came out to be $27 + 8 = 27$. Okay, then, since 27 plus 8 was really 35, all he had to do was see what number brought to the third power equalled 35. He picked up his calculator and got to work, loving that new peculiar tingling in his chest and general feeling of excitement that made his heart pound like mad.

But after writing equation after equation to no avail, David came to realize that this might be more difficult than it seemed. Still, he didn't give up. Instead, he started going about it systematically, keeping track of all the failed equations. By the time he was out of elementary and into middle school, he realized he would need a much better understanding of mathematics before he could even begin to solve this problem, and from time to time as his knowledge expanded and grew he would think about it in a new light, and his dream would be rekindled. But his was not a dream of personal glory. It was much more complicated than that, and even David himself would not be able to articulate that what he really wanted was to be connected to the flow of history in a meaningful way. He truly wanted to be a part of the chain in the progress of humanity.

When David first heard that "his" problem had been solved by someone else, he felt cheated and depressed for weeks. However, after he read about Dr. Wiles's heart-wrenching struggle, his temporary setbacks, his superhuman tenacity, and his final victory, David's initial feelings of disappointment turned to admiration for the quiet and self-effacing mathematical genius. David could wait for another opportunity to make his contribution to the world.

It was after eleven at night when David (now Blue) turned to the page in *Fermat's Enigma* that contained an amusing limerick written by some mathematicians at a symposium in Boston celebrating Andrew Wiles's greatest achievement, and he knew that this was something Louie would appreciate. Since his friend had his own phone and was a confirmed night owl, Blue had no qualms about calling so late. Actually, since the start of the semester and the rekindling of their friendship, the phone calls between them had become more and more frequent. As far as Drusie was concerned, they had the most boring conversations anyone could possibly imagine. They talked about math, mostly. One time she actually heard Louie laughing hysterically and saying something that sounded like, "The exponent was equal to the coefficient, even after the progression was factored in? God! That's funny!"

"Hey, Louie, listen to this," Blue said. "It's a limerick

about Pierre de Fermat." Blue cleared his throat and read the poem.

> *"My butter, garçon, is writ large in!"*
> *a diner was heard to be chargin'.*
> *"I* had *to write there,"*
> *exclaimed waiter Pierre,*
> *"I couldn't find room in the margarine."*

"He couldn't find room in the margarine, huh?" Louie said. "That's pretty slick."

After spending all that time writing the letter to La Casa and then reading for so long about Fermat, Blue was just too tired to complete his homework assignment for his English class that night. No, unfortunately, it was worse than that; Blue did not even *start* his homework assignment for his English class that evening. As a result, pages 103 to 107 in his English-literature textbook, which contained a short biography of William Shakespeare, remained there for another year without seeing the light of day.

A woman with the curious name of Pearl Lee Washikimas was so fascinated by the existence of countless unread pages in countless unread books that she was moved to write a poem about it in the 1930s, during the height of the economic depression in America:

> *Pages pressed together tightly*
> *In the darkness all entombed,*
> *Like a sandwich left uneaten*
> *In the lunch pail of the doomed.*

"The Unread Book"
by Pearl Lee Washikimas (1905–1948),
in *Undiscovered Poets of the Early Twentieth Century*

four

Blue usually didn't have time to check his e-mail in the morning, and, actually, before hooking up with Louie again, he rarely got any at all. But he had a few minutes to spare this morning, so he logged on and took a look. There were three letters in his mailbox. Two were spam, which he quickly deleted, since he wasn't interested in a Family Dental Plan and knew enough not to open the New XXX Babes!!!! attachment—being cognizant of the fact that even wearing latex gloves and protective goggles does not prevent the spread of computer viruses. But the third letter in his mailbox contained the kind of challenge he loved.

First of all, it was from an unfamiliar screen name— DYAD LARK—and the subject line was **In Memory of the Day, 6 March.** The message, however, was encoded like this:

55K10C81D28F135G36C138F24M76L147G127A

Blue knew the word DYAD meant a group of two—a couple or a pair—but he had long ago forgotten Mrs. Reuben's birthday, so 6 March meant simply today's date. Blue naturally assumed that this message was probably something slightly obscene or silly from Louie, a kind of reminder of the encoded messages they used to send to each other back in elementary school.

DYAD LARK? Two larks? A pair of larks? Well, there was no time to work on it now. Blue printed out the message and tossed it on the desk. Then he put the computer to sleep and went into the kitchen to get himself some breakfast.

Josh was spooning up some cold cereal, and his mother was on the back porch, starting up a load of wash. "Ah, here you are," she said, coming into the kitchen. "I've been waiting for you. There's something I have to tell you boys, and I may as well do it now."

"Well, can you hurry it up, Mom?" Josh asked, slurping away at his cereal. "I don't have much time. Remember my class won that PTA membership-drive contest? Well, this is the day we get to go to the nature museum at Lake Merritt and ride those gondolas and have lunch and stuff, and Trevor's mom is picking me up early."

"This won't take long," Sally said tersely. "I can do it

in one sentence. Your other grandmother is coming back into our lives."

Josh shot a puzzled look at his mother. "Who's my other grandmother?"

"*Mom's* mother, you dope." Blue leaned up against the refrigerator and bit at his thumbnail. "I used to call her Grammy." He looked over at his mother. "So I guess she finally apologized, huh?"

"How did you know about that?"

"Hey, Mom, I was six years old at the time! It was just before Joshpot was born. I heard you tell Dad that until she apologized and dealt with her other problems you weren't going to have anything to do with her. She was *out of the family*, as far as you were concerned."

"Blue, I had no idea you heard all that! How could you remember all that?"

Blue shrugged. "I don't know. Six-year-olds retain certain things, I guess. So—what happened?"

Sally glanced quickly at Josh, who was busy drinking the remaining milk right out of the bowl, and then signaled to Blue that she'd discuss it further as soon as they were alone.

Josh put his bowl in the dishwasher and grabbed his lunch. "Mrs. Loomis is honking. I gotta go. But where is she?"

"What do you mean? She's right outside honking!"

"No, no. I mean my other grandmother! Where is *she*? Is she coming over here? Am I going to get a new relative?"

Mrs. Loomis honked again.

"Yes, you'll get to meet her—soon," Sally said ominously. "Now get going. And please don't bang the door on your way out."

"How soon?" Blue asked, beginning to recall a few of his grammy's more memorable idiosyncrasies—like that loud, crazy laugh of hers and those occasional bouts of tears.

"She called from San Diego," Sally said, wincing at the sound of the banging door. "She assured me she's been on the wagon for almost two years now." Sally paused. "You probably weren't aware that she had this— well, this slight drinking problem?"

"Well, I guess not. Not really."

"Well, that was just one part of it. It was a combination of things—other problems, too. It just seemed to all come to a head right around the time Josh was due. The thing is, when your grandfather was alive it wasn't so bad. He kind of kept things under control. But then, well, what can I say? At any rate, she called from San Diego and said that's all behind her now— that she's been on the wagon, like I said, and that she's married now to a travel agent—"

"A travel agent?"

"Yes, that's right. I knew she'd been living with an old friend of hers in San Diego, another recent widow, who, apparently, convinced her to try AA. So that's where she met this guy. She said they've been seeing each other for over a year, and then last month they just decided to go to Las Vegas and make it legal. Now she wants us to meet him. They want to stop by in two weeks—on Sunday afternoon, actually. And then they're leaving for Europe the following day, flying out of San Francisco. She said they've been doing quite a lot of traveling."

"Wait a minute. If they're leaving for Europe two weeks from today, well, that's the same day I'm leaving."

"I suppose that's right. She said they're off to Milan on Monday afternoon—part business, part pleasure."

"Are they staying here overnight, then?"

"Oh, no," Sally said, shaking her head. "For one thing, where would we put them? Besides, I'm going to take this reconnecting thing a little slow at first. We're skating on some very thin ice here, and I certainly don't want to risk another dunking."

Meanwhile, in another part of the city, one of the eleven English teachers currently employed at San Pablo High is preparing to leave for school. Her name is Miss Lydia Wooliscroft, and she has been teaching for forty-two years. Among the students in her third-period junior English class this semester are the DeSoto twins and Omaha Nebraska Brown.

Now Miss Wooliscroft is rinsing out her coffee cup. She's hesitating for a moment before reaching for her car keys. Oh, look! She's picking up that travel brochure from the counter and gazing again at the full-color photos. And now she's rereading the text, which is printed in extra-large type in deference to the anticipated age of its readers, and which she has practically memorized.

London in the fall! What could be more glorious? Four unforgettable days in London, plenty of time to unwind from your flight, visit the museums, and shop at Harrods! Then it's on to Stratford-upon-Avon for an in-depth visit planned especially for retired teachers! Admire the desk so like the one young William sat at while attending the local grammar school. See Holy Trinity Church and pay your respects at Shakespeare's tomb (admission fee included), then it's a hop, skip and jump

by bus to Anne Hathaway's Cottage, with its
legendary thatched roof and four-poster bed!
And don't forget to ask your tour guide about
the optional visit to Charlecote Park,
traditional site of the famous deer-poaching
incident! Then we return to London for a
surprise treat! A performance of a specially
selected Shakespeare play (actual play to be
announced) in the rebuilt Globe!

Miss Wooliscroft folds the brochure and puts it in her
purse, glancing momentarily at her reflection in the tiny
mirror under the flap. Someone is *not* getting any
younger! She closes her purse with a snap. So this is it!
I'll just go ahead and do it! This will be my last year of
teaching! Next fall will find me in Stratford-upon-Avon!
She closes her eyes and clasps her hands together over
her bosom, and in a sudden burst of whimsical playful-
ness, she exclaims, "Hello, Mr. Shakespeare!"

In yet another part of the city, Dr. James Wood, age
forty-eight and a widower for several years, is also
preparing to leave for school. Among the students in *his*
third-period junior English class are Blue Avenger and

Tuesday Thomas. Like Miss Wooliscroft, Dr. Wood is also making up his mind to just go ahead and do it, but instead of being motivated by a travel brochure, he has been stirred into action by an obituary he just read in an old magazine he found wedged between the shelves in back of the breakfast cereal. And in his case, the just-do-it decision involves speaking out at last, in the fullness of his convictions, about a subject that means more to him in this particular phase of his life and on this particular day than anything else in the world.

Dr. Wood is astute enough to know that a great percentage of his students are—oh, how to put this diplomatically?—that many of his students are video-game-and-TV-addicted blockheads? No, that would be much too blunt and not in conformance with his gentle and refined style—for Dr. Wood is an Englishman by birth. Suffice it to say that most of his students have other things on their minds besides second-semester junior English. But if he can reach just one, if he can touch the head and heart of just *one* who will carry on the crusade, his mission will be fulfilled. For what is the purpose of living if not to take up the banner of our fallen comrades in just and righteous battles? And for Dr. James Wood, the cause to which he feels so committed is one that appeals to that most basic of all human desires—the longing to see fairness and justice prevail.

Before this day is over, Dr. Wood will attempt to convey to members of the next generation a belief that has been festering within him for years—the conviction that the man we know as William Shakespeare is a myth, a sham, and a fraud, perpetuated for more than four hundred years by staid tradition, economic interests, and a conservative group of closed-minded scholars who have too much invested in the status quo even to consider the possibility that they could be mistaken. Such is his noble purpose, Dr. Wood thought, smiling at his own pomposity in presuming to use those particular words in connection with his own feeble attempts in the pursuit of justice and right.

Regretfully, out of the eleven English teachers employed at San Pablo High, seven of them would be unable to define the term "horse latitudes," should anyone be inclined to quiz them. Although both Miss Wooliscroft and Dr. Wood would be able to supply the correct answer, Miss Wooliscroft's would be quite matter-of-fact and boring, whereas Dr. Wood's students would be charmed and transported by his explanation of how, in the olden days of yore, sailing vessels delivering horses to the West Indies were often delayed by the calm, windless, and hot dry weather in the waters near Bermuda and, because of the lack of sufficient food and water, were obliged to throw the horses overboard. Just think of it, those pitiful drowning horses, hopelessly struggling to survive in the sea! He would explain that the word "doldrums"—meaning low spirits, gloomy, stagnating—is another word used to describe that unique and storied region. And, who knows, should the mood be right, he might even evoke a taste of the Woodstock Nation era and recite a piece called "Horse Latitudes" by Jim Morrison (who was buried in a Paris cemetery at the age of twenty-seven) and see what his students think of *that*:

> *When the still sea conspires an armor*
> *And her sullen and aborted*
> *Currents breed tiny monsters*
> *True sailing is dead*
> *Awkward instant*
> *And the first animal is jettisoned*
> *Legs furiously pumping*
> *Their stiff green gallop*
> *And heads bob up*
> *Poise*
> *Delicate*
> *Pause*

Consent
In mute nostril agony
Carefully refined
And sealed over

Ariel Melissa Pekhaw reports in the *Poetry Club Journal* that she wrote the poem "Who was Jim Morrison?" in just thirty-two minutes! However, she is still hard at work on her memoirs, which she has tentatively entitled *In and Out with The Doors: The Real Story.* She hopes to be finished with that task "in a year, or maybe two or three—whatever."

Who was Jim Morrison? What did he do?
Well he sang and wrote poems for me and for you.
Who was Jim Morrison? Where did he die?
He died in a bathtub, that poor mixed-up guy.
Who was Jim Morrison? Why did he croak?
Alcohol, mescaline, smack, methamphetamine, coke?
Who was Jim Morrison? Anyone know?
Well, he's dead and gone now, so on with the show.

"Who Was Jim Morrison?"
by Ariel Melissa Pekhaw (1953–),
in *Ex-Groupies of Dead Rock Stars Poetry Club Journal*
(Vol. 1, No. 1, July–August 1973)

five

The students filing into Miss Wooliscroft's third-period English class had no way of knowing about their teacher's retirement plans as she stood at her usual greeting post just inside the classroom door, although Drusie DeSoto thought she noticed a slight upturn at the corners of her mouth and a certain sparkle in those pale-blue eyes. As a budding actress, Drusie was particularly attuned to the nuances of facial expressions, and she idly wondered what was up.

Miss Wooliscroft looked at the shining morning-faces of her students as she waited for them to settle down and suddenly realized how much she was going to miss them. She especially enjoyed the DeSoto twins—the girl, Drusie, such a beautiful, vivacious youngster, with her long dark hair, huge brown eyes, and full red lips! And a very talented actress, too! (A lovely Juliet in the Drama Club's summer production.) And her twin, Louie, the quiet one—definitely a late bloomer socially, but what a computer whiz! And there, by the window, Omaha Nebraska Brown—quite a unique young lady, observant, witty, wise beyond her years. Miss Wooliscroft sighed softly and fluffed the hair around the back of her neck with several short upward strokes of her hand. Well, time to get down to the business of learning.

"If we could quiet down now, class? Good. I've corrected last Friday's paragraph-practice papers, people, and most of you did very well." She started to hand out the corrected papers. "My, that's a real tongue twister, isn't it—paragraph-practice papers, people." She smiled. "But some of you are still using too many clichés in your descriptive sentences. So remember, please! Avoid those clichés!"

Louie looked up, his mind racing. Avoid clichés? What for? He loved them. They could be wonderful shortcuts. And the fact that they'd become clichés at all said something about their usefulness. He spoke up without missing a beat. "At all costs?" he asked, in a rare show of uncalled-for classroom participation, followed by an embarrassed blush.

He was rewarded by several good-natured groans.

"Like the plague?" asked the kid next to him, carrying the ball a couple of yards further.

"Now, boys," Miss Wooliscroft said with an indulgent

smile. "That's enough of that."

Although Miss Wooliscroft wouldn't admit it in a hundred years, or even two hundred years (mainly because she didn't realize it herself), uncalled-for comments from her male students were looked upon with a certain tolerance and affection that was lacking when the comments emanated from students of the female persuasion. But Miss Wooliscroft began teaching school long before those groundbreaking studies pertaining to sexual favoritism in the classroom were made. And, besides, this would be her last year of teaching. Why bother to change now?

Papers duly distributed, Miss Wooliscroft strode back to her favorite site for imparting knowledge, which was just to the right of her desk and within easy reach of her grade book, with its rows of little pluses and minuses, indicating in concrete form the strengths and weaknesses of her pupils. Now, surveying her class, she thought they looked particularly tidy and attentive this morning. She approved wholeheartedly of their new, neat uniforms and believed that they—like their counterparts in expensive private schools—would soon grow accostumed to their regulation clothing. She smiled broadly. *Accostumed!* Why, when it comes to punning, she could certainly give Mr. Shakespeare a run for his money!

Miss Wooliscroft cleared her throat. "Well, then," she said. "Let's get on with today's lesson. Did you enjoy reading about the life of the greatest dramatist of all times, William Shakespeare?"

"Oh, yes!" came one obviously overenthusiastically faked reply, followed by several appreciative giggles.

"Um-*hmm*!" came a similar echo from the other side of the room.

Miss Wooliscroft was unaware of it, of course, but there was a real-life drama of gigantic proportions going on right before her eyes: Tonia Morris and Stevie Spears were in the final stages of a nasty breakup after 139 days of a steady and exclusive relationship, during which time certain activities took place—involving private body parts—which were now bitterly regretted by at least one of the participants.

Miss Wooliscroft adjusted her glasses and opened her teacher's-edition textbook to the proper page. "Let's hurry through the basics, then. All together now! The Bard of Avon was born on . . . ?"

"April 23, 1564," some members of the class responded in a dull monotone, while a very angry and upset Stevie Spears said something else, something that had nothing whatsoever to do with William Shakespeare's birthdate. To the girl sitting in front of him it sounded something like "clucking itch."

"And he died . . . ?"

"Yes!" Louie DeSoto exclaimed, emboldened by his previously well-received contribution.

"*Mis*ter DeSoto, if you please, sir . . ."

"Yes, ma'am. Sorry, ma'am." Louie bowed his head and directed an apologetic gaze at Miss Wooliscroft from under his contact-lens-covered eyeballs—embarrassed because his second attempt at humor had fallen flat.

"He died on April 23, 1616, didn't he, Miss Wooliscroft?" a boy named Harris Beasley asked rhetorically, since he had done his homework and knew his answer was correct. (But, on the down side, there would be no letters correcting injustices or righting wrongs from Harris Beasley on anyone's desk within the foreseeable future.)

"Gee, April 23! He died on the same day as he was born, didn't he?" added Marcia Davenport, with an expression of wide-eyed wonder.

"Not precisely," Louie muttered to himself, checking his watch. Louie was anxious for school to be out that day because a friend in his second-period class had just informed him that Wylie Seratt was going to show off a new computer game called *Chimera* (produced by a company owned by Jackson Seratt, Wylie's uncle) in the school's computer lab that afternoon when classes were over. The interesting thing about *Chimera* was that it happened to be the very first computer game that Louie *himself* created—and which Wylie's uncle's company (Seratt Games, Inc.) in San Jose *finally* got around to producing! This has been a sore spot with Louie, because it all happened before he met Mr. Forni and got involved with EduGamesInc—a real company with a fine reputation—unlike Seratt's outfit.

Now Louie was wondering how come he had to hear the news secondhand, and not from Wylie himself. After all, it *was* mostly his game—if the storyline, characters, and graphics counted for anything, not to mention his new idea for explaining math concepts to little kids.

"Louie?"

"Yes?"

"I asked you about Anne Hathaway, Louie."

"Oh, I'm sorry. I guess I didn't hear the question. Would you repeat it, please?"

"Class?"

"She's Shakespeare's wife!" called out Harris Beasley.

"—eight years older than him—" added Willow Farr, the girl with the little gold ring through her tongue.

"Yeah. He was only eighteen and she was an old lady!"

"Old lady? My God! She was only twenty-six! You call that an old lady?"

"—and she was pregnant when they got married," Harris added with a smirk.

"Who said? I didn't see *that* in our book!"

"Well, *duh*! Married in November, baby in May?" Harris Beasley laughed sarcastically. "Let's just do the count here. December, January, February—"

"It could have been premature, *Har*ris. Did you ever think of that?" Drusie asked with a straight face. And then she suddenly burst into a big smile, revealing that even she herself knew the question was a facetious one.

Omaha was fascinated by the way Drusie was always smiling, since she herself rarely did. Actually, of all the girls she knew at school, Drusie DeSoto was the most interesting, for a lot of reasons. Although she was really beautiful, she didn't seem snobbish at all. And she was so outgoing, like she didn't have a fear in the world. It was hard to believe she was Louie DeSoto's twin.

Miss Wooliscroft held up her hand. "All right, class. Let's settle down now and turn to something else. What is special about the so-called First Folio?" She paused. "Volunteers? Anyone?"

Drusie and Harris—now vying for attention—both raised their hands, while in the back of the room Tonia

Morris's best friend was trying to be of some comfort, offering a fresh, unopened package of tissues to absorb the now falling tears, and fixing upon her own face a sympathetic look of utter despair—an expression that implied much more sorrow than was actually felt, for Tonia Morris's best friend thought Stevie Spears was really cool, and maybe now she'd have a chance to get a crack at him. But those who are wise in the ways of the heart, as well as experienced medical technologists in their laboratories, know that there are many kinds of tears, and Tonia's were not made of the pure, sweet mango juice of unrequited love but, rather, contained the bitter and astringent brandy of rage and anger and disgust—the usual residues of love gone bad.

Omaha Nebraska Brown was both touched and dismayed by the pitiful sight of Tonia and Stevie. She shuddered at the thought of being involved in such a public spectacle herself and resolved that it would never happen. In fact, she couldn't even bear the thought of breaking up at all, publicly *or* privately, and witnessing Tonia and Stevie's fairy-tale romance of 139 days dissolve into bitterness and disillusionment only reinforced her belief that she had made the right decision after all, as far as she and Blue were concerned. They would be friends—good and faithful friends—but with no strings attached. That's still the safest; that's still the best.

"Yes, Drusie?" said Miss Wooliscroft. "What can you tell us about the First Folio?"

"Well, the First Folio was the first time Shakespeare's plays were all printed together in one book. There were thirty-six plays in there altogether, and it was printed in 1623, seven years after Shakespeare died."

"Good, Drusie. That's correct." Miss Wooliscroft sat down at her desk. "Now, please turn to page 108. As you know, your textbook contains all of Shakespeare's 154 sonnets as well as his masterpiece—*Hamlet, Prince of Denmark.*"

Another slight disturbance at the back of the room attracted her attention. "Now, just what is the *trouble* back there?" she asked sharply.

"Nothing," one of the girls replied, while Tonia Morris covered her face with her hands and heaved silent sobs that shook her upper body in a motion that mimicked riders on the famous lurching and jerky trains traversing the heart of India.

"We will not be studying the *Sonnets*," Miss Wooliscroft continued, with one more disapproving glance aimed at the girls in the corner. "They are very difficult to understand, and scholars have debated for centuries about their meaning. Somehow, readers have never been able to connect them with events in Shakespeare's life. And even though I will *not* question you about the *Sonnets* on your exam this Friday, I would still like you to remember what you read about them in last night's homework assignment. For instance, the cast of characters—the Dark Lady, the Rival Poet, the Fair Young Man, and so forth—"

Drusie was hoping her teacher would elaborate more on that. She wanted to hear more about the Dark Lady and the Rival Poet, but that's all Miss Wooliscroft was going to say about the *Sonnets*.

"As you know from your junior English syllabus, today we are going to begin our study of *Hamlet,* and part of the mandated requirement is for you to commit a few passages of Shakespeare's works to memory. Now, since Hamlet has the most lines, we'll have to divide up his speeches, but at the end of our Shakespeare unit we will take our turns at the front and actually perform parts of the play! Doesn't that sound like fun?"

By the time the bell sounded, only Sierra Jones and Maximilian Parker were oblivious of the final breakup of Tonia and Stevie's great love affair—only because they were in the first stages of their own ill-fated romance.

■ ■ ■

A poem written by Pia Marie Skelleshaw (the young heiress of the Kansas City Skelleshaw fortune) pretty much expressed how Tonia Morris felt that day.

> *My love is like a leaky vase*
> *With roses dead and dying*
> *A candy dish with chips and cracks*
> *A love poem not quite rhyming.*
> *My love's a garbage can o'erflowing*
> *A kitchen filled with ants*
> *A backyard bog with a chained-up dog*
> *Thank God! You're gone! Good riddance!*

"Good-bye, Love"
by Pia Marie Skelleshaw (1978–),
in *Fractured Valentines: Love Poems from the Disenchanted*

SIX

Concurrently, across the hall in room 212, Dr. James Wood was about to call *his* third-period junior English class to order. On the study sheet for today, just as in Miss Wooliscroft's class, was the introduction to the Shakespeare unit as set forth in the Curriculum Guidelines issued by the Downtown Office and approved by Mrs. Manning, the principal of San Pablo High School. In all his years of teaching, Dr. Wood had been a good soldier, adhering strictly to the Guidelines, and on those occasions when he'd found himself ahead of schedule with time to spare, his supplementary material would only support and enhance what had already preceded it.

Until today.

"Good morning, everyone," Dr. Wood said pleasantly, removing his sport coat and hanging it on the back of his chair.

He was answered by a dissonant scattering of "Good morning"s from the class, while Blue made himself as comfortable as he could, settling back at his desk and stretching out his long legs. Although he had thoroughly enjoyed Ms. Chandler's English class last term (especially because Omaha was there), English this semester with Dr. Wood had become one of the most pleasant and deeply satisfying hours of his day. Blue appreciated his teacher's wry sense of humor and slightly cynical comments on the follies of the times, and on several occasions had even accepted his general invitation for students to join him in his classroom at lunchtime, although Blue noticed that most of the kids there were those shy and introspective types who didn't exactly fit in with the other inhabitants of what Dr. Wood once referred to in class as "this sometimes harsh and unforgiving jungle known as high school."

Now, on this particular morning, Professor Wood—as the kids sometimes addressed him—put his hands in his trouser pockets and looked directly into the faces of his students. "Today, as you know, we are to begin our unit on William Shakespeare. Ordinarily, we would spend the hour discussing your reading—the biography of Shakespeare in your textbook. However, I believe that the material is entirely self-explanatory. Oh, we *could* go over it, rehash it, and so forth, but I see no need for that." He paused a moment and then added, "However, for those of you who may have merely skimmed the pages, I might suggest that you read them over until you are familiar with the information—uh"—he smiled at the awkward syntaxial position in which he found himself, but then he managed to pull through admirably as he added with a sly wink, "until you are familiar with the information contained therein."

(Shakespeare scholars and others in the know tell us that William Shakespeare—whoever he was—contributed over thirty-two hundred new words to the English language. Cursory research has shown, however, that two words he *didn't* coin are the delightful newcomers "high-fiving" and "syntaxial," the latter of which is indisputably more expressive and flowing than the harsh and awkward "syntactical." Some new words have the good fortune to be immediately welcomed into the common vocabulary, such as Herb Caen's little gem, "hippie" ["young people in the 1960's, alienated from conventional society"], whereas other words, such as "edumation" ["the automation of educational intelligence systems," first coined by a certain R.L.H. of Sacramento, California], never quite catch the public fancy, in spite of the inventor's wishful-thinking protestations to the contrary. But it doesn't take a rocket scientist to coin words or phrases, such as *it doesn't take a rocket scientist*. Still, one note of caution for those who feel they are ready to take the plunge: Coined *words* have a much greater shelf life than *phrases*, which have a tendency to grow stale and trite with overuse, as any rocket scientist can tell you.)

Now Dr. Wood walked over to the front of his desk and bowed his head, thoughtfully clasping his hands together under his chin. After a minute he breathed deeply and took his usual lecture stance, arms hanging loosely at his sides, ready to break into appropriate gestures when needed.

"I just read this morning of the death of a man I admire greatly, and with your permission—and in his memory—I'd like to devote some of our classroom time today discussing the great passion of his life and the reason I think it is so important. But, first, I want to make it clear at the outset that what you're going to hear today is purely my own personal opinion and does not necessarily reflect the views of either the English department here at San Pablo High, or of the Oakland City School Board, or of the great State of California. And, of course, you will not be quizzed on it."

He was pleased to see the attention level of the class rise appreciatively, just as he suspected it would after his unusual disclaimer.

"Now, that being said, let me continue. The name of the gentleman I just mentioned was Charlton Ogburn, and although he died in October 1998 at the age of eighty-seven, I just became aware of it this morning."

Dr. Wood reached across his desk and picked up a large book bound in black, which he held up for the class to see. "This book is the result of Charlton Ogburn's life's work—*The Mysterious William Shakespeare: The Myth and the Reality*. His subject happens to be nothing less than the greatest mystery in the history of literature: Did William Shakespeare really write the works attributed to him, or were they written by another person?

"People have been asking this question for a very long time," he continued, returning the book to his desk. "And why is this? Well, to put it simply, many people—myself included—find it impossible to believe that the son of an illiterate leather-worker from a muddy little backwater town with a population of fifteen hundred souls could have written these magnificent plays and poems, when he lacked the education, the upbringing, the experience, and the knowledge to do it."

Dr. Wood shook his head ruefully. "And what is the explanation we are given? Well, William Shakespeare was a genius. William Shakespeare was divinely inspired." He raised his hands in the air and looked up at the ceiling, as if asking for an explanation from a higher authority. "It strains credulity. It is simply unbelievable."

The students were very still, sitting forward in their chairs, a little surprised at this rather unusual show of emotion on the part of their teacher.

Dr. Wood rubbed his lips with his thumb and gazed at the floor. In a moment he looked up again and asked in a now down-to-earth, businesslike manner, "So! What do we actually *know* about this man from Stratford-on-Avon, this man known as William *Shak*spere?"

He paused and raised his eyebrows. "That's right, *Shak*spere," he repeated, picking up a piece of chalk and writing the name Shakspere on the board. "Shakspere. This is the spelling that appears most frequently in the six—only *six*, mind you—purported signatures we have of the man from Stratford. Interestingly enough, not *one* of those six signatures is spelled like this." Dr. Wood then hastily wrote the name Shakespeare on the board and tapped it several times with his chalk.

Sensing a feeling of restlessness in the class, Dr. Wood put his hands behind his back and asked, "Are there any questions up to this point?"

A girl's hand went up.

"Yes, Emma?"

"Well, what about the biography of him in our book?

It says he went to a good school in Stratford, and that he went to London and acted in plays and stuff, and that he was really smart, and had lots of friends—"

"Good question, Emma. The way anti-Stratfordians answer that—and, by the way, the term 'anti-Stratfordians' refers, of course, to those folks who do not believe the man from Stratford is the actual author. At any rate, the anti-Stratfordians say we should read those biographies *very* carefully. They say we should be aware of how many times we encounter words and phrases such as 'perhaps,' 'probably,' 'it is said that,' and 'according to tradition.' And that would be a good exercise for you people to undertake. Take another look at that chapter, making note of how many times those conditional words and phrases appear. Because, in reality, the known facts about the man from Stratford are very sparse indeed."

Another hand was raised. "Well, if he didn't do it, who did?"

Dr. Wood nodded and fingered the piece of chalk he was holding. "Yes. Yes, indeed. That is the question. Who *did* do it! Throughout the years, over fifty candidates have been suggested as the true author of Shakespeare's works. Sir Francis Bacon was probably the leading suspect until the mid-1950s, and I'd like to speak about him for just a moment. First of all, you must remember that the Elizabethan poets lived and worked under strict rules of censorship, so they developed quite ingenious ways of getting around that by using literary codes and puzzles, anagrams, double meanings, puns, and plays on words. And since Bacon was fascinated by ciphers—he even came up with one himself—many people were convinced that *he* was the real author of the plays, and that the answer to the authorship puzzle was hidden away in the works themselves. And here's an interesting fact—or coincidence, as some might call it— that just added fat to the fire the Baconians were building." He paused again, then he cupped his hands around his mouth and said in a dramatic stage-whisper, "Bacon chose to reveal the secret of his cipher in 1623—the *very same year* in which the First Folio was published!"

The girl sitting at the desk across from Blue raised her hand.

"Yes, Sheri?"

"How did those ciphers work, anyway?"

"I'm afraid I'm unable to answer that, Sheri, other than to say that ciphers are like codes, substituting some letters for others, according to a predetermined plan."

Tuesday Thomas raised her hand, and after getting a nod from Dr. Wood, she said, "Ask Blue. He knows all about codes and ciphers."

Dr. Wood raised his eyebrows and peered over at Blue. "Is that right, Blue? Are you familiar with Bacon's cipher?"

Blue grimaced at Tuesday in a half-joking way, and then broke into a smile as she waggled her fingers in a silly little wave of recognition. "Yeah, I guess I am—"

"Well, then," Dr. Wood suggested, "perhaps it would be possible for you to explain it here in this room at lunchtime today for those students who may be interested."

Blue nodded and said, "Sure. I could do that."

"I can't come today," Sheri said. "Maybe on Wednesday?"

Blue nodded. "Wednesday's okay."

Dr. Wood made a little note on his desk calendar. "Good. Now, just let me say that the upshot of this whole cipher craze led to nothing but dead ends. Yes, somehow those ciphers and anagrams and suspicions of hidden messages led nowhere, and I'll tell you why. *It was because there was nothing really there.* And the *reason* there was nothing there is because I believe the man behind the pseudonym of William Shakespeare was not Sir Francis Bacon at all, but a nobleman by the name of Edward de Vere, the seventeenth Earl of Oxford."

Dr. Wood walked over to the board and wrote in his

distinctive but readable hand, *Edward de Vere, 17th Earl of Oxford.* And he finished off by underlining it with a grand sweep of the chalk.

Stepping away from the board, he took a minute to gaze at his handiwork. Then he replaced the chalk and spoke to the class, looking directly into the eyes of one, and then another of his students. "So who was this Earl of Oxford, and why did he write under an assumed name?" Dr. Wood cocked his head. "Anyone? Does anyone happen to know why he had to write under an assumed name, if the Oxfordian theory is correct? Yes, Erica?"

"Because he was an earl, and those kinds of guys weren't supposed to write plays for the common people?"

"That's absolutely correct! Good, Erica. But I'm curious. How do you happen to know that?"

Erica blushed at the unexpected attention. "I saw it on the Internet," she said. "Last night. I was checking around some Shakespeare sites and I happened to see one about that Oxford guy—"

"Really? Well, that's very interesting. I'll have to check out those sites myself one of these days. But, going back to Oxford, in his case there was even more at stake than for your average nobleman, because he was also the son-in-law of Queen Elizabeth's chief adviser! It would just be too embarrassing if people were to know that these plays were written by someone *that* close to the Queen and her court."

Another hand popped up.

"Yes?"

"Well, if Edward de Vere really wrote the plays, how did they get Shakespeare's name on them?"

"Ah!" Dr. Wood exclaimed. "The Oxfordian explanation for that is just one of the many interesting aspects of this whole mystery. Let's start with Shakespeare's two long narrative poems that are mentioned in your book, *Venus and Adonis* and *The Rape of Lucrece*. The first time the name William Shakespeare appeared in print was on the occasion of the publication of *Venus and Adonis* in 1593. And the curious thing here is that the name was *not* printed in the customary place, which would be on the title page, but instead it appeared *after the dedication* of the piece to the Earl of Southampton. And this was an indication to many that the name was indeed a pseudonym. And you must keep in mind that by this time between three and five of the plays had already been written and produced—with *no name at all* attached to them."

"But why did he pick *that* name?" Tuesday asked. "Why Shakespeare?"

"Well, the Oxfordians cite several reasons for that. One of them is that, before Edward de Vere became the seventeenth Earl of Oxford at the age of twelve, when his father died, he held the title of Viscount Bulbeck. And his crest—you know, his coat-of-arms—was a lion brandishing a broken spear, signifying that he had won the joust. A lion, shaking a spear. Shake-Speare."

"But I don't understand," Tuesday said. "How did they do that? I mean, if Edward de Vere really wrote the plays, and they have the name Shakespeare on them, how did the *real* Shakespeare, that guy from Stratford, get into the picture?"

"*Shak*spere," Dr. Wood corrected, pointing to the name on the board. "We call the man from Stratford Shakspere."

"But—"

"Let me try to explain this," Dr. Wood said with a faint smile. "It's very complicated, but I'll try to make it as simple as I can. This is the part of the scenario that the Stratfordians love to ridicule. 'We are not drawn to conspiracy theories,' they say disdainfully, as if the Elizabethan period was not submerged in intrigue and nefarious plots of every kind.

"But according to the Oxfordian theory—and let me make this clear, it *is* just a theory, since no actual smoking gun has yet been discovered—but according to this theory, around the year 1597, Queen Elizabeth and her chief minister, Lord Burghley—who was, as I mentioned before, also Edward de Vere's father-in-law—decided that it would be unthinkable for the public to know that these plays were written by one of the family. Aside from the reason that Erica cited—that noblemen just didn't write plays for the entertainment of the rowdy crowds frequenting public theaters—Edward de Vere, the seventeenth Earl of Oxford, was not just *any* nobleman, and these plays—with their biting satires of real people— were not just *any* plays. In fact, it is almost universally recognized that Lord Burghley himself is the model for the character of Polonius in *Hamlet*—as we'll see in the coming days as we begin to study that play.

"At any rate, the plan was hatched to compel Oxford to hide behind the name—or pseudonym—he had used earlier for *Venus and Adonis* and *The Rape of Lucrece*. And then, goes the scenario, someone noticed that there was an actual person—as it happened, a small-time actor— with a name quite similar to Shakespeare. And thus Oxford's previous pen name was attached to a living person. Oxfordians believe that William Shakspere was actually paid to go quietly back to Stratford-on-Avon and resume the life of a normal citizen, albeit a much wealthier one. And that would explain, of course, how he could be listed in the records as a tax defaulter on property worth five pounds in 1596, and yet was able to purchase the second-largest house in Stratford for sixty pounds the following year."

Dr. Wood searched the faces of his students. "There's one last thing that I'd like to mention in this connection," he said. "And it is this: The Stratford man's death in April of 1616 was met with complete silence. Ordinarily, the death of such a writer would be followed by a myriad of poetic tributes and public lamentations. But in Shakspere's case, there was nothing. Nothing at all. Stratfordians shrug, but Oxfordians find this very curious indeed."

Another hand went up.

"Yes?"

"Have you ever been to Stratford?"

Dr. Wood smiled a rueful little smile. "Oh, yes. Yes, I have, I'm sorry to say. And let me just remind you that Stratford-upon-Avon is the biggest tourist attraction in Great Britain after London, and we should never underestimate the huge, *huge* amount of money and power and prestige that is invested in the Shakespearean orthodoxy. To use the vernacular—that is, to use the common language of the people—committed Oxfordians have a *very* tough row to hoe."

He glanced at his watch and saw that he had ample

time to finish up. "So—what was this nobleman like, this Edward de Vere?" he asked rhetorically. "Just what sort of person was he? Well, all I can tell you is that on many occasions I have read through the night about the life and times of this remarkable man. And when you get to know Edward de Vere as I've come to know him—a first-rate scholar, fluent in several languages, a fine horseman and athlete, as well as an accomplished dancer and musician, too—hazel-eyed and curly-haired, a favorite of the Queen, quick-witted, fun to be with, a lover of travel and adventure, and a friend to actors and bartenders and others outside of the court—when you get to know him, you can't help feeling that somehow, some way, you must do all in your power to see that he is finally recognized for what he was, truly the greatest poet of all the ages. And, perhaps more important, his plays and poems take on a whole new dimension when we know so much about the life and experiences of the true author. The *Sonnets*, for instance, which have always puzzled the experts, make perfect sense when paired with the events in Oxford's life. And in this connection I'm always reminded of something an English novelist named Anthony Trollope said, which was this: 'The man of letters is, in truth, ever writing his own biography.' And in Oxford's case, we believe this is exactly the case. Ah, yes," he added, his voice beginning to crack slightly, "this man, in my opinion, got a very raw deal."

After a moment Dr. Wood walked over to the board again and printed in large capital letters the Latin phrase:

VERO NIL VERIUS

Then he stepped to one side and read aloud what he had just written. "*Vero nil verius.* Oxford's personal motto. Everybody knew it. Everyone who knew Oxford knew his motto. Translated, *Vero nil verius* means 'Nothing is more true than truth itself.' How very ironic that is! Here we have the memory of a man—a man whose very *motto* extols truth—here we have his memory besmirched for four hundred years by a foul and grievous lie."

Those students who were sitting so that the light just happened to fall on his face at a particular angle were surprised and moved to see his eyes were glistening with a hint of tears. Blue noticed this, too, and respectfully looked away. "*Vero nil verius,*" he whispered under his breath, stealthily printing the words in ink on the inside of his wrist so that he might not forget them.

Dr. Wood walked over to his desk and picked up another book, which he held up briefly for the class to see. "This book here, *Alias Shakespeare,* delves further into the Shakespeare mystery, and, as you can see, features a portrait of Edward de Vere on its cover."

He removed the cover and held it up to one side, so he, too, was able to view the picture. "I'll pass this around now, for those of you who may be interested," he said. "But let me just throw in something here about Shakespeare's portrait. In spite of the various renderings of the man called William Shakespeare in books about him and in anthologies of his works, *no actual verified portrait of him exists!* In that respect, I might add, he is much like Jesus Christ, who, as you may know, continues to have his portrait drawn purely from artists' imaginations even to this day. But the most famous supposed likeness of Shakspere is the Martin Droeshout copper-engraved portrait that appeared in the First Folio of 1623, and that's the standard one we see most often, the one that's reproduced in your textbook. But we must remember that Martin Droeshout was only fifteen years old when Shakspere died, and the engraving was made seven years after that. It's highly improbable that Martin Droeshout ever even laid eyes on the man."

Dr. Wood glanced down at the portrait of Oxford on the dust jacket. "But just look at *this* man's portrait, look at those features, and you know, you simply *know*, that you are looking into the face of the true author of those marvelous works, and it breaks my heart that he has not received the credit that I feel is his due."

Blue could feel his own heartbeat throbbing in his chest, and he found himself strangely moved and excited by the depth of his teacher's feeling about a person who has been dead for four hundred years. When the dust jacket got passed to him, he spread it open and looked at it intently. He noted the feathered black cap and the typical high, fancy collar. But, most of all, he noted the man's eyes, small, brown, piercing eyes—accusing even—that right eye especially, looking directly into his. Blue suddenly experienced what felt like the explosion of thousands of tiny stars in his arms and chest—the very same sensation he remembered feeling many years before, when the challenge of Pierre de Fermat's Last Theorem first fired his dreams and imagination.

Now the kid sitting in front of Blue was extending his hand. "Hey, pass it on," he said. Blue turned away from him, holding the cover portrait of Edward de Vere out of his reach for a few seconds longer, before finally letting it out of his grasp.

"Oh, yes," Dr. Wood was saying. "About your memorization assignment. Now, I've long been of the opinion that, as far as Shakespeare is concerned, one of the things we high-school teachers do best is instill a lifelong hatred of the poor fellow in each and every one of you."

Blue smiled, along with most of the other students in the class.

"And one of our best weapons for accomplishing this is to force rote memorization upon you." Dr. Wood looked round the room, as if for confirmation. "Right?"

"Right!" the students exclaimed, their faces reflecting a glimmer of hope that somehow they might be spared this ordeal.

"Well, it *is* a mandated requirement, and I can't get around it, but"—and here he walked to his desk and put his hand on a foot-high stack of papers—"but I'm not limited as to *what* you should memorize. So—through the years I've put together quite a wide selection of direct quotations from Shakespeare's works, arranged according to subject, together with explanatory notes when needed. Grab one on your way out—they're yours to keep—and you can read through them and memorize those bits which speak most directly to you. Fair enough?"

As Dr. Wood began to erase the board and the kids were stretching and unwinding, waiting for the bell to ring, Blue happened to glance at the girl sitting across from him. Her textbook was open and she was still gazing at the Droeshout engraving, universally recognized as the true likeness of the poet and playwright known by the name of William Shakespeare. Blue was surprised at the sudden wave of resentment he felt as he looked at the expressionless, masklike image. In fact, he could hardly stand to look at the picture of the man he now considered to be an impostor.

"Well, how about that!" Sheri whispered, leaning over toward Blue. "First day of our Shakespeare unit and already this guy is out the door—according to Dr. Wood, at least. So—I guess this is goodbye to you, Mr. Shakespeare," she added with a grin, snapping shut the book.

Blue smiled. Yes, he thought. Unless and until someone can convince me otherwise, it's goodbye, Mr. Shakespeare—hello, Oxford!

seven

There was a substitute teacher in Blue's fifth-period modern-history class and she was showing a video about the immigrant experience on Ellis Island. It was fairly interesting, but Blue had already seen it twice before. His mind began to wander, and suddenly he got an idea for a very clever puzzle. Trying his best not to attract his teacher's attention, he slowly removed the small notebook he always kept in his rear pocket and proceeded to jot the idea down. Reading it over after it was written, it occurred to him that this puzzle might present an interesting challenge for Josh.

"Hey, I got your message this morning," Blue said, as he and Louie were walking over to the computer lab after school. "I didn't have time to decode it, but it looks easy enough," he added, looking sideways at his friend.

"What message?" Louie asked. "I didn't send you anything."

"You didn't? Well, who else would send me something in code?"

Louie shrugged. "Search me."

Blue walked on in silence, wondering who in the world would be sending him a coded message. But his thoughts were interrupted when Louie remarked, "I hope Wylie really does show up. I don't know why he didn't tell me about this himself."

"Your *Chimera* game, you mean? How long has that thing been floating around, anyway?"

"Oh, man! *Too* long! It's my first commercial game, you know—before I did Boston and San Francisco, even. So I'm anxious to see it."

"You haven't seen it yet?"

"No! When Wylie's uncle started up his company in San Jose, he said he'd have it out within six months, tops. He took all my disks and stuff and told me he'd let me know when it was ready to go."

"So you haven't kept in touch with him or anything?"

"No. I just figured it was all in his hands after that. Maybe that's where I dropped the ball."

"So how did you start doing stuff for that EduGamesInc guy?"

Louie smiled. "Just lucky, I guess. Mr. Compton put me in touch with him. They were college roommates or something. And Mr. Compton knew I was starting to work on a game using a map of San Francisco—and that was just the sort of thing Mr. Forni was looking for."

"So you're getting rich, huh?"

Louie laughed. "Yeah. I'm a millionaire. Bill Gates, watch out!" Then he added, "But the *real* money is generated in those developer shops—you know, where all these computer nerds get together and come up with these fantastic new action games? Compared to them, I'm really small potatoes, man."

There were a half-dozen kids in the lab when Blue and Louie walked in, but Wylie Seratt wasn't among them. Blue sat down at one of the computers and sent the following message to Josh.

```
Hey, Josh! Here's a riddle for you!
   Oshjay, age 16, is on a camping trip
with 5 of his friends. One of the boys is
15, another is the same age as Oshjay,
and the remaining three are all 17 years
old and have their driver's licenses. A
devastating killer storm is about to hit
the campground, and although the boys
were dropped off at the site by their
parents, they now have access to a
```

12-year-old sedan in running order. The problem: Oshjay's father (just like Louie DeSoto's) has given strict instructions that under no circumstances is Oshjay to ride in an automobile driven by any friend under the age of 18, since statistics show they are the most apt to be involved in accidents. However, when Oshjay arrives home after the 20-mile automobile journey, his father is not upset. Why?

I bet you can't figure that one out! If you can, I'm still at school so e-mail me right back!
Blue

"Hi, Professor Wood," Blue heard someone say. "Come on in."

Dr. Wood, looking strangely out of place, glanced around until he spotted Blue sitting at the computer. "Ah!" he said. "I was hoping I'd find you here."

Blue started to stand up. "Hi, Dr. Wood, what—"

"No, don't get up," he said, walking over and putting his hand on Blue's shoulder. "I was just wondering—if you're not involved in something here—if you might show me how to get connected on the Internet. I guess I'm one of the last holdouts," he added with a smile. "I don't even have a computer yet. Seems like the electric typewriter was my last great technological leap, but I do want to check out some of those Shakespeare sites Erica mentioned this morning."

Blue rose out of his chair. "Sure. Look, sit down here and I'll show you. There's really nothing to it."

Dr. Wood sat down at the computer while Blue leaned over him, gently nudging him to one side as he clicked on the server to get connected to the Web. "See, you just type in the name of your search engine, like so, and now you enter the word Shakespeare."

Dr. Wood leaned closer to the screen and nodded his head. "Yes. I see. But perhaps you should write those steps down for me so I can do it myself next time."

"Sure," Blue said, removing his hand from the mouse. "No problem. But, here, you take over now. You just scroll up and down like this until you find something that interests you, then click."

Dr. Wood grasped the mouse and scrolled down, then up again, and then in little circles. "Hey," he said, smiling, "this is neat." He leaned forward and studied the screen, already clicking and scrolling like an expert.

"This is truly amazing! It's a new world, Blue. With

just a flick of the wrist I can find information here that'd take me a week to locate—"

"Hey, Blue," Louie called out from the other side of the room. "Wylie's here. Come and take a look at this."

Blue hesitated, not sure if Dr. Wood could continue without him. "Are you okay, or—"

"No, you go right ahead. I've got this thing by the tail now."

A bunch of kids were already gathered around the computer as Wylie Seratt inserted the game disk. Louie wanted to see the case it came in, but before he could ask, Wylie had already put it out of his reach and started the game.

Blue was amazed. There on the screen were the same four little characters the Famous Four featured in their Super-Duper Puppet Show in the second grade—Omo, Bomo, Nomo, and Egads. The little guy named Egads looked exactly like the puppet Blue had made, with plastic Oreo cookies for ears and a red gumdrop nose.

"Hey, will you look at that!" Blue said. "I haven't thought about old Egads for years!"

"Shh!" Wylie said. "We can't hear the dialogue."

Blue nudged Louie. "You even got his ears right," he whispered.

It took a while for Wylie to demonstrate all the features

of the game. Blue was impressed. "That's pretty spectacular," he said, as the final credits began flashing on the screen. "I'm amazed you remembered our puppets so—"

"Hold it," Louie said, quickly raising his hand. "I want to see the ending of this."

In a few seconds it was over. Wylie removed the game disk from the computer and put it back in its little plastic case, while the kids who had been crowding around the monitor started to drift away and get their stuff together.

"Hey, Wylie! Hold it!" Louie said, reaching for the disk. "I want to see that again. I think I missed something. Hand it over for a minute."

Wylie turned quickly, avoiding Louie's grasp. "What for? You already saw it once." He stood up from his seat at the keyboard and started making his way across the room.

"Well, he wants to see it again," said Blue Avenger, suddenly realizing what Louie missed seeing was his name in the credits. "Hand it over, okay? We're not going to run off with it."

Louie suddenly made a lunge for the disk and snatched it out of Wylie's hand. "Give it *here*, I said!"

Blue was relieved when Wylie didn't attempt to grab it back from Louie. He'd hate to see his friend get into a scuffle, because then Blue would probably have to step in and smooth things over before Louie found himself in way over his head. Louie was a great kid, but at times his social skills needed a bit of fine-tuning. This time, however, Wylie just shrugged and walked over to talk to the custodian, who had just entered the room with his vacuum in tow. It was almost time for him to tidy up and lock the doors.

Louie slipped the disk back into the computer. "I didn't see my name in the opening credits," he said, looking at Blue over his shoulder. "But with those other guys in the way, I could have missed it. Anyway, I'm sure it wasn't at the end."

"Yeah, I didn't see it, either." Blue was beginning to feel a queasy nervousness in the pit of his stomach, something like the way he used to feel while waiting his turn at Mrs. Field's piano recitals—before he talked his mother into letting him quit taking lessons. Blue knew how much this meant to Louie, and he was almost positive his name was nowhere on that game.

"Okay, here we go," Louie said, clicking on the mouse. "Watch these credits, now." The name *Chimera* appeared amid colorful swirls of numbers, accompanied by upbeat mariachi music. Then came the logo for Seratt Games, Inc., and below it, in extra-large font, *Jackson Seratt, President*.

"Here come the names," Louie said. A list of job descriptions paired with names quickly scrolled by: *Producer, Seymour Starrs; Art Director, Philip R. Tank; Story and Graphics, Sonny Daze; Technician, Wylie Seratt.*

"Technician, Wylie Seratt!" they both exclaimed. But there was no mention at all of Louie DeSoto.

"I don't believe this!" Louie said. "My name's not there! Who are those people, anyway? Are they for real? Seymour Starrs? Sonny Daze did story and graphics? Who's *he*?"

Louie turned from the monitor and called to Wylie, who was out in the hallway now, talking with some other kids. "Hey, Wylie! How come my name's not in the credits? What's going on?"

Wylie walked over and took the disk from Louie. "Don't ask me. Call my uncle. Call Jackson. I don't know anything about it."

"Yeah, I *bet* you don't!" Louie said, turning away in disgust and muttering, "Snake in the grass!"

Blue threw an arm around his friend. "Man, it looks like you were royally screwed. But there must be something you can do. Hey, maybe you should get a lawyer—" Blue stopped in mid-sentence as the realization suddenly hit him: *This could be a case for Blue Avenger!*

Louie's eyes were beginning to turn red with anger. "Yeah. Listen, it's late. I'm supposed to pick up my mom at four. I'll call you later."

Blue watched his friend go out the door, and then he remembered Dr. Wood, who was still peering intently at the monitor in front of him. He looked up at that moment, and their eyes met. "Blue, would you come over here a minute, please? There's something I want to show you."

Blue walked over and pulled up a stool.

"Let's see if I can get it back for you," Dr. Wood said. "Ah! Here we go." He clicked on another link and waited for the connection. "Now, do you see that? You know what that is? That's the publisher's famous dedication to Shakespeare's *Sonnets* when they came out in 1609. Look how it's written here—*Shake-Speares Sonnets*, with the suspiciously hyphenated name, indicating to many that it was, indeed, a pseudonym. And another thing: Why is it phrased *Shake-Speares Sonnets*? That's the form used when an author is dead! Otherwise it would be in the usual form—*Sonnets by Shakespeare*.

"Now look here: *To the onlie begetter of these insuing sonnets*," he read. "And look, right there—the phrase that's caused so much speculation down through the years." Dr. Wood pointed to the words on the monitor. "See there?" he asked. "It says, *By our ever-living poet*.

Well, the thing is, Shakspere was *still alive* in 1609, when those sonnets were published! Shakspere was still alive and making real-estate deals in Stratford. Not doing any writing, of course," he added sarcastically. "But why should Thomas Thorpe, the publisher, refer to him as *our ever-living poet*? That's how people refer to a *dead* man." He touched Blue's arm and looked into his eyes. "A dead man like Oxford, for instance, who died in the year 1604."

Now Dr. Wood sat back in his chair and shook his head. "Our ever-living poet," he repeated. "Yes, Thomas Thorpe was doing the best he could. I can imagine him there, racking his brain, trying to think of some way to alert us future generations that things were not as they seemed. See, there—*ever*. Could be *E. Ver*, you know. Sometimes Oxford wrote his name that way."

Blue looked sideways at the professor and squinted at him. "Verrry mysterious!" he said softly. "I zink der iss zomting verrry fishy in Denmark—"

But Blue could tell from his teacher's expression that he was more annoyed than amused by his little attempt at humor.

"Laugh if you want to," Dr. Wood said tightly. "I'm just telling you what I think. So why would *you* suppose Thorpe would include a phrase like that?"

Blue hadn't the foggiest, of course, and suddenly felt contrite for joking about something his teacher obviously considered to be serious business. Wanting to make amends and also demonstrate that he intended to give the matter some further thought, Blue pulled his pen out of his pocket and started to write OUR EVER-LIVING on the inside of his wrist—right under Oxford's motto, VERO NIL VERIUS.

Dr. Wood looked up from the monitor. "What are you doing now?"

"Huh?"

"Do you always write notes on your body?"

"No, only important stuff." Blue held out his wrist so Dr. Wood could read it. "See? Here's Oxford's motto. I copied it from the board this morning."

Dr. Wood nodded. "Yes, so I see." He stood up and shook Blue's hand, man to man. "Thanks for the computer lesson, Blue. And I'll see you tomorrow." Professor Wood felt strangely exhilarated as he walked out of the room. He couldn't have wished for a finer disciple to champion Oxford's cause than Blue Avenger.

Even though the custodian had already turned on the vacuum, Blue knew he'd at least have time to check his mail before getting chased out of the room. Could Josh figure out why Oshjay's father would not be upset? It was kind of tricky, but really not that difficult if he had read the riddle carefully. Blue quickly logged on and read Josh's note:

```
Dear Blue
I know the answer. Its easy. It was
because when Oshjay got home his father
was dead.
Josh
```

Blue felt a dull ache in his chest, and the screen suddenly became slightly blurred. That was certainly not the answer he was looking for. Poor Josh. He seemed to have adjusted pretty well to their father's death, but was it still really on his mind that much?

When Blue got home that afternoon he asked his little brother if maybe he'd like to go with him to the movies on Saturday.

EIGHT

Blue couldn't stand it anymore. He had to have a serious talk with Omaha. Since they had no classes together at all this semester and different lunch periods, he couldn't even count on seeing her at school every day. He called her before his mother got home from work.

"Omaha, I can't stand it anymore. We have to have a serious talk."

"Who *is* this?"

Oh, God. There she goes, being funny. At least she must be feeling better, finally.

"So—when? When can we talk?"

"Blue, I don't know what good it would do. I know what you want, but I'm not going to change my mind."

Blue was instantly disgusted with himself. He *knew* she was going to answer this way, but still he had neglected to rehearse a new response. So what could he say now?

"I guess you heard about Tonia and Stevie?" Omaha asked, after a short pause.

"No. Who's Tonia and Stevie?"

"They broke up today. Just before my English class. It was really terrible."

"Well, who forced them to break up? I didn't."

"They hate each other."

Blue didn't answer.

Omaha put her mouth up close to the phone, even though she was home alone. "Listen, Blue," she said. "You know there is no guy in the world I like better than you, but still—"

"Like?"

"For God's sake, Blue. I'm on the *phone*!"

Blue's whole world suddenly stood still and his breath caught in his throat. What an unexpected and wonderful thing for her to say at a time like this: *I'm on the phone!*

"Okay, then," she whispered finally. "*Love.* But that's all the more reason we *don't* have to go steady. Don't you see?"

"No."

Omaha just sighed. There was no girl in town more confident and determined than Omaha Nebraska Brown, for she felt secure in the knowledge that her insistence on independence was the best protection she could have against ever hearing the words *I have to go now, baby*—

Blue sighed, too. If there was a more miserable guy in

town, Blue would sure like to meet him.

"Okay," Omaha said, still speaking so quietly he could hardly hear her. "How's this: What if we make a deal. If ever someone should come along, some guy I like more than you—"

Just the suggestion of that possibility felt like a knife through Blue's heart.

"If that should happen," she continued—"not that I expect it will—but if that *does* happen, I swear you will be the first to know."

Blue was truly shocked. Sarcasm was the only possible response. "Oh, what a *comfort* that is! *The first to know!* Oh, I had no idea you cared about me *so much*."

Omaha almost smiled. He was so funny when he got sarcastic like that. "So will you do the same for me?" she asked. "If ever you should meet another girl that you—" She stopped in mid-sentence, her mood suddenly changing once she realized exactly what she was about to ask. She couldn't believe that the thought of him liking someone else better than her could have had such an effect on her. Was she really *that* far gone?

As for Blue, he couldn't imagine himself caring for anyone more than he cared for her. But he knew when he was beaten—at least for now—and abruptly changed the subject.

"I'm taking Josh to the movies on Saturday afternoon," he said. "You want to come?"

"So will you do the same for me?" Omaha repeated.

Blue took a long time before answering. "Okay," he said finally.

"Good. It's a deal, then."

They both paused a moment, in a kind of tribute to their pact. Even though it was not the kind of commitment Blue wanted, it was something.

"About the movies, though," Omaha said, "I have swimming practice until one. If it's after that I can go." She didn't ask why Josh had to come along. She knew Blue's mother worked on Saturdays and Blue had to look after his little brother. But she didn't mind, since Josh was obviously crazy about her, which she thought was awfully cute.

"It'll be after one, then," Blue said.

"Did I tell you I got accepted on the boys' team?"

"What?"

"On the boys' swim team. They accepted me. I'm the only girl this semester. Mr. Frazier suggested I try out. He said since I want to go to Yale it might look good on my application."

Blue felt sick. "Well, that's good, I guess."

"So that's another thing. I'll be getting rides to the meets and stuff, and if we were going steady you probably wouldn't like that, and then we'd start arguing about it, maybe, and then maybe we'd break up. Don't you understand, Blue? If you don't go steady, you can't break up."

Blue didn't want to hear any more. He wanted to get off the phone. "Well, I have to start memorizing some Shakespeare now—"

"Same here," Omaha said. "So I guess I'll see you Saturday, if not before."

"Goodbye, Omaha," Blue said, and hung up the phone. He went into the kitchen and grabbed a can of soda out of the refrigerator. Then he sat down at the table and put his head in his hands. My God! The only girl on the team! He toyed with the idea of phoning her right back and asking her if she'd met someone new yet, someone she *liked* better than him. But his better judgment prevailed, and he realized she would think it neither clever nor funny.

The day's mail was still on the table, and after a while he began flipping through the new issue of *News!* magazine. However, he missed the three-page spread featuring the movie Josh wanted to see, complete with pictures and descriptions of some of the fun spin-off products available, including a disgustingly realistic soft-plastic model of a substance which all too graphically illustrates what can happen when a concept known as the Whoopee Cushion is carried to extremes. And that was too bad—

the fact that he missed the three-page magazine spread—because, *had* he seen it, he could have made alternate Saturday movie plans for Omaha and Josh. This is the capsule review which was printed in a boxed sidebar:

> *"Three's a Gas* stars Buster B. Bodwell, the audacious new comic phenomenon from Australia, and features three delectable beauties as his three frequently frustrated girl-friends—one of which is his wife! Although the humor is scintillatingly sophomoric, it is copiously compensated for by having absolutely no expiating excuses whatsoever! This groundbreaking movie lowers the bar past all decency, happily setting new lows for rollicking, ribald humor! Double-entendres pile on double-entendres, so tote your titters to the theater and be sure to leave your good taste at the door! The five-year-old triplets (still not potty-trained!) are a squishy sensation! To use one of Buster B.'s own masterful catch phrases, "Hey, grab it quick before it slips away!""

(Cynical readers drawn to conspiracy theories may doubt the sincerity of that rave review and three-page spread. But why should they—just because the company that produced the movie and licensed the spin-offs is owned by the corporate parent of the very magazine that reviewed it? So what ice does that cut?)

As Blue continued to flip through the pages of the magazine, a loose, postage-paid subscription-order card for a new publication called *Mr. WiseGuy* slipped to the floor, and when he reached down to pick it up, he thought he noticed some irregularities in the quoted subscription prices. He folded it in half and slipped it into his shirt pocket. There was a distinct possibility that a letter from Blue Avenger would soon be landing on the desk of the unsuspecting publisher of *Mr. WiseGuy* magazine.

The doorbell rang after dinner that night. It was Uncle Ralphy with a Mac G-3 and a nineteen-inch monitor still in their boxes sitting there on the porch beside him.

"Hi, kid," he said when Blue opened the door. "I got your message about the Samwich Wagon. Tough luck. Listen—I'll keep my eyes open. Maybe something else'll turn up. In the meantime, though, I've got something for you. Give me a hand here, will you?"

They carried the boxes inside and set them down in the front room.

"Yo, Sally," Uncle Ralphy called out as he and Blue started to unpack them. "Where do you want this junk?"

Sally walked into the room and said, "Oh, hello, Ralph." Then she noticed the new computer and monitor. "Oh, my! Well, I guess we can put it on the desk in the dining room—exchange it for the old one. Are you lending it to the boys, or—"

"Nope. It's theirs," he said. "I made a deal."

"Hey, cool!" Josh said, fingering the keyboard. "And look at that monster monitor."

"Don't touch it," Blue said. "Look at your hands. What *is* that stuff?"

Josh stared at his hands a minute and then quickly held them up right in front of Blue's face. "Rattlesnake guts!" he said, wiggling his fingers. "And lizard's gizzards!"

"This monitor's going to be a tight squeeze all right," Ralphy said, after a short, dismissing glance at Josh. "But it'll fit." He unplugged the old computer and monitor and set them on the dining-room table while Blue started to clear off the desk. He picked up the printout with the encoded message he had left there in the morning, folded it, and stuck it in his pocket.

"Hey, I got an idea!" Josh said. "Maybe Blue could move out, and then we could put it in his room!"

"Looks practically new," Blue said. "And a Mac, too. A lot better than the ones we have at school. It's just great! God, wait till Louie sees it! You didn't *buy* it, did you? Where'd you get it, anyway?"

"Got it from Nick Basso—an old customer of mine." Uncle Ralphy looked at Blue. "Hey, you met him once, kid. Remember that guy in the shop who was complaining about those big crooks in Washington—and you got right back at him by saying maybe some other form of government would be better than ours? Remember how he backpedaled his way out of that one!"

Blue grinned. "Yeah."

"Well, that's the guy. He bought this thing and never could figure out how to get it going. I told him maybe he should read the instruction book, but he didn't want to do that." Ralphy laughed and shook his head. "Finally, he got so frustrated he was ready to chuck the thing. So we worked out a trade. I got the computer and he gets a year's worth of free trims."

"Well, that's very thoughtful of you, Ralph," Sally started to say.

"Nah! I figure I got the best of the deal. The guy's practically bald." He reached over and gave Blue a little punch on the shoulder and Josh a fist rub on the head, but not too hard.

After Uncle Ralphy left, Blue was lying on his back on the couch in the front room, holding the paper with the encoded message from DYAD LARK aloft with his raised left hand.

"I went on a gondola ride today," Josh said. "At Lake Merritt."

"That's nice," Blue said, beginning to get really frustrated with DYAD LARK. He knew it would be impossible to figure out the code without some sort of key, and he felt that was the function of the screen name, DYAD LARK. Trying to break a code containing just a series of numbers mixed with letters without a key to give it meaning would be an exercise in futility.

"My teacher fell in the water and almost drowned."

"She did not."

"The gondolier jumped in after her."

"He did not."

"And then his accordion fell in, too, and all the people on shore starting yelling and clapping and hollering, 'Sink the accordion! The accordion from hell! Sink the accordion!' "

"Josh, will you be quiet. I'm trying to figure something out here."

"Later, Ms. Hamster told us that everybody thinks the accordion is *Italy's* national instrument, but it really is France's. Did you know that? I bet you didn't know that the accordion is *France's* national instrument! So you don't know *every*thing, do you?"

Blue closed his eyes a minute and tried to think. Could it possibly be a message from Omaha? No, not likely. For one thing, she doesn't have a computer. And if she *were* to send him a message in code, she'd tell him about it. Hey, maybe they could give their old computer to Omaha! He'd ask his mom later, after she got out of the shower. Omaha's been wanting to get on-line. Plus, it'd be great to be able to send e-mail to her, especially from Venice—

"Trevor Loomis was sitting next to Megan Ames on the gondola and she dared him to kiss her, so he did. And then, when the ride was over, old Megan ran over to Ms. Hamster and tattled on him. 'Trevor kissed me on the gondola!' she said. And Trevor was there and he said, 'No, I didn't! I kissed her on the *lips*!' " Josh started laughing. "Get it? He didn't kiss her on the *gondola*!" Now he was laughing even louder. "Where's her gondola, anyway? Hey, brother Blue! Did you ever kiss Omaha on the gondola?"

"Keep Omaha out of your stupid, idiotic kindergarten jokes, please. And your teacher's name is not really Ms. Hamster."

"Yes, it is! Ms. Ima Hamster! That's her name. Really. Really, it is. That's her real name! Don't you believe me?"

Blue sighed and shook his head. Was he like that at Josh's age? Not likely! He looked again at DYAD LARK. Could it be an anagram? He had been accustomed to working anagrams since he first learned to read, and if they were not too long, he didn't even need a pencil. DYAD LARK—how about ARK LADDY? Well, that didn't make much sense. He tried moving a D from LADDY and adding it to ARK. Now it became DARK LADY. Since Blue had not read his homework, he was unable to connect DARK LADY to Shakespeare's *Sonnets*, although it did occur to him that Tuesday Thomas might refer to *herself* as DARK LADY. Tuesday Thomas! Maybe he was getting somewhere now! He looked more closely at the code:

55K10C81D28F135G36C138F24M76L147G127A

Let's see, he thought. Numbers of two or more digits followed by a single letter, the numbers ranging from a low of 10 to a high of 147. And there was no letter past the letter M in the alphabet. Blue had long ago memorized the number equivalents of letters. The letter M corresponded to the number 13, but he didn't know if that would be of any help deciphering this code or not.

As he lay there thinking, his eyes happened to wander off of the code on the printout and focus on the penned-in letters on his inner wrist.

VERO NIL VERIUS
OUR EVER-LIVING

His eyes lingered there, and soon he started to notice something very peculiar. Two V's in each phrase, two R's, the O's match—

Blue jumped off the couch and grabbed a pencil. He could feel his heart thumping in his chest as he methodically crossed out the letters in the two phrases. He couldn't believe his eyes. Except for the final S in VERO NIL VERIUS and the final G in OUR EVER-LIVING, he had an anagram!

Yes! Except for the final letters in each phrase, Edward de Vere's family motto, VERO NIL VERIUS, could be made into an anagram for OUR EVER-LIVING, the words used by Thomas Thorpe in his dedication of *Shake-Speares Sonnets*—the words Dr. Wood suspected of being the publisher's way of telling us that the poems were *not* written by a man still living—as William Shakspere was—but that the real author was Edward de Vere, the seventeenth Earl of Oxford!

Blue let out a yelp and called to his mother and Josh to come and see what he had discovered. Josh couldn't have cared less, of course, and after Blue had spent several minutes trying to point out the significance of his find to his mother, the initial charge of excitement was gone, like an obscure joke that must be explained. "Oh, *I* see!" Sally said finally, but Blue knew she was just trying to be nice.

Then he got the idea to call Dr. Wood, but there were over a dozen "J." or "James Wood"s listed in the directory and he couldn't call them all. He'd just have to wait until morning.

Even though it was after eleven when Blue turned in, he soon realized that he was too excited to sleep. So he switched on his light and retrieved the postcard from his shirt pocket—the postcard that had fallen out of the magazine that afternoon. Then he quietly made his way to the dining room and sat down at the new computer. He looked at the postcard again and quickly did a few calculations to verify his suspicions and get the numbers right. Then he went on-line and located the name and address of the publisher of *Mr. WiseGuy* magazine.

It took him longer than he thought it would to compose the letter:

```
Archibald Stern, Publisher
Mr. WiseGuy Magazine
845 Third Avenue
New York, NY 10022
```

Dear Mr. Stern:

I recently came into possession of an invitation to subscribe to your magazine in the form of a postage-paid "business reply card" which I am enclosing for your perusal. As you can see, your so-called "MONEY-SAVING DEAL" gives me "two options" for subscribing to Mr. WiseGuy, for which you will "gladly bill me later":

Money-Saving Deal!

Simply Check the Plan You Desire and Drop This Card in the Mail <u>TODAY!</u>

Regular Price
Thirty-nine (39) weeks at 63¢ per week.

$ave $$

Two full years (104 wks!) for only $72.80!

This Offer Will Expire Soon! Send <u>no money</u> now! (We will gladly bill you later.)

As the chief Mr. WiseGuy, Mr. Stern, you
must think we are all Mr. StupidGuys who
can't add, subtract, multiply, or divide,
since your "$ave $$" option costs MORE than
your "Regular Price" one!

Allow me to explain: The cost for one
issue at your Regular Price is 63 cents,
while the cost for one issue at your $ave
$$ price is 70 cents! In other words, the
person who chooses to "$ave $$" will
actually LOSE $7.28 over the course of
two years!

Oh, sure, I realize that $7.28 won't buy
a whole lot in today's market, but just
for fun let's multiply that amount by
1,000,000 and see what we get!
$7,280,000! Now, that's a lot of money!
Pretty amazing, isn't it?

I believe I may want to speak to some of
my attorney friends about a possible
class-action suit unless you can assure
me by return mail that this reprehensible

```
subterfuge foisted on an unsuspecting
public will be corrected immediately.

Sincerely,
Blue Avenger
```

Blue read the letter over a couple of times and then
decided maybe he was being a bit too hard on Mr. Stern.
It was possible that he didn't even *know* about the offer.
Maybe it was just an honest mistake on the part of some
mathematically challenged underling. At any rate, Blue
decided to add a P.S.

```
P.S. If you would like to plead
ignorance in this matter, Mr. WiseGuy, I
will entertain your explanation, if it
is presented in a civilized and
businesslike manner.
```

A few minutes later, as Blue watched the finished
letter crawling its way out of the printer, he wondered
why he still felt empty and vaguely dissatisfied. Then he
suddenly realized that, though he couldn't be sure his
letter would accomplish its purpose, writing it was
merely a means of marking time until he could really sink

his teeth into righting *larger* wrongs. And, oddly enough, the two injustices he had in mind were cut from the same cloth—although they were oceans apart and separated by four hundred years of history.

But hadn't he just discovered an anagram to beat all anagrams? Could anything be too difficult for Blue Avenger now?

Earlier that same day, at the DeSoto home, Louie was impatiently waiting for his father to come home from work. He wanted to check with him before he went ahead and called Jackson Seratt.

"So you turned *all* your stuff over to him?" his father asked, after Louie had explained what happened. "*Every*thing? Your notes and everything?"

"Well, yeah. I had no reason *not* to. I mean—"

Mr. DeSoto checked his watch. "Well, okay. Seratt may still be in. Get me his number. I'll give him a call."

Louie stood pacing nearby as his father punched in the number. "Hello? Mr. Seratt? This is Elias DeSoto, Louie's father. Yes. Well, Louie tells me he saw his *Chimera* game today and that—"

Soon it was obvious to Louie that Jackson Seratt was doing most of the talking. His father would start to say something and then he'd stop talking and listen. This went on for several exchanges.

Louie was becoming extremely frustrated.

"Well, I know Louie spent a lot of time working on—

"Well, no, but—

"No. No, he didn't."

Louie couldn't stand it. "What's he saying, Dad?"

Mr. DeSoto, still listening, put his finger over his lips. Finally, he said, "Yes. I see. But just the same, I'm going to talk to my lawyer tomorrow." Another pause. "Well, we'll see about that, too! Goodbye, Mr. Seratt."

"So what'd he say?" Louie asked with a slight tremor in his voice.

"He just says it's his. Says his people worked on it—"

Louie hit his thigh with the palm of his hand. "Rotten to the core!"

"Listen," he father said, "I'll talk to this lawyer friend of mine tomorrow. Name's Cameron Sweet. He works over in Legal, and he doesn't mind dispensing advice in cases like this. You know, when someone's just asking for clarification. Don't worry. We'll try and straighten this thing out."

"Louie?" It was his mother calling to him from the kitchen. "Louie, will you come here a minute?"

Louie started walking toward the kitchen. "What? What do you want?"

"How about asking David over for dinner tomorrow? I don't know if you realize it or not, but you boys will be leaving for Venice in just two weeks. We should talk to David—"

"Blue, Mom! Blue!" Louie was in an extremely bad mood. "He changed his name, remember? He doesn't like it when people still call him David."

"Well, whatever his name is, will you ask him over for dinner? We should make some lists, figure out what you should pack—"

"Okay!" Louie interrupted. "I'll ask him!" *Jackson Seratt! My God! What a disgusting little creep he turned out to be!*

nine

Blue was so anxious to tell Dr. Wood about the anagram that on the following morning he got to school extra early and waited for him in the faculty parking lot, and when his teacher finally drove up and parked, Blue was standing right there alongside the car.

Dr. Wood opened the door carefully and started to step out, but Blue stopped him in his tracks.

"Boy, do I have something to show *you*!" Blue said, holding the car door open, but also not giving Dr. Wood enough room to stand up.

"May I at least get out of the car?" his teacher asked with raised brows and a curious smile.

"Oh, sorry." Blue stepped aside while Dr. Wood stood up and locked the door.

Blue had his little pocket notebook opened to a blank page, and he started printing out the two phrases just the way he had them on his wrist.

"Now, watch this!" he said, holding the notebook

under Dr. Wood's nose. "First, I'm going to cross out this final S from VERO NIL VERIUS, and the final G from OUR EVER-LIVING, like so." And then he proceeded to cross out the other letters in sequence, stopping after each step to glance meaningfully at his teacher.

"My God!" exclaimed Dr. Wood. "It's an anagram!" He stared at Blue in amazement and took the notebook from his hand. "Let me see that!"

Blue nervously began flicking his fingers one by one with his thumb while crowding in close and watching as his teacher repeated the process.

"Well, you're right!" Dr. Wood said. "This is *really* something! How did you happen to discover this? It's amazing!"

Blue was simply overjoyed. The lettering on his inner wrist had mostly been washed away when he showered, but there were still a few traces remaining. He held up his arm for Dr. Wood to see. "I was just lucky, I guess. Since I just happened to have the two phrases written together here, when I looked at them, the anagram practically jumped out at me."

"Well, as soon as I get a chance I'm going to call an old friend of mine back east who's active in the Shakespeare Oxford Society. I want to see if this thing has ever been pointed out before, and if not, I'll certainly see that it is, and that you get proper recognition for it." Dr. Wood looked at his watch. "It's still early. Walk over to my classroom with me, will you? I want to give you something."

Blue waited while Dr. Wood unlocked the door to his classroom and then followed him inside. He really didn't know what to expect, so he was surprised and honored when Dr. Wood picked up the thick black book called *The Mysterious William Shakespeare: The Myth and the Reality* by Charlton Ogburn—the book that he had held up in class the day before—and solemnly handed it to him like an offering. "I want you to have this, Blue," he said. "I didn't mention it in class, but it happens to be an autographed copy. My only request is that you study it in the pure and honest spirit with which it was written."

Blue nodded, momentarily unable to speak, wondering why he felt, once again, like a make-believe superhero in his own comic strip.

"Did you hear that, kids?" Mrs. DeSoto asked. "It's up to forty-three million now, and *some*body is going to win it!"

She was sitting in the back seat of the car with Drusie, while Blue was up in front with Louie. They had just picked up Mrs. DeSoto from the elementary school where she taught third grade, and now they were headed down the freeway to the DeSotos' house. The radio was tuned to Drusie's favorite station, mostly music with brief news breaks.

"So here's what I'm going to do," Mrs. DeSoto was saying. "I have extra Lotto cards at home, one for each of us, including your father, of course," she added, motioning to Louie and Drusie with a wave of her hand. "And after dinner we'll have a little session and choose our lucky numbers. Then, tomorrow, I'll turn them in at Gene's Quickmart and pay the five dollars. *But,*" she added with a warning smile, "if one of us wins, we split the loot! Don't forget that!"

"Only one thing, Mom," Louie said from the driver's seat. "We can't play. Remember? Underage?"

"Oh, pooh-pooh! There's a simple way to get around that! I'll just let you kids pick the numbers and then I'll enter them all under *my* name."

Blue turned sideways in his seat and smiled at Drusie and her mother. He didn't know Mr. DeSoto too well, but the guy must be a genius. With a mother like that, how else to account for a brainy kid like Louie and a— ah, well, he didn't know exactly how to describe Drusie.

"But, Mom, if all the tickets are in *your* name, when

one of us wins you won't *have* to split the loot!" Drusie said, smiling back at Blue and bouncing around in time to the music.

Blue suddenly noticed some unusual commotion a distance ahead of them on the other side of the divided freeway. "Hey, look at that!" he said.

A small open trailer carrying a load of firewood had broken away from the badly dented pickup truck that was towing it, and now the loose trailer was careening diagonally across the freeway, slowly losing speed and heading directly into the oleander bushes growing along-side the center divider.

"Wow!" Drusie exclaimed, turning her head and look-ing out the back window. "It's lucky no one was hurt! Did you *see* that thing?"

"That's why I just *hate* freeway driving!" Mrs. DeSoto said.

"Oh, yes, it can be dangerous all right," Blue agreed, feeling guilty for his unkind thoughts about her mental capacity and attempting to make amends by polite conversation.

The radio was still playing, and now a female vocalist started screaming over and over something about how she wanted to "jasey bacum yow-oweee!" At least that's what it sounded like to Blue, but, apparently, Drusie knew the song, because she started to join in every couple of words. *"Gimme jaasey ahh neeeja yowy."* When the song was over Louie reached down and shut the radio off.

"Hey!" Drusie said.

"Sorry. Driver's choice." Louie turned to Blue. "An old family thing," he explained.

Blue shrugged. "Whatever works." He moistened his lips. Lately, since being around Louie and computers so much, he had begun to think a lot in computer-game terms.

"Hey, Louie," he said. "That loose trailer back there gave me an idea—"

"Yeah? What about?"

"For a new little-kids' computer game, actually. See, you could have this trailer full of chickens, for instance, and it becomes unhooked from its pickup truck just like that one did, and it sails across the freeway, and suddenly the air could be filled with chickens—red hens clucking hysterically, roosters with big tails and those things sticking out of their feet—those talons, I mean—and cuddly little baby chicks flying through the air like—like so many yellow tennis balls. The kids could count them, make groups and stuff like that."

"Sounds good," Louie said dully. "Why don't you write one?"

Drusie leaned forward and put her hands on the back of Blue's seat. "Yeah, Louie! You could call it *Freeway Chickens*. And it could come in two versions—girls' and boys'. You can do that, can't you? Fix it so you just click on the version you want?"

Louie didn't answer.

"Like, in the girls' version," Drusie went on, talking faster now, "the chickens could all wear these cute costumes, they could dance and go on dates—"

"And in the *boys'* version," Blue broke in, thinking of Josh, "all the chickens suddenly have to go to the bathroom—"

Drusie whooped with laughter.

"Makes a real mess," Blue continued. "Stuff hitting windshields, cars skidding around—"

"And lots of sound effects!" Drusie added, with more laughter. "But, back to the girls' version, the chickens could all do the chicken dance! Remember that one we used to do at Martin Luther?" Drusie stuck out her elbows and did her chicken imitation. "Cluck, cluck, cluck!"

Blue was not to be outdone. "That's good, but, for the boys' version, the roosters could suddenly sprout antennae and several more legs. Maybe the hens could develop big humanlike breasts and wear high heels. Or is that too advanced for little kids, Louie?"

Louie just kept on driving.

Now Drusie was getting caught up in the boys' version. "Hey, the roosters *could* get a bit menacing and threatening. The cars could retaliate by trying to run over the chickens. Guys with machine guns could suddenly appear, leaning out windows and shooting—"

"So there you go, Louie!" Blue said, turning his head again and smiling back at Drusie. "All plotted out for you. Simple as that!"

Louie answered only by saying, "Jeez!" under his breath in a really disgusted way, and turning the radio back on.

"Well, what's wrong with *him*?" Drusie asked, rolling her eyes at Blue while motioning toward Louie with a quick movement of her head.

Actually, there was nothing wrong with Louie. He was just thinking that people who come up with great ideas for computer games (or novels) and think they're doing people a big favor by telling them about it, should just shut up and write it themselves if they think it's so easy.

Little Sheree Siam Kapwilla (who's all grown up now, but still obliged to spell out her unusual name when ordering subscriptions or mail-order items over the phone) once wrote a poem in the second grade about freeway driving:

My Daddy ~~likes~~ likes to drive on freeways

But Mommy ~~likes~~ likes the streets

But I don't care how we get there

When we go to ~~grandmas~~ Grandma's house I get

lots of tre~~x~~ats.

"Driving Cars"
by Sheree Siam Kapwilla (age 7)
*(From Mrs. Reuben's corrected stack of "Our Poems"
for the children to recopy in time for Open House)*

ten

As soon as they got home, Drusie changed out of her white blouse and blue skirt into a short pink cotton T-shirt and a pair of jeans. Then she got three cans of soda out of the refrigerator and went to join Blue and Louie in Louie's room, where Louie was complaining about Shakespeare.

"I'm having a devil of a time trying to memorize that stuff," Louie said. "And what's the purpose, anyway? A complete waste of time, in my book. I spent over an hour last night with this meaningless crap and I still haven't nailed it."

Drusie was sitting on the floor now, leaning against Louie's dresser, with the cat in her lap and a can of soda in her hand. She was just about to take a sip when Louie made his unfortunate remark. "Meaningless crap?" she repeated incredulously, and with such force that the cat suddenly leaped up and made it all the way to the bed in one jump.

"Whoa, kitty!" Blue said. "Did you see that? Jungle cat!"

"Yes, I said meaningless, asinine, nonsensical, half-witted, dopey *crap*!"

"And that's putting it mildly," Blue said with a straight face.

Drusie, more calm now, smiled and stood up, fetched the cat, and went back to her spot and curled up on the rug again. Blue wondered if Omaha had a pink cotton T-shirt. (He knew she had a pair of jeans.)

"You know something, Louie?" Drusie said rather haughtily, running her hand through her hair. "You only show your ignorance when you talk about Shakespeare like that."

"Oh, is that right?" Louie reached for the textbook lying open on his desk. "Okay, then, listen to this. This is part of what I'm supposed to memorize." He cleared his throat, preparing to read, but first he said, "Oh, yeah, this is from act one, scene four. Hamlet speaking: *The king doth wake to-night and takes his rouse, / Keeps wassail, and the swaggering up-spring reels; / And as he drains his draughts of Rhenish down, / The kettle-drum and trumpet thus bray out / The triumph of his pledge.*"

Louie leaned forward and looked directly into Drusie's eyes. "Now," he challenged, "what's *that* supposed to mean?"

Blue laughed, but Drusie didn't think it was funny. "So what do the notes say? Or did you bother to read them?"

"Nah," Louie said, putting the book back on the desk. "I didn't read them."

"Well, then, how do you expect to understand what you're reading?"

"That's it exactly!" Louie said loudly. "I shouldn't have to read *notes* in order to understand what I'm reading!"

"Yeah, right!" Drusie said sarcastically. "Stephen King doesn't have *notes*!"

Louie exhaled through his mouth and said sharply, "I don't read Stephen King that much anymore and you know it."

Drusie wasn't ready to give up yet. "It's no different from math, in a way, you know."

"What's no different from math?"

"Shakespeare! I mean, let's say you give a second-year algebra book to somebody who's never been exposed to math—somebody from, oh, I don't know—"

"Mars?" Blue suggested. "Somebody from Mars?"

Drusie rolled her eyes and feigned exasperation. "Oh, all right. Mars. Anyway, even if this Martian is a born mathematical genius he won't be able to do the problems, because he doesn't understand the symbols. Don't you see? It's the same exact thing with Shakespeare. You just have to learn the jargon, that's all."

Drusie suddenly stood up and headed for the door. "Listen, I know just what you need. I'll go get it."

She was back in a minute with a small paperback book, which she gently tossed in Louie's direction.

"What's this?" He read the title. "It's just a copy of *Hamlet*."

"Yeah, but this one is special. Give it here. I'll show you. That part you recited, it's in act one, right?"

"Act one, scene four."

Drusie found the passage and started reading. *"The king is celebrating tonight: Drinking deep, making merry, and rollicking to wild dances. And as he drains his tankards of Rhenish wine, kettledrums and trumpets blare out in celebration of his toasts."*

"Let's see that," Louie said. "Where'd you get that?"

"Where do you think? I bought it." Drusie handed him the book, holding the pages open to the part she had just read.

Louie read it over for himself. "Humph," he said. "Shakespeare on one side, English on the other. Cool. But, still, for me, he's just not relevant, and until somebody can prove that his plays actually have something to do with *my* life—with *our* lives today—I mean, just look at his plots, for God's sake!"

Drusie took careful aim at Louie's wastebasket and sent her empty soda can flying through the air in a slow, high arc, scoring a direct hit. "Oh, puh-*leeze*, Louie! What do you know about Shakespeare's plots? You don't know *anything* about Shakespeare's plots."

Louie shrugged and snorted and wiped his hand across his mouth. "Well, I know all I want to know. And I know he's not worth the struggle." He looked at Blue. "What about you?"

Blue gazed down at his hands, feeling his knuckles and examining his palms. "You know, I really can't say yet. With a reputation like his, I mean, there must be *some* reason for it."

"Sheez!" Louie breathed. "*You* can keep looking for the reason, but I'm just going to do what it takes to pass this class and that's it."

"Listen, Louie. I feel just like you, in a way. I mean, I can't see what his plays have to do with my life, either. From what I know of them, anyway. Now, if something or somebody can point out the similarities, I might be persuaded to change my mind." And then, just to be funny, Blue cupped his hands around his mouth and said, "Yoo-hoo? Anybody listening out there? Anybody hear that? Shakespeare? Shakspere? Oxford? Anybody?"

"Hey, cut that out," Louie said, half-jokingly, not bothering to ask who Shakspere and Oxford were. "You're giving me the willies."

"One of Shakespeare's ghosts will probably be coming round to set you straight," Drusie said.

"Yeah. Right." Louie got up from where he was sitting at the end of his bed, walked over to his desk, and turned on his computer.

Blue scooted his chair a little closer to Drusie. "Did Miss Wooliscroft say anything at all about the authorship question?"

"Authorship question?"

"Yeah. Like who *really* wrote Shakespeare's plays. Dr. Wood talked about that for almost the entire period yesterday."

"Well, Miss Wooliscroft didn't even mention it."

"Dr. Wood thinks the name William Shakespeare is just the pen name of this nobleman named Edward de Vere, the seventeenth Earl of Oxford." Blue paused. "And now I do, too. It may sound kind of stupid, but actually I'm more interested in *who* wrote them than in the plays themselves. Strange, huh?"

"Very strange. So how come everybody else in the world doesn't have a problem with it?"

Blue was surprised to discover that he didn't know

how to answer that. Although he believed with all his heart that Oxford was the real author, he just didn't have enough ammunition at this stage of the game to mount a successful campaign. So, for the time being, he took the easy way out. "Remind me to tell you about him sometime," he said.

And that's when Blue resolved to conduct his own investigation into the Shakespeare mystery in an orderly and systematic manner. And he would begin by keeping a notebook, which he would call the Shakespeare Mystery Notebook.

"I think Dad's home," Louie said. He stood up from the desk and walked to the doorway.

"Dad?"

Blue heard footsteps, and in a moment Mr. DeSoto appeared at the door.

"Did you get to talk to the lawyer?" Louie asked.

"Yes, yes, I did." Louie's father noticed Blue, sitting over by Drusie. "Oh, hello, David," he said, at the same time acknowledging his daughter with a nod and a smile.

Blue stood up. "Hi, Mr. DeSoto."

"But did you talk—" Louie started.

"Yes, I did. We had quite a nice chat. The first thing he wanted to know was—did you have a contract? He wanted to know if you and Jackson Seratt had anything written down. Any kind of agreement, you know—"

"Well, no—"

"That's what I told him. And then he asked if there was any way of proving that you really *did* give him disks and other materials. Was anyone there? Were there any witnesses?"

"No. I guess not. But I *did* give them to him! I mean, that's obvious, isn't it? He made the whole game out of them!"

Blue and Drusie exchanged looks.

Mr. DeSoto put his hand on Louie's shoulder. "According to Cameron, it appears the guy's got you over a barrel. Since there's no real, tangible evidence linking you with the game, there's nothing we can do, except chalk it up to experience. I'm really sorry—"

"Yeah," Louie said. Suddenly feeling utterly defeated, more depressed than angry, he sat back down at his desk and idly ran his fingers across the computer keys. "Well, thanks, Dad. Thanks for trying, anyway." He forced a smile, just to show he could take it on the chin. "No use crying over spilled milk, huh?"

Blue stared at the floor. There must be some way to get Louie the credit he deserved, something short of kidnapping Jackson Seratt, tying him up in the basement, and pulling out his fingernails one by one until he 'fessed up. But that definitely wasn't Blue Avenger's style. So what was that Mr. DeSoto had just said? There's no real *tangible evidence* linking Louie with the game. That sounds just like the Shakespeare mystery, since there's no tangible evidence—as yet—linking Oxford with Shakespeare's plays and poems. So I guess *my* work's cut out for me. Just keep my eyes peeled and my ears alert for some of that tangible evidence!

Mrs. DeSoto fixed spaghetti with meat sauce for dinner. "Spaghetti!" she said with a wink. "Since you boys are going to Venice!"

Louie rolled his eyes. "Brilliant idea, Mom," he said, adding under his breath, "Jeez!"

"So—what's the weather like over there in March?" she asked brightly. "I imagine you might need your raincoats and umbrellas—" She suddenly put her hand to her mouth. "Oh, yes. That reminds me, David. Mr. Forni called today and asked that I be sure to—"

"He likes to be called Blue, Mom," Drusie said, reaching for the bread basket. "He's Blue Avenger now." She took a piece of French bread and passed the basket to Blue. "Bread, Blue?" she asked. And then she giggled a little. "Bled Brue? Blue Bleard?"

Blue thought he might be blushing. "That's okay,

Mrs. DeSoto," he said. "I know it's hard for some older people to start—"

"*Non*sense! Blue it is! But what I started to say, David—"

Drusie laughed loudly and hit herself on the forehead with the palm of her hand.

Mrs. DeSoto continued without a pause, "—is that Mr. Forni suggested that you skip travelers' checks, but be sure to get an ATM card in your name, so you can withdraw small amounts of Italian money as you need it. Louie already has his. Oh, and he made a point of saying that the McDonald's there takes cash only. Also, he wanted to make sure that you knew his company was only prepared to pay for your airfare and hotel room. Your food and entertainment and so forth are your own responsibility."

"Oh, yes," Blue said. "Yes, I do know that. And I've got my ATM card now, so I'm all set."

"How come *Louie* gets his own ATM card?" Drusie interrupted, feigning outrage. "And how come *I* can't go to Venice, too? Just because I'm not some computer whiz—" She playfully threw a small, hastily made bread-ball across the table at Louie. It landed right in his plate.

"Drusie!" Mrs. DeSoto scolded.

"Whoops, sorry," Drusie said, holding up her open

palm to show there were no hidden bread-balls. "It slipped."

Blue laughed outright, and even Louie smiled.

Mr. DeSoto, working on his third glass of red wine, seemed to be enjoying all this family camaraderie with good humor and patience. "At least she didn't blame the slip on Omo," he said, making quotation marks in the air as he said *the slip*.

Blue looked up. "Omo? Hey, that's the name of—"

"It's the name of one of Louie's imaginary friends," Mrs. DeSoto said, looking over at Louie fondly, as if he were still a toddler. "When he was two or three years old, he played with these little imaginary friends he made up—"

Louie sighed and sank down in his chair. "So what other kind are there, Mom?" he asked, beginning to drum his fingers on the tabletop.

"He even used to hold the screen door open for them whenever he came into the house," Mrs. DeSoto said, blithely ignoring her son's sarcastic retort. "I'd say, *Louie, close that door, you're letting in all the flies*. And he'd say, *Wait—my little friends aren't in yet!* It was so cute. I'll never forget their names. Let's see, there was Omo, Bomo, and Nomo. Isn't that right, Louie?"

Louie just scratched his ear and shook his head, but Blue was instantly alert. This might be the evidence he was looking for! "So *that's* where you got the names for those puppets we made, back in the second grade! Where are they now, Louie? Whatever happened to them?"

Louie shrugged. "I don't know. What happened to yours? Whatever happened to Egads?"

Blue tried hard to think—to remember the last time he saw little Egads. Finally, he just shook his head. "I don't know," he said. "The last time I remember seeing it was after we gave the show. That's the last time I remember seeing it." Blue was glad he didn't tell Louie why he was so interested in the puppets. It would only have made him feel worse about *Chimera*.

Mrs. DeSoto brought the blank Super Lotto tickets out to the table along with the spumoni ice cream and coffee. "Get us some pencils, would you please, Drusie?" she asked.

Then she made a little production of passing out the forms. "As you all probably know, the jackpot is up to forty-three million dollars now. So here's the deal. We all get a chance—there's five of us present—and we're going to sign a little paper here that specifies that if one of these tickets wins we split the jackpot even-steven. Let's see. Five into forty-three million is about eight million. Right, Louie? We'll each win over eight million dollars. Is that okay with everyone?"

Louie closed his eyes and shook his head hopelessly. "Mom," he began wearily, "do you realize what our chances of winning are?"

Mrs. DeSoto looked at Louie with genuine annoyance. "Louie, my boy, do you know that there are two kinds of people on this earth?"

"Yeah. Smart, and dumb."

Blue was mildly shocked at the latent disrespect inherent in Louie's response to his mother, although she chose to see it in a different light.

"That is *not* funny! The two kinds of people I'm referring to are those whose glass is half empty and those whose glass is half full. Your glass, Louie, is half empty!"

Mrs. DeSoto turned to the others. "We're playing the six-pick here. So concentrate for a few minutes and then pick out your best six lucky numbers."

After a short pause that included a bantering exchange between Drusie and her father regarding some possible methods of choosing lucky numbers, the five Super Lotto tickets were duly marked.

"Okay, pass them back over to me now," Mrs. DeSoto instructed. She began checking over the blacked-out numbers, counting to be sure that six were chosen on each card. She didn't want any mix-ups here.

And then, "What's *this*?" she practically shouted. She held up a card in front of Louie. "Louie, is this *yours*?"

Louie looked at the card with growing interest. "Nope," he said. "It's not mine, but I like it!"

"Uh-oh," Blue said. "I guess that's mine. Is there something wrong with it?"

"Actually, yes!" Mrs. DeSoto said. "Just *look* at it."

She sounded distressed, but Blue couldn't figure out the reason for her discomfort. "Well, I just picked numbers one through six—"

"Exactly! That's just it, David! You picked numbers one, two, three, four, five, and six!"

"What's wrong with that?" Louie said suddenly, grinning at Blue—as he himself would have said—like a Cheshire cat. "Those numbers have just as much chance of winning as any others."

"Well, no, they don't! That combination of numbers will never win! That would be practically impossible! The winning tickets *always* have the numbers scattered all around."

No one spoke. The only sound was the rhythmic ticking of the antique clock on the wall. Drusie was sitting with her elbows on the table and her chin in her hand. Mr. DeSoto looked down at his coffee cup and rubbed his nose gently with the tip of his index finger. Blue looked at Drusie, then at Louie, pursed his lips, and raised his eyebrows.

Mrs. DeSoto shook her head and slowly tore Blue's Lotto card in half. Then she handed him a new one, all the while looking at Louie. "The winning numbers are chosen randomly," she said firmly. "Do you think I don't know what *random* means, my little computer genius?" she asked in a pleasantly sarcastic tone. "Random is *never* one, two, three, four, five, and six—all in order like that! Random means all scattered around." She turned back to Blue. "So here's a new card, David, honey. Please do it over again, *correctly* this time, if you don't mind."

Blue politely took the card, all the while watching in amazement as Mrs. DeSoto flew through the air and landed headfirst in an old rust-colored bin in his brain labeled GOOFY.

All the same, the experience gave Blue a wonderful new idea for a future Blue Avenger mission as soon as he had the time—and that would be to do his best to expose the lottery for the wildly misunderstood and downright heartless scam that it was.

As it happened, Blue thought about the lottery again that evening—but in a slightly different context—when he heard on the news of the freak accidental death of a fifty-four-year-old man who was struck on the head by a stone kicked up by a commercial-sized lawnmower in the park. "A one-in-a-million chance," said the newscaster. "It shouldn't have killed him, but it did." So, in a way, Blue thought, that man had won the lottery. For what is the lottery if not beating the odds, and how many men were dealt a deathblow on the head by a wayward stone that day? We play the lottery constantly in a million ways we can never know, so we're bound to have our share of winning. Didn't I win the lottery on that wonderful day when I first saw Omaha? And what about—oh, God, how can I think this way?—but what about that moment when Dad got killed? That was like the lottery, too. The lottery of death. But I don't want to think of death now. What's another, more pleasant win? How about when the computer randomly chose me to be in Dr. Wood's class instead of Miss Wooliscroft's, where I wouldn't have heard about a man named Edward de Vere? Yes, we are always winning the lottery. It's only the prize that varies.

Just before he went to bed that evening, Blue made the first entry in his Shakespeare Mystery Notebook, using *The Mysterious William Shakespeare: The Myth and the Reality* as his main source:

SHAKESPEARE MYSTERY NOTEBOOK (ENTRY #1)

For the sake of clarity in this notebook I will use the following names to denote the three principal characters:

WILLIAM SHAKSPERE: the man born in Stratford-on-Avon in 1564

OXFORD: Edward de Vere, the seventeenth Earl of Oxford, born in 1550

WILLIAM SHAKESPEARE: the author of the works, whoever he was

The exact date of William Shakspere's birth is not known, but the baptismal register of the Stratford parish church in Stratford-on-Avon records the christening of "Gulielmus filius Johannis Shakspere" on 26 April 1564. Neither one of William Shakspere's parents could read or write. He may or may not have attended the local grammar school. (The school records for that period have been lost or destroyed.) Shakspere's only son died at age eleven. His two daughters never learned how to read or write. (If Shakspere really was Shakespeare, it's hard to believe that he could have neglected this vital part of his own daughters' education.)

Oxford was born on 12 April 1550, at Castle Hedingham, in Essex, England. At age fourteen he received a degree from Cambridge University. One of his tutors was his uncle, Arthur Golding, the translator of Ovid's <u>Metamorphoses</u> into English, a work which greatly influenced Shakespeare's poems and plays. It has even been suggested that young Oxford assisted in this translation. Besides his complete mastery of Latin, Oxford was also fluent in French and Italian.

eleven

On Wednesday morning, at the end of his third-period English class, Dr. Wood made the following announcement: "Remember, in this room at noon today Blue Avenger will be explaining the Baconian Bi-lateral Cipher. Everyone is welcome. I'm sure it will prove most interesting." And then he looked up at the huge damp circles on the ceiling, which were growing larger by the minute. "But if the rain keeps up like this, we may very well need our life preservers."

On his way out of the room, Blue hesitated for a moment by his teacher's desk. "It's bi-*literal*, Dr. Wood," he said softly.

Dr. Wood looked up. "Ah, yes. So it is."

Blue was slightly taken aback at the scene that greeted him when he entered room 212 at the appointed time that afternoon. For one thing, the chairs were all scattered around in disarray, and although he didn't count them, there were sixteen kids either sitting or milling about, and—to Blue's surprise—two babies. However, one of the babies wasn't real. It was merely a pretend baby made out of rolled-up newspapers held together by a baby blanket and tied up with a pink ribbon. This was "Ruby," the pretend baby that Celeste Ramsey and Danny Davis were supposed to be "parenting," a one-week assignment commissioned by Ms. Upton— the new social-studies teacher at San Pablo High—in a well-meaning attempt at "getting these kids to experience firsthand the self-sacrifice and continuing demands of parenthood," as she had cheerfully explained to her rather skeptical fellow teachers.

At the moment when Blue entered the room, Daddy Danny was dangling his baby out of the window, holding on to the pink ribbon by only two fingers, trying to get Mommy Celeste's attention. It was still raining, and Ruby was getting quite soaked. But Mommy Celeste had not yet noticed these shenanigans, since she was in the midst of the group of girls gathered around little Gus, the real baby, who was squalling loudly and would simply not be comforted by Joannie Green, the real mommy, no matter in which position she held him or how much she jiggled him. Joannie Green was not attending school this term because of the baby, but she thought it would be fun to visit Dr. Wood's class at noontime today, just like she used to do last year.

Suddenly there was a scream from the back of the room. "Acchhh! Dr. Wood! There's some water dripping on me!" Another scream and some wild laughter followed. "It's getting my lunch all wet and soggy!"

"Oh, it's dripping over here, too, you big idiot," said Sheri, the girl who had first asked about the cipher. "Just get one of those pans from behind Dr. Wood's desk." Then she stuck her head back in her book and muttered to herself, "What an idiot."

"Maybe he's hungry," suggested one of the girls gazing down at the real baby.

"No," Joannie said, with an air of indisputable authority. "I just fed him before I got here."

"How *did* you get here?" one of the girls asked. "Did Leroy bring you?"

Joannie bent her head down toward the baby she was holding. Then she raised one arm as high as she could and awkwardly tried to rub her nose against her shoulder. "No," she said, sniffing slightly. And the girls moved their feet around and exchanged knowing glances.

During all of this, Dr. Wood was standing by his desk with a sandwich in one hand and a carton of milk in the other, having what looked like a very serious discussion with a new exchange student from Ireland. Now Blue approached his teacher and stood there patiently until Dr. Wood noticed him.

"Ah! Our speaker is here! Good show! Listen, listen, everyone—"

Except for baby Gus, the room quieted down immediately, since the kids knew Dr. Wood's rules: He would stand for a certain amount of chaos, but when he addressed them, they'd better listen or they'd jolly well be looking for an alternate lunchtime site.

"Those of you who are interested in hearing Blue explain Bacon's Bi-literal Cipher, just grab a desk and form a little semicircle up here by the board."

Drusie and Tuesday separated themselves from little Gus and dragged their desks over to the area Dr. Wood had indicated, and in a few minutes Blue had an audience of eleven kids plus his teacher. As Blue was looking around for a piece of chalk, Tuesday cupped her hands around her mouth and called out to him, "Hey, get any interesting e-mail lately?"

He leaned toward her. "So it was *you*!"

Tuesday grinned. "Having problems, huh?"

"Well, you've got to admit, it *is* pretty obscure."

"Really? I wouldn't think so. It's stuff we've been reading about. Well, maybe you need another clue. I'll see what I can do."

Blue nodded and then turned to face his audience. "Okay, here's the deal. Francis Bacon came up with the idea for this cipher about four hundred years ago, and what it is, actually, is just a code. Code words—well, letters, really—are hidden in what appear to be ordinary sentences. And here's the way he did that."

Blue turned to the board and began to write the letters of the alphabet in capitals in a line across the board, up through the letter M, when he ran out of space. He again turned to the kids. "This is going to take a minute, so— uh, excuse me." He made a little apologetic shrug, turned back to the board, and started a second row.

The students not interested in Blue's presentation were talking in little groups or quietly reading at their desks, some of them still munching on chips or drinking sodas. The real baby had quieted down temporarily, and the pretend baby was now hanging by its long pink ribbon from a hook in the ceiling, drying off. Once in a while Daddy Danny would give it a little push, swinging it back and forth like a pendulum. Mommy Celeste had been so wrapped up in the real baby she still hadn't noticed what had been going on with little Ruby.

Blue had finished writing the letters of the alphabet in two long rows across the board, and now he began to write a series of five small letters, made up of only a's and b's, under his large capital letters. When he was finished, the board looked like this:

A	B	C	D	E	F	G	H	IJ	K	L	M
aaaaa	aaaab	aaaba	aaabb	aabaa	aabab	aabba	aabbb	abaaa	abaab	ababa	ababb

N	O	P	Q	R	S	T	UV	W	X	Y	Z
abbaa	abbab	abbba	abbbb	baaaa	baaab	baaba	baabb	babaa	babab	babba	babbb

"Now," Blue said, "please notice the I and J double up, and so do the U and V. I guess that's because in Bacon's day they didn't use a whole lot of J's or U's. I'm just guessing. I don't know."

Then he pointed to the series of small letters under the capitals, the little a's and b's. "These a's and b's here are like the codes, or ciphers, for these big letters here," and he indicated all the big letters with a sweep of his hand. "If you don't understand right now, just keep listening. You'll get it in a minute, because this cipher is *really* easy once you catch on."

The air was suddenly pierced by Mommy Celeste's clear high-pitched shriek. "*Danny!* What are you *doing*? Get the baby off of there right now!"

"What for? She's drying off—"

Dr. Wood stood up and faced the back of the room.

"All right, now," he said. "Blue is trying to explain something here. Let's quiet down, please."

"Get her *down*!" Mommy Celeste hissed, quickly glancing at Dr. Wood and then putting her hand over her mouth.

"Uh," Blue said, "where'd I leave off? Oh, yeah. What's absolutely required in this kind of cipher are two different types of fonts. But they can't be *too* different. In fact, ideally they should be so much *alike* that only those looking for a difference will actually find it. Now, one type of font will stand for the letter a, and the other will stand for the letter b. And since I can't write in different fonts too well, I'll use capital letters to represent a's and small letters to represent b's. So, to help you remember that, I'll just write it on the board." And he wrote:

a = CAPITAL LETTERS   b = small letters

Just then someone in the back of the room made a big audible sigh and whispered, "What is he *talking* about?"

Blue looked up, alarmed. "You don't get it?"

Several people in the semicircle immediately came to his defense.

"Go on," someone said. "We're following."

"Yeah, just pay attention back there."

"Shheez!"

Blue hesitated. "Well, okay. Anyway, as I was saying, I'll use capital letters and small letters in place of two fonts. So now we're ready to go. Let's relay the simple one-word message *fly*, since that's the one Bacon used in his own example."

Blue pointed to the letter F on the board. "We'll start with the letter F. You'll see that the code, or cipher, for F is aabab." And here Blue pointed to the little row of letters under the big capital F.

"Listen now, because this is important. All we have to do now is *write something—anything at all*, actually— being sure to alternate our two fonts according to the cipher. You got that? The *words* in the sentence you write don't matter. It's *how* you write the letters that counts. If I remember correctly, the sentence Bacon used was something like *Do not go till I come*."

Then Blue wrote that sentence all in capital letters high above what he had already written. Next he counted off the letters in groups of five and drew a long line to indicate the breaks.

DO NOT|GO TIL|L I COM|E

"Each of these little groups of *five letters* will become *one letter* in code. Now, stick with me," he said, grabbing an eraser in his left hand, "because here comes the fun part. The first letter in the word *fly* is F, so we want to write the cipher for F, which is aabab. Looking at our code here, capital letters indicate a. The first letter in the cipher for F is an a. So we leave the first capital D in our sentence DO NOT GO TILL I COME. The second letter in the cipher for F is another a. So we leave the O in the word DO a capital."

Blue could tell there was some disturbance going on at the back of the room, but he decided to just ignore it and continue on, until Mommy Celeste screamed again.

"*Danny!* Stop that! *Stop tossing the baby around!*"

"Oh, she *likes* it! Watch. Hey, Phil, *heads up!*"

But poor Phil was caught off guard. "Whoops," he said. "Dropped her." He reached across the aisle for Ruby, who was now beginning to come undone. "Sorry," Phil said, clumsily retying the pink ribbon.

But now the real baby had lost his pacifier and was starting to cry again. Joannie, suddenly looking very tired, pushed her hair back behind her ears and reached for a large blue diaper bag.

"Oh, God," Phil said, only half joking. "Let me out of here! She's going to change him!"

"Very funny!" Joannie shot back. "Somebody

once changed *you*, you know!"

Dr. Wood stood up again. "This is your last warning, kids," he said. He looked at Joannie and lowered his voice. "Is everything all right back there?"

Joannie bent to pick up the baby's pacifier. "I think I'd better go," she said. "He won't stop crying." Except for the baby's whimpering, the room was very quiet as she gathered up her stuff.

"I'll go with you," one of the girls said.

Joannie stopped at the door and nodded at Dr. Wood. "Goodbye," she said. "It was nice seeing you again."

"Yes," he said. "It was nice seeing you, too."

Blue waited a moment before starting up again. "Now we come to the third letter in the cipher, which is a b. How do we indicate a b? By a *small* letter, right?" He erased the capital N and replaced it with the small letter n. "Then we need another capital letter for the fourth a in the cipher, and finally another small letter for the final b." He made the necessary changes. "So the words 'do not' look like this." He finished writing on the board:

DO nOt

"And those five letters, written as they are, really stand for the letter F. Now we can do the same thing for the letters L and Y, to spell out our secret word FLY."

Blue turned back to the board and altered the sentence until it looked like this:

DO nOt Go TiLl I coM

"You'll notice there's no final e in the word 'come.' That's because our word FLY is complete without it. So we'll just add a small e to complete the word."

Blue put the chalk back and brushed the white dust off of his hands. "Well," he said, shrugging and looking at Dr. Wood, "I guess that's it. Except maybe to add that Francis Bacon was way ahead of his time, since today's computers are based on his idea of using just two symbols—you know, his two different fonts. Computers today do more or less the same thing by using just zeros and ones."

"Thank you, Blue," Dr. Wood said. "That was very well done."

Blue shrugged, slightly embarrassed. But he was pleased to get the compliment, especially from Dr. Wood.

A few minutes later, just before the bell sounded, Mommy Celeste was distressed to find that little Ruby had disappeared. Daddy Danny insisted he didn't know what had happened to her, but it seemed mighty suspicious that his friend Phil was reading the sports section and Danny himself had the comics.

Louie and Drusie were home alone after school on Wednesday afternoon when the phone rang. As usual, Drusie got to it first, mainly because Louie never considered it a contest.

"It's for you!" she called out. "It's Mr. Forni. He's calling from Elk Grove."

"I'll get it in here," Louie said, picking up the extension in the kitchen. "Hi, Mr. Forni. This is Louie."

"Well, hello, Louie. How are things going there?"

"Fine."

"I probably should talk to your folks about this, but I wanted to at least explain the situation to you first, and then if they have any questions—"

Louie caught his breath. Oh, no! The Venice trip is off. "Well, they're not home right now, so—"

"That's all right, Louie. You can relay the message. It's just that something's come up here, and it appears that I'm not going to be able to go with you fellows to Venice—"

"Oh—" Louie said, a wave of disappointment starting to build up in his chest.

"—but wait. Listen. I realize it's awfully short notice,

but if it's all right with your parents, there's no reason why you can't go without me. After all, it's really quite simple. You change planes in New York and Rome and then fly direct to Venice. I can arrange for someone from the hotel to meet you at the airport, so that shouldn't be a problem. And remember, you'll have access to a computer and the Internet, so you can keep in touch with your family by e-mail. I gave you the name and address of that place, didn't I?"

"Yes. Agostino's. It's on that e-mail you sent me with all that other information."

"Good. Well, I guess it all depends now on how your parents are going to feel about it."

Drusie, curious about the call, was now in the kitchen and mouthing the words "*What?* What's *wrong?* What's he saying?"

Louie turned away from her. He was certain that he and Blue would have no problem at all being alone in Venice for four days. "Well, my parents aren't home now. But I'll ask—"

"Yes," Mr. Forni said. "You ask them. I'm on my way out now, but I'll be in the office all day tomorrow. You have that number?"

"Yes. I do. I have it right here."

"Good. Well, I'm sure you guys would be able to

handle it just fine. So why don't you talk it over with your parents, and talk to your friend, too. Maybe this can be worked out after all."

"Sure. Okay! I'll talk to my parents as soon as they come home. We'll call you—"

"Oh, yes. There's one more thing. If someone over there can use my plane ticket, they're certainly welcome to it. And the same goes for my room there at the hotel. We managed to negotiate a special price for the two rooms, and I don't want to get into a hassle over that now. Maybe one of your parents would want to go. Whatever you decide will be okay with me."

"Okay! Gee, that sounds really great. That's really nice of you. Thanks, Mr. Forni. Sorry you can't go, but I guess that's how the ball bounces—"

"Yes, that's true. Talk to you tomorrow, then."

"Right."

Drusie had her brother by the arm even before he hung up the phone. "So what did he say? What did he say? He can't go, right? And he wants to give his ticket away, doesn't he? Doesn't he? Oh, Louie, can I go? Can I go? Please, please, please, please—"

When Louie called Blue to tell him about this change in plans and to check to see if he would still be allowed to go, Sally was not home from work yet. Blue knew, however, that one of the perks of being an all-around good kid—one who is clean-living and drug-free—is that your mother would have no qualms about letting you go to Venice for four days without adult supervision.

"I'm sure it'll be okay," Blue said. "But why don't you call me back later, just to make it official?"

"Okay. And hey—guess what? Now Drusie's begging to come along."

"Oh, yeah? Will your parents let her?"

"It could go either way. Time will tell. Anyway, I'll call you back later."

After dinner, while waiting for Louie's call and before starting his homework, Blue made the second entry in his Shakespeare Mystery Notebook:

SHAKESPEARE MYSTERY NOTEBOOK (ENTRY #2)

There's so much interesting stuff in Charlton Ogburn's book that I'm having trouble deciding what to put down in this notebook. But here goes:

Of all of Shakespeare's nonhistorical plays, only one, The Merry Wives of Windsor, is set in England. The rest all take place on the continent, and at least a dozen of them are set wholly or partly in Italy.

There is no evidence whatsoever that William Shakspere ever journeyed outside of England. On the other hand, there are detailed records of Oxford's travels to the continent during the years of 1575 and 1576, when he was twenty-five years old. In Italy, he visited the cities of Padua, Verona, Venice, Milan, Florence, Rome, and Naples, even going as far south as Palermo, in Sicily. This is all documented in letters that have survived to this day. Also, there is an unsubstantiated report in the State Archives of Venice which suggests that he may have even built himself a house in that city.

While Oxford was in Italy he had some financial dealings with two Italian men whose names were Baptista Nigrone and Pasquino Spinola. In Shakespeare's play The Taming of the Shrew, the name he gives to Katharina's father (a character who seems to be inordinately concerned with money) is Baptista Minola. Question: Did this come about by coincidence, design, or the

unconscious workings of the human brain?
Something to ponder!

Blue was still pondering when the phone rang.

"So—were you right?" Louie asked. "Can you still go?"

"Yep."

"That's great! When Forni first called, I thought for sure it was curtains—until he suggested we could go without him."

"So what about Drusie?" asked Blue. "Did your parents decide about her yet?"

"No, they're still talking about it." Louie laughed. "Can't you hear them? Actually, they've been talking about the movies."

"The movies?"

Louie laughed again. "Yeah. My mother wants to know how can they let her go off to Italy when it's common knowledge that the world is full of boys with only one thing on their minds—and that's how they can manage to lose their virginity before prom night."

"Say that again—"

"See, my mother's been reading the blurbs on the back of movie videos."

"What was Drusie's answer to that?"

Louie laughed. "First she did her usual *Don't you trust*

me? routine, and then she followed that up by saying, 'Besides, they probably don't even *have* proms in Venice.' And my mother said, 'Well, why wouldn't they?' And then they got into this big argument about whether or not they have proms in Venice. I'm telling you, it's crazy over here." Louie paused a minute. Then he said, "Uh-oh! Something's up! Drusie's really mad now. She's heading for her room." Louie lowered his voice. "No! Hold it! My mother's speaking to her. Just a minute, now—well, well! It appears that Drusie's little bluff has done the trick. She's coming back." Louie put his mouth closer to the phone. "We'll return to this exciting *live* broadcast after these short announcements. Do you suffer from night sweats? Do you find yourself making trip after trip to the bathroom? Do you—"

Blue laughed. "Oh, cut it out, Louie. What's happening now?"

"Wait a minute. My mom and dad are discussing something between themselves. Drusie's pouting in the corner. Hold it! I do believe Drusie has won again! You've got to hand it to her. She does it every time. There they go. She and my mom are off to the kitchen. Oh, just a minute, Blue. My dad wants to speak to you."

Blue heard the phone changing hands. "Hello, Blue. How are you?"

"Fine, thanks—"

"Well, we've just been trying to come to some decision here about this Venice thing. Actually, to tell the truth, we were a bit hesitant about Drusie, allowing her to go along, you know what I mean?"

"Uh—"

"But it appears to have been decided." Mr. DeSoto cleared his throat. "Now, Louie here assured us earlier that he'd keep an eye on her, so we wondered if you—" He laughed, just a little nervous laugh. "Well, her mother and I were just thinking that, if you could kind of watch out for her, too—you know, keep an eye on her?—"

"Oh, sure. I understand."

"Well, that's good, then. You see, her mother suggested that if the *both* of you could, you know—"

"Keep an eye on her? Sure, Mr. DeSoto. I understand."

"Now, you won't forget, will you? I mean, I have your word on that—"

"Certainly! Sure! We'll watch out for her. Both Louie and me. We'll watch out for her."

"Okay, then. That's fine. One more thing, though. I'm not going to mention this little conversation to Drusie. You know how she is. She almost had a fit when she heard us ask Louie to look after her. And, actually, she doesn't need *looking after*, just—"

"I understand. Just keep an eye on her. We can do that—"

"Well, good! So that's settled! Drusie seems very happy and excited about going."

Blue was happy, too. Drusie was a lot of fun, and it was good to know that she would be going along to Venice with them, even if he *was* expected to keep an eye on her.

Blue still had two quizzes to study for that evening, but first he wanted to write a letter to Mr. Chase R. Wanner, president of the Wanner Cornstarch Company:

```
Mr. Chase R. Wanner, President
Wanner Cornstarch Company
Wanner, NJ 07017


Dear Mr. Wanner:


Hello. My name is Blue Avenger. As you
may recall, my recipe for a weepless
lemon meringue pie (THE LAST MERINGUE:
BLUE AVENGER'S WEEPLESS WONDER LEMON
MERINGUE PIE) was featured in the Ask
Auntie Annie column in February of this
year. The reward promised to me for this
```

achievement was twofold: First, my recipe
was to be featured on boxes of your
cornstarch as soon as you ran out of all
your old boxes, and, second, I was to
receive from your company a lifetime
supply of Wanner Cornstarch. (Naturally I
wouldn't expect to receive a lifetime
supply of <u>Kingsford's</u> Cornstarch, would
I? Ha-ha.)

I don't quite know how to say this, since
I do not wish to appear greedy or unduly
avaricious, but I just can't believe that
a three-ounce sample package of Wanner
Cornstarch constitutes a "lifetime
supply," especially since I am only
sixteen years old and have (should I be
blessed with a reasonably long life) at
least a trainload of lemon meringue pies
left in me.

I fully understand that calculating how
much cornstarch could reasonably be
considered a "lifetime supply" could be
daunting, and that this problem just may

be the cause of the delay. At any rate, I
trust that you and your fine staff are
doing your utmost to solve this conundrum
and that I can look forward to receiving
my shipment of cornstarch any day now.

Yours sincerely,
Blue Avenger

P.S. How is your supply of old boxes
holding out? My mother is anxious for the
day when she can see my recipe in print
whenever she passes the baking supplies
aisle at the supermarket.

Not bad, Blue thought, after printing the letter and reading it over. Now for a quick call to Omaha.

After a few moments of small talk, he related the latest Venice news—Mr. Forni couldn't go, so it would be just Louie, Drusie, and him.

"*What?*" Omaha exclaimed. "You're going to *Venice*, with *Drusie DeSoto*?" And no sooner had she spoken those words when, unbeknownst to her, the layer of ice surrounding her heart slowly and barely perceptibly began to show signs of cracking.

And our man Blue, like a wild beast in the forest smelling blood at last, replied soothingly, "Only for four nights, that's all."

Omaha got home from swimming practice early and was waiting for Blue on Saturday afternoon. Her mother had some shopping to do, so that left her home alone with some extra time to think. That spontaneous outburst of undisguised panic that had escaped from her lips when she heard about Drusie was unforgivable! But now she could be on her guard. She was prepared to show not one iota of jealousy. After all, wasn't *she* the one who didn't need the security of going steady—a term that made her cringe. And on top of that, she was still dealing with that business about her father. She was her mother's daughter, after all. And if Margie could have made such a mistake about a man, well—maybe the same could happen to her! Well, couldn't it?

Blue had arranged to drop his mother off at work that morning so that he could use the car. They probably could have taken the bus to the movies, but he wanted to bring the old computer over to Omaha anyway and thought that would be a good time. Josh came up to the door, too, but Omaha led him directly to the kitchen and sat him down by the little TV set and gave him a plate of cookies. Then she went back to join Blue in the den, where he was busy setting up the computer.

"I talked my mother into signing up for an Internet service," she said, handing him a cookie.

"That's great! Now we can exchange e-mail while I'm away—"

"—in Venice!" Omaha said brightly, obligingly finishing his sentence for him.

"With Louie and Drusie DeSoto!" Blue added, just as brightly.

"Yes!" she agreed, doggedly playing the game.

"But only for four little nights," Blue added in a playful falsetto, looking into her eyes and touching his finger to the tip of her nose.

In years to come, Omaha would recall that it was the look in his eyes that caused the dam to burst. At any rate, she suddenly threw herself into his arms and clung to him like a kitten refusing to be placed into a cage for a trip to the vet. "Oh, Blue—Blue!" she wailed. "Please, *please,* don't take her on a gondola in the moonlight! I can't stand the thought of you sitting beside Drusie DeSoto in a gondola in the moonlight!"

And suddenly the ice began to melt completely from Omaha's heart, and her plan to "just go it alone" (the decision she had lived by ever since she made it during her plane ride home from Rome) seemed to float off into the air, like this: just go it alone.

Oh, weary world, take note—for this is another shining moment for Blue. He knew that now, faced with the specter of a possible romantic encounter between him and Drusie DeSoto, Omaha would most certainly agree to a more formally committed relationship that would automatically preclude such an assignation. All he had to do was ask. But the name of that game is coercion, an activity deemed totally unacceptable to Blue Avenger— secret champion of the underdog, modest seeker of truth, fearless innovator of the unknown—whether in or out of uniform.

He held her close like that for some of the most glorious seconds in his entire life. And the kiss (or kisses?) that followed can only be described as Pure Bliss—capital P, capital B.

"Come on, you guys!" Josh said a few minutes later, walking into the room while chewing on the last cookie from the plate. "We're going to miss the beginning of the movie!"

What was *wrong* with Omaha, anyway? Did her sense of humor really go out to lunch? Aside from a retired rocket scientist and a contingent of old folks from Fair Acres

Retirement Home (who got shuffled by mistake into the theater showing *Three's a Gas* instead of the revival of *On Golden Pond* they paid to see, and who therefore walked out en masse after they finally realized what had happened)—aside from those people, Omaha was the only person in the theater who hardly cracked a smile during the entire movie, let alone roar with laughter.

But she was sorry—she just couldn't see anything funny about a pile of brown stuff (that just fell out of a baby's diaper, hint hint) traveling down the conveyor belt at the supermarket, even though the cashier happened to be Buster B. Bodwell, the funniest new comic around, who was sure to greet *that* surprise in his own special hilarious way. ("Falling-down funny! Buster B's a comic genius!!!")

As for Blue, well, he was suffering the consequences of reading too many books from his father's bookshelf, because the sad truth is that, after reaching a certain level of mental maturity, it takes much more than nicknames for sexual organs and the bizarre exhibition of human bodies or bodily functions and/or the products thereof to cause that unexpected surprise or twist of events which results in genuine laughter. In other words, at sixteen, poor Blue was beyond vulgarity, although he did manage to see a rare bit of unintentional humor here and there along the way.

And Josh? Well! Here we have a different story! Josh was practically rolling on the floor during the entire movie, for it was, indeed, tailor-made for his still-developing ten-year-old brain.

So there stood Omaha after the movie was over, leaning up against the wall in the crowded lobby, waiting for Blue and Josh to come out of the men's room and wondering, What's *wrong* with me, anyway? What kind of a stupid sourpuss am I, for God's sake? Everybody else thought it was funny!

And then she heard it—a snatch of a conversation just in passing from a woman zipping up her red windbreaker. "I'm just sick and tired of complaining about it," the woman said in a slightly nasal, whining tone of voice.

Omaha looked up as the two women headed for the exit. *I'm just sick and tired of complaining about it.* Omaha smiled, faintly at first, wondering why that little phrase seemed so odd. *I'm just sick and tired of complaining about it.* Omaha's smile became bigger, and in another second she was laughing—not a simple, surface, flash-in-the-pan guffaw laughter, but a much more subtle and satisfying one, brought about by her recognition of the unique and circular humor contained in that woman's innocent complaint. By the time Blue and Josh came by, Omaha was bent over with tears of laughter welling up in her eyes, but now (for those students of the psychology of laughter who might care to delve further into Omaha's psyche) the more immediate cause of the manifestation of the aforementioned reflex was her feeling of relief and self-reassurance that her humor detector was, indeed, in splendid working order. She was *not* a stupid sourpuss.

"Hey! What's so funny?" Josh asked.

"Yeah," Blue added, starting to laugh himself at the sight of her.

"Well, I'm just sick and tired of complaining about it" was all she could choke out before collapsing against Blue's arm in another fit of uncontrollable laughter.

"I don't get it," said Josh. "Come on, let's go. I'm hungry."

Blue definitely would have "gotten it," but her words were so scrambled with her laughter that he couldn't make out exactly what she was saying. So he patted her shoulder and smiled benignly at her and said, "We've got a nice lemon meringue pie waiting at home. I baked it fresh this morning."

"Oh, wow!" Josh exclaimed. "A genuine Blue Avenger Weepless Wonder Lemon Meringue Pie! How could I be so lucky!"

Later, after they had their pie and Josh went off to play computer games, Omaha asked Blue how his *Hamlet* memorization assignment was going.

"Oh, we don't have to do *Hamlet* if we don't want to. Dr. Wood put together about twenty pages of Shakespeare quotations and we get to choose from there what we want to memorize." He glanced around the kitchen. "There it is, on the counter there, right behind you. I was looking at it this morning, while my crust was baking."

Omaha picked it up. "Oh, I see. He's got them separated by subject." She flipped through the pages. "There's a whole bunch on love in here," she said.

"I know." Blue hesitated, then recited, *"What is love? 'Tis not hereafter, / Present mirth hath present laughter. / What's to come is still unsure. / In delay there lies no plenty, / Then come kiss me, sweet and twenty. / Youth's a stuff will not endure."*

Omaha smiled. "Blue, you're blushing," she said, studying the quotations more carefully now.

He touched his face. "Am not," he said, getting up and putting what was left of the pie back in the refrigerator. He leaned over her shoulder. "See anything interesting in there?"

"Wait." Omaha was reading something to herself, silently, her lips barely moving.

"What is it?" asked Blue.

"It's just—"

"What?"

"Well, it's Shakespeare's way of saying something that—well, it's something that I noticed just before my father left us. I noticed how extra *polite* he and my mother were acting. It just wasn't normal, you know?" Omaha was surprised to hear herself talking about something so personal, but, in a way, it was a relief to be able to bring it out in the open—to talk to Blue about it.

"Read it—if you want to, I mean."

"Okay. But Dr. Wood made a little note here. He says what Shakespeare means by *enforcèd ceremony* is strained politeness, but that's pretty obvious. Anyway, it goes like this: *When love begins to sicken and decay, / It useth an enforcèd ceremony. / There are no tricks in plain and simple faith.*" She looked up at Blue. "*Julius Caesar.* Act four, scene two."

At first Blue didn't know what to say. Then, finally, he just said in a quiet voice, "So that's how they were acting, huh?"

Omaha nodded. "It's funny that Shakespeare noticed it, too, way back then in Elizabethan times. I guess some things never change. Listen, do you think I could get a copy of this?"

"Sure, I think so. Dr. Wood had a big stack of them

on his desk. I'll get one for you next week."

Omaha kept scanning the entries under love, running her finger up and down the page. "Oh, wait, here's another one." She looked up at Blue and smiled. "When you were a little kid did you ever play with snails?"

"Play with snails?" he repeated, with a bemused little smile. "What do you mean?"

"Oh, you know, like when you barely touch those little feelers they have and then watch how fast they can pull them in? Listen to this. *Love's feeling is more soft and sensible / Than are the tender horns of cockled snails.*"

Neither of them spoke for a moment, picturing the tender horns of cockled snails. Pretty soon they both smiled. "Good old Oxford," Blue said.

twelve

It was almost five o'clock on Sunday afternoon, a week after Blue had taken Josh to the movies.

"I think they're here!" Josh said suddenly, letting go of the curtain and hopping up and down with excitement. He'd been looking out the living room window sporadically for the last half hour, and now, at last, he saw a car pull up in front of the house.

Sally and Blue both rushed to his side. "That's them, all right," Sally murmured. "Oh, Lord. Why am I so nervous about this?"

Blue touched her arm. "Hey, it's okay, Mom. Relax."

"Look! He's opening the door for her," Josh said, moving the edge of the curtain with his finger to make a small peephole. "What a gent!"

"Quit fooling around with the curtain, Josh," Blue said. "They'll see you."

"No, they won't. They aren't even looking this way.

Hey! Look! They have a dog! They have a little dog, Mom!"

"Yes. I can see that," Sally said dully, immediately thinking of her sinuses. "One of those little mutty kinds, too. Well," she sighed, "I guess we may as well go outside and greet them."

Josh led the way, running out the door onto the small porch and taking the three cement steps in one giant leap, landing spread-eagled on the short, narrow walkway leading down to the front sidewalk. "Ow-wee!" he screamed, slowly rising and examining the slight tear at the knee of his pants and his scraped palms.

"Oh, *my*! Are you all right?"

Josh looked up to see a slim lady with tousled, carrot-red hair—dressed in tight blue jeans and a green "Murphy's Pizza" T-shirt—standing over him. Holding the small moplike dog under her arm, she bent down on one knee and extended her hand to Josh, saying, "Here. Let me help you up."

Josh grimaced with pain and shook his head. "No, that's okay," he said. "I'm okay." He looked up at the woman and tried to smile his most charming smile. "I'm Josh," he said. "This may sound very weird, but I believe I am your grandson."

"Yes. I believe you are." She smiled, too—her best

grandmotherly smile. "Would you like to call me Grammy?"

Josh grinned. "Sure." Then, ever the little joker, he added, "So—did you bring me a present, Grammy?"

She looked at him in alarm. "Actually, no—"

Josh favored her with his typical "har-har-har" laugh. "Just *kid*ding, Grammy-O. Just *kid*ding!"

"Why, you little son-of-a-gun," she said to him in a raucous whisper. "I'll get you for that!"

In less than a minute, Josh and Grammy had bonded beautifully.

Blue and Sally had reached the sidewalk now. "Hello, Mother," Sally said, not quite sure how to handle the situation. "It's—it's been a long time, hasn't it?"

Blue watched, slightly embarrassed, as the two women clasped hands and exchanged brief kisses on the cheek, with Grammy still managing to hold the little brown-and-white dog under her arm all the while.

"Yes, it has, Sally. And it was all my fault," Grammy said, winking at Blue as she spoke. "And this must be David!" She reached out her free arm and gathered Blue in close to her, this time, however, crushing the dog in the process until he squealed his displeasure. "Vixen!" scolded Grammy. "Hush!"

By now the travel agent had locked the car on the

driver's side and had come around to join the others on the sidewalk. He was a dapper older gentleman with a slight paunch and a trim, gray mustache. He was wearing a white cap with the words "Golden Getaways Travel" spelled out in red on the brim.

Grammy took him by the hand and gently pushed him forward. "Say hello to Byron, everybody, your new—well, I mean, my new—that is—" Grammy stammered. "Well, let me just say this is Byron, my husband." She paused a minute and then planted a big kiss on the side of the little dog's nose. "And this is our baby, Vixen."

There was a general hand- and paw-shaking all around, until finally Sally said cautiously, "Shall we go inside?"

Sally's initial plan had been to go out to dinner, since she had spent most of the day sprucing up the house and didn't exactly feel like cooking. However, after they'd discussed the matter, it was decided they would have to dine at home, mostly because the visitors had brought along the little doggie they had just adopted five weeks ago—a two-year-old Shih Tzu named Vixen—and Grammy didn't want to leave him home alone.

"We have a nice fenced backyard," Sally suggested, once they were all seated around the table. "I'm sure he'd be happy out there."

Grammy pursed her lips and slowly shook her head back and forth. "Ohh, no. That won't work, I'm afraid. Vixen is a *house* dog. He doesn't like to be outside."

"No," Byron agreed. "We don't dare let him out of our sight, even for a minute," and then moved his eyebrows suggestively and added cryptically, "if you know what I mean."

Grammy picked the dog up and gave him a big smooch on his ear. "He's just our widdle-waggie-Wixen, aren't you, Mommy's widdle-bit of sugar-poo?" She set him down again and pushed him gently under the table.

Josh caught Blue's eye and gave a little shrug of disbelief at what he'd just heard.

"If he's a male, how come his name is Vixen?" Blue asked, vaguely disturbed by the obvious blunder.

"Well, you know," Grammy said, "I never really thought of that. I just like the name Vixen, I suppose."

"So, Byron," Sally said, "I understand you're in the travel business."

"Oh, yes," he answered proudly. "I've been in the travel business for more than forty-five years, if you can believe that." He looked over at Grammy, as if for confirmation.

"Don't look at me, honey! Forty-five years ago I was still in diapers!" She tapped Josh on the elbow. "Do you believe that, Josh?" she asked, straightening her shoulders and looking down at him in a pretense of gravity.

"Oh, *sure*, Grammy!" he said. "If you still wore diapers in your twenties!"

"Well, you certainly asked for that one, didn't you, dear?" Byron asked. Then, obviously uncomfortable with the direction the conversation was taking, he said, "Not to change the subject, but—"

Josh burst out laughing. "Good one!" he exclaimed. He looked at the blank faces staring back at him. "Well, don't you get it? Not to *change* the subject? Diapers? *Change* diapers? Boy, you guys are sure dense."

Blue groaned, while Byron was trying to decide whether or not to take credit for an unintended pun.

Josh, still holding on to his fork, started gesturing wildly. "Man, there's this *great* movie you guys should see! It's called *Three's a Gas*, and it's about these three five-year-olds who still wear diapers—well, actually they don't really *need* to wear them, it's just part of the plot, because Buster B. Bodwell is trying to keep them from being adopted, and he thinks that if they still wear diapers nobody will want them, so in this one part, this one kid's diaper is so soaking wet that it falls off right by where this lady is washing her car, and she grabs it by mistake, thinking—"

"Josh!" Sally said sharply. "That is *not* dinner talk!"

Byron cleared his throat. "Yes. Well, the best thing

about the travel business is that it allows me to indulge in my favorite passion—which is, of course, travel! In fact, we're off again tomorrow—to Europe this time."

Sally spoke up now. "Yes, Blue and I were remarking on what a coincidence that was, since he is leaving tomorrow morning also—for four days in Venice."

"Who's Blue?" Grammy asked.

"Oh, that's my stupid—" Josh began.

"I'll explain it later," Blue said firmly, cutting Josh off with a piercing glance.

"Venice!" Byron was saying. "Marvelous! Where will you be staying?"

"The Hotel Bartolomeo," Blue said. "We'll be there four nights, Tuesday through Friday."

"Ah, the Hotel Bartolomeo, just off Campo San Bartolomeo. I know the place. It's small, but a good, clean bargain hotel. We'll be flying into Milan on Tuesday, and although I've got several irons in the fire, we have no *definite* plans during our first week in Italy. Maybe we can arrange to stop by and see you in Venice before—"

"Oh, that would be wonderful!" Sally broke in, a bit too enthusiastically. She looked at Blue, somewhat sheepishly. "Not that I'll be worried about him or anything like that—"

"Oh, *right*, Mom," Blue said, trying to hide his sudden

feeling of reciprocal affection under the guise of sarcasm. "Not that you'll be *worried* about me or anything."

Even though she had never heard of Josh Schumacher, by a strange coincidence Sparkie Leah Wilseam (another poet with an unusual name) wrote a lovely haiku entitled "Dinner Talk."

> *Witty, erudite,*
> *Books and movies, snow piled high*
> *Never diapers.*

"Dinner Talk"
by Sparkie Leah Wilseam (1980–),
in *2001 Best Haikus from North Dakota*
(Privately Printed)

tHIrteen

Blue didn't know what to do. He was dying to call Omaha—and perhaps even take a quick run over to her house—on this, his last night before his trip. But he felt he really shouldn't leave his mother to hold the fort alone with Byron and Grammy.

However, after dinner, after the others had gone into the living room, Blue stayed behind to clear the table. And on one of his trips to the kitchen he paused to give Omaha a call.

"Oh, hi," she said. "I was about to call you. How's it going with your other grandmother?"

"Just fine. It's going good."

"So—I guess you're all packed—"

"Yep! I'm all packed. I'd sure like to see you tonight, but I don't know how I can get away—at least not before they leave, and I don't know what time that'll be."

"I could come over there, maybe," Omaha said, only in the way of a suggestion, of course. "Maybe my mother could drop me off, and you could take me home after they leave—maybe."

"Hey, sure! Do that! We've just finished dinner, so come on right now, if you can."

"Okay. I'll see you in a few minutes then. Uh, you're sure it'll be okay with your mom?"

"Oh, yeah. It's fine. Come on. I'll be waiting."

Of course, neither Omaha nor Blue had any way of knowing what was about to transpire in the front room that evening.

Blue was still putting dishes in the dishwasher when the doorbell rang. He quickly dried his hands and left the remaining kitchen chores undone.

"Grammy, Byron—this is my friend Omaha," he said, as the two of them walked into the living room.

Byron stood up to be properly introduced as Grammy made a quick grab for Vixen, who started yapping and wiggling around like a fish out of water as soon as he saw Omaha.

"Sit down, Omaha," Sally said warmly after all the introductions were over. "We were just talking about Venice."

No one noticed the wooden stake turning and twisting in Omaha's heart. "Oh," she said, smiling weakly.

"I've never been there."

Suddenly Vixen made a flying leap off the couch, where he was sitting beside Grammy, and made a bee-line for Omaha.

"Vixen!" Grammy shouted. "Sit!"

Omaha bent down and attempted to pet the little dog, who was jumping and twirling around in circles. "It's okay," Omaha said. "He must smell Stinky."

"Well, he certainly *doesn't*!" Grammy said crossly. "He just came from the groomer's!"

Omaha looked up, puzzled. Then she caught on. "Oh, no!" she said with a little nervous laugh. "That's my cat. My cat's name is Stinky." Omaha blushed. "I guess it's not a very nice name, but she actually does—whoops! Whoa there, Vixen!"

Josh suddenly started giggling, covering his mouth with his hand and pointing at the dog, who had now somehow mistaken Omaha's ankle for a hairless female Shih Tzu.

Byron quickly jumped up from his chair and snatched up Vixen before the love affair got too serious. "Stupid dog!" he muttered under his breath, giving the animal a little smack on the behind.

Omaha took it all in stride. She kind of brushed the dog hair off her pants leg and pretended nothing untoward had happened.

"Yes, Venice is a beautiful place," Byron said, all the while keeping a firm hold on Vixen. "You should keep in mind that the city as a whole is very small. Actually, it's only about three miles long and a little over a mile wide. But it's unique in that it's composed of more than a hundred islands joined together by about four hundred bridges."

Josh was not listening to the travel agent's description of Venice. Instead, he was watching Vixen, who had managed to inch his way out from under Byron's hand and had just slithered quietly to the floor. Now he was crouching alongside of Grammy's sandaled foot.

"Now, here's the beautiful thing about Venice. Besides the entrances from the street, the houses that face on canals all have docks, so you can park your little boat or gondola right at your back doorstep!"

After several moments of single-minded determination, Vixen had finally succeeded in straddling Grammy's ankle. Josh leaned forward in anticipation. Oh, darn! Grammy gently kicked him off with her other foot, and now he was lying on his back wriggling around with his legs in the air.

Josh, intrigued with Vixen's antics, had almost completely blocked out Byron's droning on about Venice, until he was suddenly jolted to attention.

"Oh, by the way, David," Byron was saying, "if you're like most first-time visitors, you'll be confused by the word *ca'*. For instance, you might see a sign that says Ca' d'Oro, or Ca' Pesaro. Well, that *ca'* is simply a contraction of the Italian word for house—*casa*. So Ca' d'Oro is the house of gold, and Ca' Pesaro refers to the house of the Pesaro family, and so forth."

Josh recognized an opening when he saw it. Using every ounce of self-restraint he possessed, he kept a straight face all the way to the end of his question. "Are there any *Ca' Ca'*'s, perchance?" And then he collapsed like a house of cards, shaking in laughter at his own wonderful cleverness.

Byron looked a bit stunned, while Grammy let out a genuine, appreciative "Ha!" Sally just shook her head and sighed; Blue and Omaha had both seen it coming a mile away, so the necessary element of surprise was somewhat muted.

"One thing I would recommend," Byron said once things had settled down again, "is that you purchase a long-term pass for the waterbus—*vaporetto* in Italian—that traverses the Grand Canal—"

But wait! Vixen was off his back now, once again settling himself on his location of choice—Grammy's right ankle. Josh was frantically trying to signal over to Blue so he wouldn't miss the show, to the great annoyance of Sally. "What *is* it, Josh?" she barely whispered. Josh just shrugged and gave her his innocent look.

Meanwhile, Grammy was having quite a struggle. "No!" she said in a subdued but insistent voice. She suddenly raised the leg Vixen had attached himself to and started shaking it vigorously.

Josh covered his mouth with his hand and made little sputtering noises.

"Vixen! No! Mind your manners!"

The dog only stepped up his lovemaking antics.

Josh threw back his head and howled with laughter, while Sally turned away in disgust. Blue checked to see how Omaha was taking it, and was not surprised to see her watching the action with interest, showing no particular emotion.

Byron didn't make a move this time. He just said between clenched teeth, "I *told* you we should've had that dog fixed! And I can't believe you want to risk taking him on this trip! He's going to be *entirely* your responsibility, Gert. That's all I can say!"

Grammy had reached down now and was trying to break the hold poor Vixen had on her leg, but Vixen had other ideas. He only accelerated the pace.

"Go get your*self* fixed!" Grammy shot back at Byron.

"See how *you* like it!" She finally stood up from the couch and started to walk toward the small fireplace with little kicking steps, like a beginner in dancing class, with the tenacious dog still clinging on, now more from fear than *amore*.

"Let *go*, damn it!" she hissed, raising the leg with the dog attached a foot off the floor and shaking it like a mop.

Josh actually rolled off of his chair then and curled up in a fetal position, little squeaks of laughter coming out of him as if he were a slowly deflating rubber ball.

"Joshua! Get up off the floor!" Sally said. *"This instant!"*

Obviously, this job now cried out for Blue Avenger. He quietly walked over to Grammy and encircled the dog's belly with his hands. While the top hand faked affection by patting and stroking, the fingers of the bottom hand did the dirty work. With a yelp, Vixen loosened his grip and threw in the sponge.

Omaha stood up and made a suggestion. "Maybe Blue and I could take little Vixen for a walk, do you think?"

"A splendid idea," Byron said, quickly snapping the leash on Vixen's collar, while Grammy carefully repositioned herself on the couch and tried to regain her dignity. To Sally's surprised relief, she didn't even ask for a drink.

■ ■ ■

Blue and Omaha sat on the swing on Omaha's front porch for quite a while after he took her home that night, even though it was very late and he had to get up at four-thirty in the morning so he'd be ready when the DeSotos came by to pick him up.

They were obliged to whisper, of course, since the sound of their voices would carry through the night air right into the bedrooms of the neighboring homes. Omaha loved sitting out on the swing with Blue, because she could enjoy his company and his closeness without having to worry about—well, about things getting out of hand. So far they had managed to honor their agreement not to let this happen, but it certainly wasn't getting any easier.

The important thing was that they both agreed, on principle, that there were certain limits, certain boundaries, they would not cross. But the problem was, the boundaries they initially set were subject to change. "Can we go *this* far?" they asked each other. "This far and no further?" And on some nights, perhaps one or the other was vulnerable, was confused and mixed up and wondering, Well, why not? What difference would it make? What *real* difference? But by some lucky stroke of fate or design (or, as some would say, *un*lucky stroke), the night when both were of the same mind had not yet occurred. One or the other would suddenly remember their bargain and would abruptly change the environment or mood with purposeful resolve.

Perhaps Blue's wish for a more committed relationship was driven by a mostly subconscious desire to fully possess this girl, this Omaha, to make her truly his own. And perhaps Omaha's reluctance to agree to this was also driven by a subconscious desire, a desire deep within her, to—oh, how hopelessly old-fashioned and dumb and boring—to wait until they were ready to actually share their lives completely, contrasted with an occasional date, a late-night telephone call, a stolen hour in a secluded place, a constant worry about an unwelcome pregnancy. And because life is not easy and nothing is simple, often the two of them would find they were actually wishing for each other's subconscious desires—the one to possess and the other to wait for a better and more fulfilling time.

So these are the things they discussed, between lovely and passionate kisses and the almost overwhelming feelings of joy from holding each other close for long, long minutes they wished could last forever.

But still and all, how pleasant it is to contemplate that, amid all the noise and clamor and rush to selfish fulfillment, somewhere there does exist—if only in our dreams—an intelligent and thoughtful pair of lovers like Omaha Nebraska Brown and Blue Avenger.

Now, at last, it was time to part. But only for five nights, counting the one on the plane.

Omaha was too proud to mention again her one fervent wish—that he not sit beside Drusie in a gondola under the moonlight. But Blue remembered, and even though neither one of them actually spoke the words, both the request and the promise to honor it were floating like a zephyr in and around their heads, and it was as binding as if it were written in stone and signed in blood.

Just before turning in for the night, Blue thought he might try to memorize another Shakespeare quotation, and as he was flipping through the pages of Dr. Wood's printout he happened upon one from *Henry IV* that rang so true it took his breath away. *And I will die a hundred thousand deaths / Ere break the smallest parcel of this vow.*

fourteen

Three tired travelers finally arrived at the Venice airport late Tuesday afternoon after more than fifteen hours in the air and two plane changes. Louie had spent most of the time absorbed in his guidebook, while Blue had managed to read through Dr. Wood's Shakespeare quotations several times and memorize a goodly portion of them. Drusie watched the movies and read magazines.

They were met at the airport by a dark-complexioned middle-aged Egyptian named Ahmed. They knew he was their man because he was holding up a piece of paper on which was written the single word LOUIE. After the introductions, the first thing Ahmed did was take Drusie's bag from her, saying, "Please, madam? Allow me? Now, follow me, please, to the bus."

"I thought we were supposed to get to Venice from here by boat," Drusie said in a low voice as they hurried along behind Ahmed.

"No, according to the guidebook it's faster by bus, and cheaper, too," Louie said.

"But isn't Venice an island?" Drusie asked. "Oh," she added, "unless there's a bridge—"

"Yes, there is a bridge. It goes from the city of Mestre on the Italian mainland to the Piazzale Roma in Venice."

"What's the Piazzale Roma?"

"*Piazzale* means like a square. Like a *piazza*. It's Venice's bus stop and parking lot. No vehicles can go beyond there. There are only two squares in Venice that are called *piazza*. One is this *Piazzale Roma* and the other one is the largest square in Venice, *Piazza San Marco*. The others are all called *campo*, or, if they're real small, *campiello*."

Blue decided to try out his Shakespeare. "Hey, Drusie," he said, gesturing over to Louie. "He is very great in knowledge and accordingly valiant."

It took her a minute to catch on. Then she smiled and said, "Forsooth, 'tis true."

Ahmed led them to an orange bus which was parked alongside the curb in front of the airport. They followed their guide inside and down the aisle of the bus to the very last row of seats. Ahmed reached over and punched all four of their tickets by inserting them in a small canceling machine. Then they placed their suitcases in the storage area provided and set their backpacks down on the floor and held them between their knees.

Since Drusie was on vacation, she was dressed in shorts and a long-sleeved T-shirt, although she had a pair of jeans in her backpack in case the weather turned cold. But now, at 5:05 P.M. on the outskirts of Venice, the temperature was still pleasantly warm. Had she looked around her, however, she would have noticed that she was the only *signorina* headed for Venice who was so attired. As it turned out, Ahmed took it upon himself to educate her on this point.

"Excuse me, madam—"

"Hey, Ahmed, it makes me nervous when you call me madam." She extended her hand. "My name is Drusie."

Ahmed took her hand and smiled. "Drusie."

"And I'm Blue," Blue said, also extending his hand. "I'm a friend of Louie's," he added, and then felt stupid for stating the obvious.

"Louie, Drusie, and Blue," Ahmed repeated. "Americans from California?"

All three smiled and nodded yes. Blue noticed for the first time how really white Drusie's teeth were, and that a little dimple appeared on the left side of her face whenever she smiled. But it didn't mean anything. He was still in love with Omaha, and it would take more than white teeth and a dimple to change that.

Ahmed, who was sitting next to the window beside Louie, leaned over so he could speak directly to Drusie. The bus was well on its way by then, and he had to speak quite loudly in order to be heard. "Drusie, in Venice there are many churches."

"So I've heard."

"Yes. But have you also heard that you are not allowed in the church if you are wearing"—Ahmed gestured to her legs—"if you are wearing pants so short as that."

Drusie looked down at her legs and then at Ahmed. "But maybe I'm not planning to *go* to any churches—"

Ahmed opened his eyes wide. "You don't wish to see the great art in the churches of Venice?"

"Well, yeah, I guess, but—"

"The Venetians are very strong in their preference for modest dress, so I would recommend that, if you wish to have a pleasant stay, you will consider what I say."

Both Louie and Blue turned to see how Drusie was taking this bit of unsolicited advice. After thinking about it for a moment, she reached down and unzipped her backpack. She fished around for her jeans and got them out with two or three good jerks, stuffed back her pajamas, which had fallen out, and rezipped her pack. Then, right there on the bus, she stood up and pulled her long pants on over her shorts, even though she practically fell on Ahmed's lap several times while doing it.

"How's that?" she asked after she had completed her task.

Ahmed nodded. "Very good," he said.

After their bus had arrived at Piazzale Roma, Ahmed led them down some steps to the *vaporetto* stop, where they quickly boarded the waiting waterbus. "We get off just after we pass under the Rialto Bridge," he told them. "It is about ten minutes." Then he handed each of them a small ticket and told them that since it was a round-trip *vaporetto* ticket and only used once, it was still valid for another ride.

"Do we owe you for these?" Louie asked, holding up his ticket. "For the bus tickets and for these?"

"No," Ahmed said, looking somewhat surprised at the question. "No, these are included in your paid bill at the hotel."

Leaning against the guardrail along the side of the boat, the three travelers crossed the wide Grand Canal with the soft Venice breeze caressing their faces and playing in their hair. Soft breezes blow in Oakland, California, too, but somehow it was not the same.

Approaching the first stop, Drusie noticed the sign posted on the floating combination waiting room and dock. "What's the Ferrovie?" she asked, pronouncing the Italian word the best way she knew how, which happened to be incorrect.

Blue was curious, too, but he was content to let Drusie ask the questions.

"It's the train station," Louie said. "That FS on the building up there stands for Ferrovie dello Stato, Italy's state railway."

"Permesso!"

One of the young workers on board the *vaporetto* was making his way through the crowd over to the exit gate next to where Blue was standing. When the waterbus was within a few feet of the dock, the young man skillfully tossed the loose end of a sturdy rope around a low pile emerging from the water adjacent to the floating dock. Then he gracefully secured the rope with a kind of simple figure-eight knot and pulled it tight as the operator of the *vaporetto* inched the craft alongside the dock, accelerating the engine in loud staccato bursts. The gates on either side of the waterbus were made of horizontal metal bars about a foot apart, and when the boat came to a stop, the young Italian (Drusie was certain he was Italian, an extremely *cute* Italian) grabbed the waist-level upper rung and slid the gate open with a clang, making about a four-foot opening through which passengers could enter or exit directly onto the floating combination dock and waiting area.

Our three Americans watched the docking operation in a kind of otherworldly trance, brought about partly because they hadn't been to bed for over thirty hours and they couldn't remember when they had had their last meal, and partly because they were, after all, in Venice.

"Your first time?" a voice asked.

Drusie turned to see who was speaking to her. It was a short, gray-haired woman with a round, pleasant face.

"This *is* your first trip to Venice?"

Drusie smiled. "Yes. How did you know?"

The woman gestured over to the young man who handled the rope. "You'll never forget that, as long as you live—the way he tossed that rope." The woman nodded and patted Drusie's arm in a motherly fashion and then made her way through the crowd to the covered middle section of the boat and took a seat next to a man reading a newspaper.

Drusie glanced again at the young Italian and was surprised and pleased to see he was watching her, and when their eyes met he smiled at her in an unmistakably flirtatious manner. And she smiled back.

In a few minutes they were on their way again. "Oh!" Drusie breathed, about to vocalize exactly what her brother and Blue were thinking. "Just *look* at those beautiful old houses or palaces or whatever they are, all those pretty reddish-browns and beiges and pinks and ivory colors, and the different heights and sizes! Look how they're all joined together side by side like that, except for when those other canals come curving in between them to join up with ours. Oh, look at those *balconies*, and those windows—all those arches and pillars reflecting in the water! And they're so *old*! Oh, my God, what's *that* one?" she said, out of breath now, and pointing at a huge and stately three-story Baroque palace on her right.

"Ca' Pesaro," Blue said, reading the banner strung across the front. "Gallery of Modern Art and the Oriental Museum."

"What's the *ca'* mean?" Drusie asked.

"It's the abbreviation for *casa*, the Italian word for house," Blue chimed in before Louie could respond, for that was one question he *could* answer.

"Whoops! That was close!" Blue said suddenly, as a sleek black gondola barely made it out of their way in time. "Look at that thing bobbing around in our wake!"

At the sight of the gondola, Blue's mind was suddenly filled with thoughts of Omaha, and a wave of sadness washed over him. Oh, how he missed her, and how he wished she were beside him now, holding his hand and sharing with him these first, unforgettable moments of Venice.

The Hotel Bartolomeo was a short but confusing walk from the Rialto Bridge *vaporetto* stop. Again they followed Ahmed, first along a wide walkway bordering the Grand Canal, and then turning to their right into a narrow alleyway bounded on both sides by high stuccoed buildings, and then left onto another wide walkway leading directly into a very crowded and spacious rectangle-shaped *campo* with a large statue of a man in its center.

Ahmed stopped a few feet away from the statue and set Drusie's suitcase down on the pavement beside him. "We are now in Campo San Bartolomeo. Can you guess who that is?" he asked, pointing to the statue.

"Uh, San Bartolomeo?" Drusie ventured.

"Aha!" Ahmed exclaimed, laughing. "As you Americans say, *gotcha*!"

"So who is it?" Louie asked, since it was his business to learn all he could about this place in the short time allotted to him.

"That is a statue of Carlo Goldoni, Venice's most famous playwright." He picked up the suitcase. "Okay, then, the hotel is through that little alleyway directly ahead of us. But first, look there, to your left. Do you know what that is?"

Blue looked to his left and saw, a short distance off, the wide steps that led up to the Rialto Bridge. "The Rialto Bridge?" he asked.

"Correct! And the reason I point that out to you is this. Tomorrow, when you find yourselves lost in *la bella Venezia*, merely follow the yellow signs you see high on the sides of the buildings which direct you *Per Rialto*—to the Rialto. And when you are back at the bridge"—Ahmed snapped his fingers—"you are no longer lost! Okay? You understand?"

They all nodded. "Yes. Thank you. We understand," they said.

Once they were inside the small lobby of the hotel, Ahmed greeted the clerk on duty and then plopped himself down on one of the large, comfortable chairs behind the counter. "They are here, Mario," he said with a tired laugh. "The Americans have arrived."

Mario asked for their passports and then turned and removed two of the keys that were hanging on the wall behind him. He handed one to Louie and the other to Drusie.

"Your rooms are on the third floor," he said, indicating the stairs behind him. "Your room key also opens the toilet and shower across the hall. Breakfast is included. The hours are seven-thirty to nine. If you have any problem just let me know."

Ahmed raised his hand in a slow wave and smiled from his chair behind the counter as the three Americans began to make their way up the narrow staircase.

Yes, their eyes were bloodshot and tired and they couldn't remember when they had had their last meal; nevertheless, they quickly checked out the two rooms, located the toilet and shower across the hall, and promptly decided to go out and see Venice.

Forty-five minutes later, just prior to sundown in Piazza San Marco, in the heart of Venice, Louie DeSoto fell in love for the very first time in his life—an all-consuming, flat-out, head-over-heels, six-ways-to-Sunday love. Her name was Angela, and she was Italian.

When he first saw her, she was crawling around on her hands and knees, surrounded by pigeons, not more than twenty yards away from the shining golden splendor of the façade of the Basilica di San Marco, with its breathtakingly beautiful mosaic scenes in the huge archways looming overhead, the replicas of the four famous gilded-bronze horses looking down at the awestruck admirers below, and the crowning glory of its Byzantine cupolas reflecting the final rays of the setting sun. But to Louie, one single lock of Angela's golden hair was far more beautiful than all the mosaics and gilded Byzantine cupolas in the world. And the sight of her there, down on all fours, put the replicas of the magnificent horses of Venice to shame. For Louie, the most challenging and terrifying event in his entire life was about to transpire, but was he not in Venice—where even the most impossible love-dreams can come true?

At times like this, one must work alone, unhindered by sisters or friends. He spotted Blue and Drusie, now standing several feet away from him, looking this way and that, almost overwhelmed by the magnificent panorama of Piazza San Marco at dusk.

"Hey!" Louie said, with unmistakable urgency in his voice. "Drusie! Blue! Listen!"

"What?" asked Drusie.

"What's wrong?" asked Blue.

Louie's mouth felt tight and dry. He quickly moistened his lips and began to speak. "You see that girl over there, down on the pavement? I'm going to go over and talk to her now, and I want you to leave me alone. Do you hear? *You don't know me!*"

As Drusie and Blue stared at him in amazement, he turned on his heel and made his way through the

dwindling crowd toward the object of his desire. Gathering up every ounce of his courage in a grand do-or-die effort, he got down on one knee and looked into her eyes—one of emerald green and the other an amber brown. "Lost your contact, huh? Need some help?"

FIFTEEN

"So what *happened* to you last night, Louie?" Drusie asked.

They were drinking *caffe latte* and eating marmalade croissants out of a basket while squeezed in the corner table of the small room reserved for breakfast at the Hotel Bartolomeo. They had a feeling of being rushed, since every seat was taken and a few people were milling about in the hallway, obviously waiting for an opening.

For a moment Louie could only sit there with a silly grin on his face.

"*So?*" Drusie insisted, as Blue nodded sympathetically at his friend with a knowing I've-been-there-done-that look.

Louie didn't answer.

Drusie looked at Blue. "What time did he get in, anyway?" she asked.

"Don't ask me. I was already asleep. I hardly remember even opening the door."

"It wasn't late," Louie said. "It wasn't *that* late."

"So what's her name?" Blue asked, refilling his cup by simultaneously pouring from two pitchers, one filled with hot milk and the other with strong coffee. "You can at least tell us that, can't you?"

"Her name is Angela," Louie said slowing, savoring the word with just a hint of self-parody—for, though a part of him knew that what he was feeling was genuine, another part just couldn't believe it was happening to him. "And that's all I'm going to say. My lips are sealed."

"Good!" Drusie said, feeling out of sorts for some reason. "And by the way, you owe Blue one hundred thousand of those *lire* things."

"*Lire* things?"

"We stopped at an ATM on our way back here to the hotel last night," Blue said. "The money came out"—he snapped his fingers—"just like that! The machine's right out there in the *campo*. You can't miss it. Anyway, I withdrew three hundred thousand lire and lent Drusie one hundred thousand so she'd have some money. Then we went back to that McDonald's we saw on the way to San Marco and had something to eat."

Louie reached for his wallet and took out his ATM

card. "Listen, Drusie, how about giving me some of that money and you can take the card and get some more today. You know the code?"

"T-W-I-N?"

"That's right."

Drusie slipped the card into the waistband money-holder she wore under her T-shirt.

"Wait a second," Blue said, reaching for his wallet. "Why don't I lend you a hundred thousand, too? It's enough to buy an awful lot of hamburgers. And then Drusie can pay me back for both of you when she makes her withdrawal."

"Okay, thanks," Louie said, taking the money.

"I think we'd better get out of here," Drusie said. "People are waiting to sit down. So what are we doing now, anyway? What's the plan?"

Louie wiped his mouth with his paper napkin and checked his watch. "Uh-oh. My plan is I've got to get going. I'm meeting Angela at nine this morning on the Rialto Bridge."

"Hey," Blue said. "I thought we were going to look for that bookstore. I want to check my e-mail." He stood up and smiled back at a woman his mother's age who was sitting at the next table.

"You don't need me," Louie said. "The address is on

that information sheet I sent to you."

"Well, I'd rather you came, too, but I guess if you've got other plans—"

"You can borrow my map. I have it marked on there."

Blue looked at Drusie. "You want to come?"

"Sure. But I want to go upstairs first."

"Shall we all try to meet for lunch?" Blue asked as they were climbing the stairs to their rooms. "We could meet at that same McDonald's."

"Uh, don't count on me," Louie said.

Drusie paused in front of her door. "You could always invite her along, you know. Don't we get to meet her?"

"We'll see," Louie said lightly. "Time will tell." He looked at Blue. "You have the key?"

Blue nodded and opened the door. Louie rinsed off his hands in the little sink and checked himself out in the mirror, baring his teeth and turning his head from side to side. "Well, I'm off," he said, giving Blue a little salute and hurrying out the door.

After a few moments Blue remembered the map. "Hey, hold it!" he called out. "You forgot to give me the map!"

But it was too late. Louie was already down the stairs and out the door, whistling a merry tune and walking on air.

■ ■ ■

Blue decided to wait for Drusie downstairs in the lobby. He was surprised to see that Ahmed was still there, sitting at the desk in front of a computer monitor. Somehow he was able to work the keyboard with his left hand in spite of the cigarette dangling from his fingers, hold a phone up to his ear with his right hand, confirm reservations in French, and nod a greeting to Blue—without missing a beat.

While Ahmed was thus engaged, Blue stepped up to the large wall-map of Venice and tried to locate the Rialto Bridge. Ahmed hung up the phone before he could find it.

"You work long hours," Blue commented.

Ahmed knocked the ashes off his cigarette and considered Blue's statement as if it had never occurred to him before. Finally, he nodded. "Yes," he said. "I do."

A group of people chattering in Italian came down the stairs and handed their room keys over to Ahmed. *"Grazie. Buon giorno,"* he said, smiling and hanging the keys on the wall behind him. One of the men, who was carrying a little white dog under his arm, asked Ahmed a question, and Ahmed reached under the counter and handed him a phone book. The man looked at it briefly and put it back on the counter. *"Grazie,"* he said, and went out the door to join the others.

Ahmed leaned back in his chair and took a deep drag on his cigarette. "Yes. I'm here all night, and sometimes in the days. This is my other home, it seems."

A young couple wearing backpacks entered the lobby and looked around tentatively. "Possible to make reservations for Saturday, mate?" the man asked.

Ahmed extended his index finger and moved it back and forth several times. *"Completo."* After they left he looked at Blue and shrugged. "Those Australians—they should call ahead," he said, "especially for Easter weekend." He smiled and motioned to the phone with his head. "Like the French."

"I wonder if you can help me find something," Blue said, looking at the map again. "It's a place called Agostino's. I think they sell old books and stuff."

Ahmed put the phone book back under the counter and extinguished his cigarette. He studied Blue carefully. After a minute he asked, "You have business there?"

"Not exactly. Well, yes, I guess I do. They're supposed to have a computer there that Louie and I can use. They rent computers."

Ahmed nodded. "Ah. I see."

Blue got out the information sheet and read the address. "Campo San Polo. Is that hard to find?"

Ahmed got up and approached the wall map. "I have

heard some rumors about Mr. Agostino." He again studied Blue's face, as if looking for clues.

"Really? Like what?"

Ahmed shrugged. "Shall we say his suppliers are sometimes rather difficult to track down?"

Blue thought for a second about the implication of that remark. Then he said, "Well, that won't concern us, since we won't be buying anything from him. We'll just be using his computer."

"Very good." Ahmed pointed to a place on the map. "All right, look closely. You cross here, at the Rialto, go this way, then that way. See here—this Campo San Polo? It is near there. You can ask when you get in the area."

"Okay, thanks. I guess I can find it." Blue looked up. There was Drusie now, waltzing down the stairs with that unmistakable sure-footed exuberance that had *future movie star* written all over it. Blue smiled with pleasure at the sight of her, even though she was just not his type and Omaha still had nothing to fear.

"Did that guy with the little white dog come downstairs?" Drusie asked as they were leaving the hotel.

"Uh-huh. Why?"

"Wasn't he *so* cute?"

"Kind of old for you, wasn't he?" Blue teased.

"Very funny. Anyway, he was standing around waiting for those other people when I came out of the bathroom, so I just went over and told him what a cute little dog he had."

"Oh."

"I guess he didn't speak English too well, because he just smiled at me and said *'Grazie.'* "

They had walked through Campo San Bartolomeo now and were headed for the Rialto Bridge when Blue spotted a display of Venice maps and a selection of travel guides for sale in a small kiosk filled with souvenirs, mostly little glass objects made in Murano.

"Wait," he said. "I think I want to get a map here." He ended up buying a guidebook, too, and Drusie couldn't resist getting a tiny pink glass duck.

A moment later they were on the bridge and were able to squeeze in among the people who were lined up against the railing, gazing down at the wide expanse of the Grand Canal until it curved gracefully out of sight some distance away. Drusie lifted the little camera that was hanging from her neck and started snapping pictures.

"I'm really sorry now I didn't bring the camcorder," she said, as Blue began to unfold the map. "Look over there, Blue—the way those old buildings reflect all ripply in the water! And look at those *vaporetto*s chugging along, and all those boats carrying boxes and vegetables and stuff. Hey, look! There's one full of garbage!" She pointed to their left. "See the *vaporetto* stop where we got off last night. Listen! Hear that accordion? It must be a gondola! Hey, the singer's not too bad. Look! Here it comes under the bridge!"

Blue looked up for a second from the map he was studying, trying to hold it steady against the breeze. "Yeah. I see."

"I'm *really* sorry I didn't bring the camcorder. Just because Louie said it was too big and old—"

Blue held the map to one side and turned to look at her. "Old? How old?"

"Oh, my mother got it when Louie and I were toddlers," Drusie answered, still snapping away on the camera. "She said we were so *cute*."

"Listen!" Blue said, getting her attention with a little nudge of his elbow. "Do you think she ever took a video of Louie holding the door open and calling for his little friends? You know, like she was talking about at dinner last week."

"Gee, maybe. You mean like Omo and those guys? God, it's been so long since we've looked at those videos. And I've heard that story about Louie so many times it's sickening, so I just can't remember if she taped it or not.

Anyway, what difference does it make?"

"Well, don't you see? If there's a *video* of Louie calling to his little friends, we can show it to that Seratt guy, and—"

"You're right! That would *prove* that those were really Louie's characters!"

"So can you find out? Can you e-mail your mother and ask her?"

"No. She doesn't do e-mail. But my father does. I can ask him, and he can have her check them out. She used to write the dates and subject matter and stuff on them, and anyway she'd probably remember if she *had* video-taped that. But like I said, we haven't looked at them for years. Jeez, Blue! What a brainstorm!"

"I don't want to say anything to Louie yet, though. We should wait until we see if there really is such a video. We don't want to get his hopes up for nothing."

"Yeah, you're right."

"Let's get going," Blue said finally. "After we get on the other side, we should go straight for a little while and then turn to the left."

But Drusie wanted to stop again shortly after they had climbed down the long flight of steps on the north side of the canal. "Look at that funny little statue!" she said, grabbing hold of Blue's shirt and dragging him over to it. "He's all hunched over! It looks really old, doesn't it?

What's that supposed to be that he's holding on his back? Can I see your guidebook for a sec? Maybe it tells about it in there."

"Ah, let's see here," Blue said, turning to the section describing the Rialto Bridge and environs. "That's the *Gobbo di Rialto*. And he's holding up a flight of stairs, which is seen as an allegory for the heavy taxes the Venetians had to pay. And it *is* old! Sculpted in 1541. *Gobbo* means 'hunchback.' "

"Wow—1541! That was there before Shakespeare was born," Drusie whispered.

"It was also there before Oxford was born," Blue added. "You know, he may have even seen it when he was visiting here."

And then, reflecting on what he had just said, Blue suddenly felt almost transported for a moment—almost like his whole life had been suspended in a chilling, miraculous void. He knelt down and reached through the bars of the little enclosure and slowly ran his hand along the shoulder and arm of the stone figure. "He might have even touched this very statue."

"Ooh, that kind of gives you a weird feeling, doesn't it?"

"Yeah, it does," he said softly. "It's *very* weird." He kept stroking the rough surface of the little statue—

savoring the sensations he was feeling, but at the same time attempting to analyze and demystify them, to understand exactly what he was experiencing, and why.

Drusie had stepped back a few feet now to take a picture, but still Blue kept his hand where it was, touching the very surface that Edward de Vere might have touched over four centuries ago. It's just a moment in time, he finally decided. A fleeting moment that has nowhere to go. It's just an emotion—a one-sided bit of self-indulgence—it's all in my mind. And yet why do I feel this *connection*, so much like the way I felt when I first saw his likeness on a book cover—

Suddenly Drusie was kneeling beside him, reaching her hand through the bars, too. "Do you think he really *touched* it?" she asked. "And if he really *was* Shakespeare, that means we're touching the same spot that was touched by the greatest poet of the ages! That is really *something!*"

And then it happened. For a few fleeting seconds her hand touched his as they knelt by the statue together, kneeling so close that he could feel the warmth of her body—this beautiful, wonderful (yes, wonderful) girl and him, sharing a moment so rare and moving he would remember it forever.

Blue stood up so suddenly he almost lost his balance.

He was shocked and appalled by what he was feeling now. And then, almost mockingly, Shakespeare's words echoed in his mind:

> *Sigh no more, ladies, sigh no more,*
> *Men were deceivers ever,*
> *One foot on sea and one on shore,*
> *To one thing constant never.*

After several minutes Blue was back on an even keel. A momentary lapse, he told himself. Just one of those things. Omaha has nothing to fear.

Pretty soon Blue gave up on the map. The street names were either too hard to read or nonexistent. They had crossed a myriad of bridges and traversed a maze of sidewalks and alleyways—some lined with shops and restaurants, and others merely windowless expanses of peeling stucco. At last they came upon a bridge that appeared to Blue to be of some significance. He squinted at the faded street name painted on the side of the building in front of them and announced victoriously, "Wait! I think we're almost there!"

He unfolded the map again. "Uh-oh. Now I see where I went wrong. Remember way back there when we made that first left turn after the *Gobbo*? Well, I overshot our street. That's why we ended up way up here." He pointed to a spot on the map. "See? We were supposed to be somewhere around here. Between here and here. Wow! Did *we* come the long way!"

Drusie laughed. "Really? I would never have guessed it."

They walked on just a few yards farther and suddenly a large *campo* opened up before them. They stopped to look around the busy square filled with people of all ages, from little old ladies wearing heavy knit sweaters to little boys scurrying around chasing soccer balls.

"Oh, there's the place!" Drusie exclaimed. "See that little sign? You can barely read it, but I'm sure it says Agostino's."

"Oh, yeah. I see it now. Let's go."

Twenty minutes later Blue was seated at a computer, while Drusie was in the adjacent room with her hands clasped behind her back, peering at the old books and sheet music carelessly crammed on the floor-to-ceiling shelves. She soon realized she was truly in another country when she didn't see even one title printed in English. Meanwhile, Blue was checking his mail. He read the one from Omaha first.

```
Dear Blue!
   I hope you get this. I haven't sent
much mail yet, but I think I'm doing it
right. (Thanks for the computer!) Did you
have a good flight over? What's it really
like over there? Is the hotel okay? I
checked the weather report in the Star,
and it didn't have Venice, but it said
Milan was 78 degrees and clear. So I
suppose it's about the same in Venice.
Sounds really nice. I hope you're taking
lots of pictures.
Love, Omaha
P.S. Shall I abide in this dull world,
which in thy absence is no better than a
sty? Write to me!
```

Blue smiled and reread her postscript. Although he
didn't have Dr. Wood's Shakespeare quotations with
him, he remembered one that would do just fine:

```
Dear Omaha,
   How like a winter hath my absence
been from thee! I DO miss you and wish
you were here. And thanks for the mail!
```

```
It's Wednesday morning and I'm at this
store where Mr. Forni arranged for Louie
and me to have access to a computer.
Only Louie's not here. You won't believe
this, but he met a girl in St. Mark's
Square yesterday and made a date to
meet her again this morning at the
Rialto Bridge!
   Everything's okay so far. Our hotel is
nice, and there are plenty of McDonald's
around. Mr. Agostino, the guy running
this place, is a very tainted fellow, and
full of wickedness, according to my
friend Ahmed, the clerk at our hotel.
```

Blue paused, wondering whether he should put "very tainted fellow, and full of wickedness" in quotation marks. He decided not to. She would recognize it from Dr. Wood's quotations.

```
   At first Agostino wasn't going to let me
use the computer because I wasn't Louie,
and that's whose name he had in his book.
But then he finally did. He was busy in
this little dinky back room smoking his
```

big cigar and talking with some British
guy when we came in, and this kid at
the front had to call him to get his
permission and so forth. Now he's back
there again and the door is open so I can
see them looking through some kind of old
papers and stuff, but the Brit keeps
saying they're too expensive.

Oh, I almost forgot. There's also this
woman named Tina here. She just sits on a
stool by the window looking really bored
and eating little bits of beef jerky from
a cellophane bag. When Mr. Agostino came
over to check me in, I noticed he went
over and patted her leg and whispered
something in her ear which produced quite
a giggle. I have a feeling there's a
little hanky-panty (as Josh would say)
going on around here. (God, I hope
Agostino doesn't see this or I'll get
drawn and quartered. Last night I read in
Louie's guidebook that they really used to
do that in Venice, you know.) I can't take
pictures because I forgot to bring my

camera. But you can remind me to bring one
when I come back here with you someday.
    Thither write, my queen, and with mine
eyes I'll drink the words you send!
Love, Blue

The next message was signed "Your friend, DYAD,"
but of course Blue knew who it was from:

Hi, Blue
    hE HAs BeeN lIviNG In a SHOEbOX aLL
tHiS TIme!
Your friend, DYAD

Dear DYAD,
    If you say so! Thanks for the tip. I'll
see what I can do with it.
Your friend, Blue

There was one more message. It was from Dr. Wood:

Hello, Blue!
    This is just a short note to let you
know I'm now on-line! Got a big fancy

computer (fax included!) last weekend and am having a ball surfing the Web. Your brother, Josh, gave me your e-mail address. He's quite a kid, isn't he? I hope you're enjoying yourself in Venice. As you probably know, our friend Oxford was there for quite a while in the year 1575. Did you know you can get Shakespeare's ENTIRE WORKS on the Web? They're in the public domain, so it's perfectly legal. Did you ever read "The Merchant of Venice"?

Best regards,
James Wood

Dear Dr. Wood,
   E-mail from Dr. Wood! What a surprise! All goes well in Venice. I'll try to write more later. (Oh, yes—don't believe a word of what my brother, Josh, says!)
Blue

He thought he'd better write something to his mother and Josh and decided to take the easy way out.

```
Dear Mom and Joshpot,
   Having wonderful time. Wish you were
here.
Love, Blue
```

Blue realized he needed a copy of Tuesday's latest message so he could figure out the code later, and he really wanted to keep a copy of Omaha's letter, too. He checked the printer for paper and clicked it on, but as soon as it started to print, Mr. Agostino suddenly appeared from the back room and shook his finger at him. "The printing is not included," he said brusquely. "The printing is extra." He pointed first to a faded price chart hanging on the wall and then to the kid sitting at the cash register. "You pay the boy," he said. Then he went back to his little room and closed the door.

After Blue finished printing, Drusie sent her father a message with her inquiry about a possible video of Louie. When they left the store, Tina was still sitting on her stool, looking out the window and looking very bored.

"Did you notice how short her skirt was?" asked Drusie after they had left the shop.

Blue laughed. "Tina's, you mean?"

"Who else! It was six inches shorter than my shorts,

for God's sake. Good thing Ahmed wasn't there."

"Well, maybe she doesn't go into churches."

Drusie rolled her eyes. "Yeah, maybe, but what do you think was going on with Agostino and that English guy in the back room? I know it had something to do with *Romeo and Juliet*, because I kept hearing little snatches—like that famous one where Romeo talks about every cat and dog—"

"I don't know that one. Dr. Wood has a lot of *R & J* in his little booklet, but I don't remember anything about every cat and dog."

Drusie laughed. "Neither could Roger Bates—you know, that guy who played Romeo opposite me last summer? Anyway, the speech goes, *Heaven is here / Where Juliet lives, and every cat and dog / And little mouse, every unworthy thing, / Live here in heaven and may look on her, / But Romeo may not.*" Drusie paused. "Jeez, you don't suppose they had some ancient quarto or something back there, do you? After all, Agostino *is* in the old-book business."

"Could be. But listen, I want to go back and check the mail again later today. His sign said they're open between seven and nine in the evenings. So let's go back then. I'm really anxious to hear what your mother says about Omo."

"And anxious to hear from Omaha again, perhaps?"

Drusie asked with a knowing smile.

"Perhaps," Blue said, smiling back. "So—what do you want to do now?"

"See more of Venice, I guess. You know, I'd really love to run into Louie and Angela. Do you think we will?"

Blue couldn't say, since, as a first-time visitor, he had no way of knowing that Venice is peculiar that way. As it happened, Drusie was the first to spot them. It was mid-afternoon in the Piazza San Marco, and Louie and Angela were waiting in line to purchase elevator tickets for the ride to the top of the Campanile, the famous tower in the southeast corner of the square.

"Look! There they are!" Drusie said. She quickly ducked behind Blue and peeked over his shoulder, whistling softly between her teeth. "Can you believe that's really Louie there, *holding hands* with a girl? And look at her! She's not even that pretty—I don't think, do you? Do you think we should go over and surprise him?"

"No." Blue shook his head. "No," he said softly. "I think we should leave him alone."

"Don't you even want to spy on them for a while?"

"No."

Drusie stood still for a moment, her attention suddenly drawn to the clock tower on the side of the square opposite the Campanile. There, at the very top, two large, dark male figures had begun to strike the hour on the huge bell that was hanging between them. "Four o'clock," she said. "No wonder I'm so tired. Let's go back to the hotel and rest up before we have dinner and try to find Agostino's again."

"Okay," Blue said. "But it won't take as long to get there next time. I know how to find it now."

Louie was held spellbound by the magnificent view of the city from the top of the Campanile, but now Angela wanted to take him to visit the Ghetto of Venice.

"We'll go on the *vaporetto*," she said. "We can get on here at San Marco and travel almost the entire length of the Canal Grande. It's a beautiful ride, with many fine houses and palaces. I will never tire of it. Then we will get off at the San Marcuola stop and walk to the north into the Cannaregio *sestiere*, or district, and soon we are in the Ghetto."

"Lead the way," Louie said. "I'm at your beck and call."

Angela smiled. "My beck and call?"

"It's just a saying," Louie said, still trying to picture her in the half-inch-thick glasses she told him she had worn until just the year before, and understanding all too well the peculiar feelings of isolation and loneliness that come with being the smartest kid in the class.

"We have quite a long ride," Angela said, as they boarded the *vaporetto*. "So let's sit inside."

After they found a seat she began to tell him about the Ghetto. "The Venice Ghetto is important because it is the first Jewish ghetto in the world," she said. "The Venice Council of Ten decreed back in the early sixteenth century that all the Jews in Venice would be confined to that one area at night. During the day the Jews were allowed out, but they still had to wear identifying badges and caps all the time. And the only work they were allowed to do was in medicine or trading textiles or moneylending."

"Where'd they get the word 'ghetto'?"

"It comes from *geto*, the Venetian word for 'foundry,' since that's where the Venice foundries were in those days. Anyway, as more Jewish people kept coming into Venice—and since they were all confined to that one area—the only thing they could do was build their houses higher and higher. So, even now, the tallest houses in Venice are still in the Ghetto."

"I'll have to be sure to mention that in my game," Louie said.

"Yes." Angela nodded. "That would be good." She looked out the window for a minute and added as kind of an afterthought, "No wonder Shylock was so pissed off."

Louie, taken by surprise at her choice of words, looked at her and burst out laughing. "Where'd you learn that?"

"What?"

" 'Pissed off.' "

She shrugged. "It's just an expression you use in America, isn't it? So that's why I felt kind of sorry for him."

"Who?"

"Shylock. In *The Merchant of Venice*. Didn't you ever read it?"

"No," Louie said. "I'm not really into Shakespeare that much."

"Well, you should read that one. It's got some beastly anti-Semitic stuff in there, but our teacher said it was reflecting the attitude that a lot of the British people had at that time." She suddenly stopped talking and pointed to a large impressive palace on their right. "See that? That huge building with those two rows of arched windows? That's called 'The House of the Thirteen Windows.' Or the Ca' Moro-Lin. In Shakespeare's time it was really two separate houses, and in one of them a member of the Moro family murdered his wife—whose name was Desdemona—and that's partly where Shakespeare got his plot for *Othello*." Angela smiled at him with slightly raised eyebrows and a humorously scolding look. "But, then, you probably haven't read that, either."

"Nope," said Louie, with an exaggerated apologetic smile of his own. "Not yet. But I suspect I'll probably have to get around to it one of these days soon."

SIXTEEN

Mario was on duty when Blue and Drusie got back to the hotel, and he handed Blue a message slip along with his key. "It's a local call, so you may use that phone," he said, pointing to the telephone on the end of the counter.

"What is it?" asked Drusie. "Is everything all right?"

Blue quickly read the note. "Everything's fine," he said. "My grammy's in town and wants me to call her."

Drusie vaguely remembered that on one of the legs of their flight Blue had mentioned his grammy and how she had just come back into their lives. "Where is she?"

"It says the Bauer-Grunwald. No doubt that's one of the nicer hotels. Her husband's a travel agent, you know. I guess I'd better give them a call."

A few minutes later he had his grammy on the line. "Hello, Blue, darling," she said, pleasantly surprising him by remembering to call him Blue, even though he had just mentioned it to her once last Sunday night in Oakland. Now she was telling him that she and Byron had taken the train from Milan the day before but were too "bushed" to call him. They were finally all rested up, and did he want to go out to dinner a little later—say about seven.

"Just a second," Blue said, covering the mouthpiece with his hand. "Do you want to go out to dinner with them?" he asked.

"Sure."

"Well, Grammy, my friend Drusie is here, too, and—" Blue paused long enough to allow Grammy to invite Drusie, then said, "Okay! Great! So you guys will come by here around seven?" He paused again. "Between six-thirty and seven-thirty? Okay! See you then!"

He hung up the phone, saying, "It's all set." And then he hesitated, wondering whether he should tell her about Vixen now, or let her be surprised. He decided on now. "Did I tell you they have their little doggie with them? His name is Vixen, and—dog lover that you are—I'm sure you're going to really flip over this one!"

But as it turned out, Vixen was conspicuous by his absence.

Blue didn't ask about him until they were all seated in the restaurant and had placed their orders. "Where's Vixen, anyway? Did you leave him in the hotel?"

Grammy gave Byron a not-too-pleasant sideways

glance. "Vixen is at the vet's," she said tersely.

"Oh, is he sick?" Drusie asked in alarm, for she had so looked forward to meeting him after Blue's glowing description.

"No, he's not sick!" Grammy said, again casting a withering look at her travel agent. "The truth is, he's been *fixed*."

"Ooh," Drusie said, scrunching up her nose. "Poor little thing."

"Poor little thing, my foot," Byron muttered, dabbing his mouth with his napkin.

"He's obliged to spend the night at the vet's," explained Grammy, "but I'll pick him up first thing in the morning—and then Vixen and I will bid a fond farewell to Byron as he leaves for a lovely cruise on the Brenta and a two-night stay in Padua."

"You don't *have* to miss the cruise, Gert," Byron said, his face turning crimson. "All you have to do is *board* the dog for a couple of nights. It's just *not* that big a deal!"

"I am *not* going to board my dog, Byron! He's suffered enough already!" Grammy turned to Blue and Drusie. "We've been invited by an old friend of Byron's on a lovely cruise, but, unfortunately, Vixen is not included, and I simply *refuse* to leave him at the vet's."

"Well, wait!" Drusie said. "You don't have to do that!

I'd be more than happy to baby-sit him! And Blue will help me, won't you, Blue?"

"Well—I don't know. Maybe they won't allow us to keep him in the hotel."

"Sure they will! That little white dog stays there! Anyway, we can ask Ahmed when we get back."

A minute later, while Byron and Grammy were involved in their own discussion, she quietly tapped Blue's arm. "We're not going to make it back in time to check the e-mail tonight, you know," she said softly.

Blue nodded. "I know. I was thinking about that, too. We'll do it first thing in the morning."

When the four of them got back to the hotel, Ahmed was leaning back in his chair behind the counter, smoking a cigarette and reading the paper. "No problem," he said in answer to Drusie's question about the dog.

Grammy was very pleased. "That is *so* sweet of you, Drusie, my dear!" she said, giving her a big, exuberant hug. "We can have Vixen here by nine in the morning, if that's not too early for you—"

"That's perfect," Drusie said. "It'll be fun. And, besides," she added, winking at Blue, "*Teen* mag says a little dog can be a great ice-breaker when you're trying to meet guys. But"—she shook her index finger—

"German shepherds and pit bulls are a no-no, since they tend to have the opposite effect."

"Well, that's fine, dear," Grammy said vacantly, since her mind was busily occupied comparing the tiny lobby of the Hotel Bartolomeo with the grand and spacious one of the Bauer-Grunwald.

After she and Byron had gone, Ahmed put the newspaper on the counter and reached for Drusie's key. "Louie came in earlier," he said to Blue. "Your key is in the room."

"Thanks," Blue said, and headed up the stairs.

But Drusie lingered behind. "Hey, Ahmed, what's *ragazzi cattivi* mean?" she asked, pointing to a headline in the newspaper.

"Ah, that!" He shook his head. "Some new mischief the kids are doing in the stores. The boys think it's entertaining to slip small merchandise into tourists' pockets when they're not looking, and then, when the people leave the store, it makes the alarm go off. The boys keep score. It's like a contest. Very stupid."

Blue was already on the first landing. "Coming, Drusie?" he called down.

"Good night, Ahmed," Drusie said, suddenly bounding up the stairs, passing Blue halfway up on the second floor and beating him to their rooms on the third. She sat down on the floor with her chin in her hand. "What took you so long?" she asked.

Drusie waited while Blue tapped on his door, and when Louie opened it, she said, "Hi, stranger! Can I come in?"

Louie shrugged. "Sure."

"So how's the big romance going?" she asked, plopping down on one of the beds. But before he could answer, she had another question. "You went up on the Campanile today, didn't you? We were spying on you—"

"We weren't spying on you," Blue said quickly. "Drusie just happened to spot you and Angela in the ticket line."

"So who *is* she?" Drusie asked. "And why are you so secretive about everything?"

"Who's secretive?"

Blue was curious, too. "Is she Italian? Where does she live?"

"She *is* Italian, but I don't know where she lives. I don't know anything about that. She didn't tell me yet." He laughed, a private little laugh that made Drusie turn away in annoyance.

"But she's a really, *really* special person! I can't tell you how great she is! I still don't know how I was so lucky to meet her—"

"Hey, that's easy," Blue cut in. "You just won the lottery, that's all."

"What?"

"Oh, nothing. What were you saying?"

"Well, besides being really smart—and beautiful, too—she really *loves* this city. When I told her why I was here—you know, about EduGamesInc and all—she just couldn't wait to take me around to all her favorite places."

"So what was she doing crawling around on the pavement with all those pigeon droppings?" Drusie asked, idly examining her fingernails.

"I bet she lost her contact!" Blue said quickly.

Louie laughed that little secret laugh again. "Yeah, that's right. She thought it was funny when I asked her if her eyes were really green or brown. It turns out her contacts are green and her eyes are brown."

"If she's Italian, how come she's a blonde, and where did she learn her English?"

"What do you mean, how come she's a blonde? There are plenty of blond Italians, especially here in the north. And she learned English both at home and at school. Her parents are bilingual. Her dad's a lawyer, and she really respects and admires him a lot. But haven't you noticed how many people here speak more than one language? It's pretty amazing." Louie stretched and sighed. "I told her I was going to put her name in the credits of my game as my on-site Venice consultant. And I will, too." He paused a minute and then looked at Blue. "By the way," he said with a mirthless smile, "that reminds me. I figured out your anagram for Jackson Seratt. And ain't it the truth!"

Drusie and Blue exchanged glances, but of course they didn't mention Blue's idea about the video.

"I'm supposed to meet her tomorrow at ten in the morning at the Accademia."

"What's the Accademia?" Drusie asked.

"It's the name of both a bridge across the Grand Canal and, according to Angela, one of the finest art museums in the city. I'm supposed to meet her on the bridge, and then we're going to the museum."

"Well, I get to baby-sit Blue's grammy's dog!" Drusie said. "So there!"

On Thursday morning, while Blue was waiting for his turn to shower, he decided to use the time to decipher the message he had received from DYAD LARK the day before— the second message from her that was supposed to be a clue to help him decode the *earlier* encoded message which she sent on the sixth of March. He removed the latest printout from his wallet and took another look at it:

```
hE HAs BeeN lIviNG In a SHOEbOX aLL
         tHiS TIme!
```

Blue immediately recognized it as a possible Baconian Bi-literal Cipher, and that would make sense, because Tuesday might be trying to pay him a backhanded compliment—showing that she had indeed paid attention to his noontime explanation. And he was correct in that assumption. By the time Louie was back from his shower, Blue had figured it out. The word revealed in the coded sentence was SONNETS.

Sonnets? What could that mean? He was as much in the dark as ever.

When Elias Walker Peshami, a brilliant but naive English major at UCLA, saw an advertisement for a sonnet-writing contest in the Sunday comics section of the newspaper, he thought it might be fun to pull the judges' legs by dashing off the silliest, most stupid sonnet he could think of and entering it in the competition. The only rules were that each entry must conform to the usual sonnet pattern of fourteen lines in iambic pentameter, and that the rhyming scheme must follow that of Elizabeth Barrett Browning's famous Sonnet Number 43, the one that begins "How do I love thee? Let me count the ways." Elias pressed his tongue firmly in his cheek and wrote the following:

Honk! Look up! We're migrating from the east
Tern part of the USA to the West!
Heard of us yet—we silly geese all dressed
In clothes—not in a roasting-pan all greased?
At Thanksgiving you must (before the feast)
Compliment your hosts: "What a lovely vest
Your goose is wearing! Yes! It is the best,
With matching shirt and pants all nice and creased."
Look up, you residents of western states!
We naked geese are heading straight toward you!
You'll have to dress us. Better make us cute!
Buy us plaid scarves and belts for our fat waists,
Some football jerseys, a chartreuse tutu,
A sleigh to ride, and a Santa Claus suit!

"Sonnet from the Porch Geese"
by Elias Walker Peshami (1982–)
Sonnets from Our Hearts

Elias was astounded several weeks later when he was notified that his poem was a winner. "Heartwarming and original," said the congratulatory letter sent to Elias (as well as to every other entrant in the contest with a legible name and address). And, what's more, his poem was going to be featured in a book called *Sonnets from Our*

Hearts bound in "rich-looking Letherlike® with gilded letters," which Elias would be able to purchase for a limited time for the low price of only $39.99. "A cherished keepsake for yourself," the letter stated, "as well as a wonderful gift idea for family and friends."

seventeen

Grammy and poor little Vixen were sitting on the small brown couch in the lobby of the hotel when three members of the old Famous Four came downstairs at nine o'clock.

"Oh, have you been waiting long?" Drusie asked, falling to her knees in front of the dog and putting her hands around his little neck and rubbing behind his little ears. "Oh, he's just *darling*! And so *tiny*!" She kissed him on top of his head and then bent back a little so she could look into his soft brown eyes. "And look at that darling little face. I wonder what he's thinking now!"

Blue suddenly burst out laughing. This dog actually looked embarrassed! Blue could almost hear him saying, Hey—it wasn't *my* idea, you know, so please stop looking at me like that!

Grammy opened her purse and pulled out a small opened bag of BesPet Dog Food. "Take this, please, Blue," she said. "It should last for a day or two." Then she handed him a few Italian bills. "And here's enough money to get him another bag. Now, it *must* be BesPet," she said, "or he simply refuses to eat. Oh, and I should warn you it is not that easy to find here in Venice, you may have to shop around a bit. And, please, get the puppy-kibble size, because regular dog food is too large for his little mouth. Isn't it, sweetie-poo? But you don't have to get it until tomorrow, in case you have other things to do today," she said, as if that somehow made it less of a chore.

Grammy rummaged around in her purse again. This time she extracted a large Baggie containing several smaller Baggies and a box of tissues. This one she gave to Drusie.

"Drusie, honey," she said, "here's his little clean-up kit. He's a good boy, and only does his big duty once a day, and always after breakfast. You should take him outside, but be sure to clean up after him. Venetians love dogs, but have *very* strict rules about picking up their debris."

Blue smiled when he heard the word "debris." Here was yet another synonym for "excrement," one that was somehow overlooked during the discussion sparked by his friend Mike Fennell's four-letter Bringaword vulgarity in Ms. Chandler's English class last semester.

But now Grammy was kissing the dog again. "We'll be

back here at the hotel Saturday morning to pick him up. But don't worry. I know you have a plane to catch that afternoon. We'll be back in plenty of time. And, oh, I almost forgot. Be *very* careful of his stitches, will you? He's supposed to have them out in two weeks, but we don't want anything to go wrong."

Blue nodded. "Okay, Grammy. We'll take extra-good care of him. Don't you worry about a thing!"

Drusie took the bag of dog food from Blue. "I'll take care of this," she said. "And Vixen will stay in my room, if that's okay with you."

And thus the die was cast, the stage was set. There would be no turning back.

On their walk over to Agostino's, Blue tried to fill Drusie in on the Shakespeare mystery as best he could. It came out in fits and starts, however, because she was forever stopping along the route to admire a particular building or something wonderful she saw in a shop window. And, naturally, she was disposed to snap pictures from every bridge they crossed. But Blue managed to hit the high points, and even if he didn't have her completely sold on Oxford, he had, at the very least, given her something to think about.

For the most part, Vixen was behaving himself

admirably, except when they happened to pass another dog, of course. But barking like a maniac—while rearing up on his two back legs and straining at the leash until he could barely breathe—was probably the natural thing to do, since all the other dogs they passed did the exact same thing. In time he seemed to tire, though, so Drusie picked him up and carried him the rest of the way.

Only Mr. Agostino and Tina were in the store when they arrived, and when Tina spotted Vixen, she immediately jumped down from her stool and fell on his neck and covered him with kisses. Blue began to suspect that the attraction he noted between little dogs and females might be gender-related, perhaps connected somehow to the mothering instinct.

"Can I carry him, please?" Tina asked Drusie, in slow, uncertain English, holding out her arms in expectation.

"I guess so," Drusie replied. "But be careful." She pointed to the dog's underside. "Operation," she said with a grimace. "Yesterday."

"Oohh," Tina crooned, nodding her head in sympathy. "But he is so light! I think he must weigh not even one kilo—how do you say in English? One pound?"

"Well, he probably weighs more than a pound," said Drusie, "but he *is* small."

Blue was about to explain that a kilo was equal to a

little over two pounds, but since no one asked him, he just let it go. Besides, the way Tina was grasping little Vixen's head between her hands, touching foreheads, and making little kissy sounds at him, she probably wouldn't have heard him anyway.

Mr. Agostino sidled up next to her and made some comment in Italian that Blue suspected had to do with Vixen's surgery, judging by the way Tina put her hand over her mouth and turned away with an embarrassed laugh. A few minutes later she slipped the dog his first little bite ever of beef jerky.

Both Blue and Drusie held their breath while she logged on and checked her mail.

Dear Drusie,
    Your mother and I were happy to hear that you and Louie are enjoying yourselves in Venice, and please give our best to Blue. I can't imagine what it must be like to be in a place with absolutely no automobiles at all. (When I told your mother that, she suggested I take her there and see for myself!)
    But as to your question about a video of Louie holding the door open, your

mother says unfortunately she does not
have one. She said she was never able to
get the camcorder ready in time, and
Louie always refused to repeat it for the
camera once his little friends were
safely inside.

Write again when you have time. Isn't
e-mail wonderful? Do you know that I can
remember the days when computers were as
big as a house? Love from your mother
and me,
Dad

"So much for that brilliant idea," Blue said with a disappointed sigh.

"Yeah, I know. It *was* a good idea, though. Listen, I want to send a couple of messages to my friends. Are you in a big hurry to check yours, or—"

"No, you go ahead," he said, in spite of the fact that he couldn't wait to hear from Omaha.

Although Blue hadn't noticed him coming in, the same Englishman who had been there yesterday had returned, still wearing the same slightly wrinkled blue suit and checkered tie. Now he and Mr. Agostino were in the back room again, sitting across from each other at a little table. But this time they had the door slightly ajar, and Blue—not more than a couple of yards away—could see they were both intent on examining what looked like some very old and possibly water-damaged books. At one point the Englishman carefully raised one of the books up closer to the light, and Blue could see it was not a printed book at all, but looked more like some kind of handwritten notebook or diary.

And then Blue saw the man slowly turning the pages and reading a snatch here and there, in a kind of musing voice, but what made Blue really sit up and take notice was when he thought he heard him say—now he couldn't be positive about this because he could only make out snatches of the conversation—but he thought he heard him murmur the name "de Vere." Blue strained to hear more.

"Yes, hmm, this is very interesting—written right here, let's see, so forth and so on—yes—de Vere mentions Romeo and Giulietta—city of Verona. Now, was Verona in the Brooke version, or did that come from da Porto's book, do you know?"

Blue couldn't hear Mr. Agostino's answer.

Now the Englishman began speaking a little louder. "Yes, you've got some quite interesting material here," he said, putting that particular book down and picking up another. "Now, you understand I'm not interested in the entire bundle, just certain portions, and I'm going to have to do some phoning around before I can make you a definite offer."

At that point Mr. Agostino suddenly came out of the back room and got a pack of cigarettes out of his coat jacket, which was hanging on the back of a chair not far from where Blue was sitting. Blue quickly averted his eyes and leaned forward, pretending to be looking at Drusie's monitor. Mr. Agostino returned to the back room, but this time he shut the door behind him.

Drusie looked up from the monitor. "Blue, what's wrong?" she whispered. "You look kind of funny."

"I'll tell you later," he whispered back.

In a few minutes Drusie was finished at the computer, and she and Blue exchanged places. He was still shaken by what he thought he'd heard, but what could he do about it? He couldn't just waltz in there and say, "Excuse me, but you don't happen to have something there that could prove Edward de Vere was really Shakespeare, do you? Oh, you do? Well, may I have it, please? Thank you very much! The world's been waiting for this!"

Blue checked his mail and, of course, read Omaha's letter first:

Dear Blue:

The big news here today is that my
mother has forgiven you, even though in
my opinion there wasn't that much to
forgive. Anyway, we finally had a long
talk about my father (even though I had
resolved not to discuss it) and now she
thinks it was a GOOD thing that I went
to see him because now I can see him in
a more realistic light. I told her it
feels something like when I stopped
believing in Santa Claus. It's pretty
devastating at first, but it's nice to
know the truth.

You talked about Louie, but you
haven't mentioned Drusie yet. How doth
she fare? Hath simple friendship
blossom'd into love / By accident of
fickle fate?

Ha-ha! Fooled you! That's not
Shakespeare. I made it up myself.

Coach Conley called a special
practice meet yesterday even though
we're on vacation and I beat Bret Olsen

```
in the 200-meter freestyle. Afterwards
he said he had the flu. (He didn't look
sick to me, at least BEFORE the race.)
   Write to me!
Love, Omaha
```

Blue quickly suppressed the little twinge of guilt he felt
upon reading Drusie's name. That little episode by the
Gobbo really was just kind of a fleeting, freaky aberration
thing that was full of sound and fury, signifying nothing.

Before composing his answer, he read her note over
again very carefully, checking for every nuance, realizing
that he was—metaphorically speaking—drinking in the
words. And although he wasn't aware of it just yet, his
admiration for the genius of Shakespeare was firmly
planted and already starting to grow.

```
Dear Omaha:
   I'm glad I'm back in good favor with
your mother, and congratulations on
winning the race.
   Grammy and Byron have arrived in
Venice and little Vixen has been fixed,
if you get my meaning. Drusie has
agreed to baby-sit him until Saturday
```

morning so Grammy and Byron can go on a
little cruise. My job is to buy his
dog food.

   You sure fooled me with your
Shakespeare imitation! Now here's one
for you: "Of all the fair maidens I
ever didst saw, / The fairest by far is
mine own Omaha."

   I can't believe it's Thursday
already. I guess I'd better check
my other mail and go do a little
sightseeing. Will I hear from you
tomorrow, my sweet? Until then, fair
thoughts and happy hours attend on you!
Love, Blue

Ah, what's this? A long one from Dr. Wood. Looks
like more material for my notebook.

Dear Blue,
   Hello again. Here is something
interesting about Oxford and Venice
that I got off the Web. (Of course, as
we both know, just because it's on the
Web doesn't make it true, so I'm going

to check into it further.) But it seems that the testimony of a Venetian choirboy named Orazio Cogno before the Venice Inquisition on 27 August 1577 reveals that our man Oxford heard him sing in the year 1575 at the Church of Santa Maria Formosa in the campo of the same name, which was noted for its attraction to players, magicians, acrobats, and general merry-makers. Oxford invited the teenaged choirboy to accompany his party back to London, where he became a page in Oxford's household and had an opportunity to sing for the Queen on several occasions before returning to Venice.

Question: Is it possible that Oxford left some evidence in Venice that could reveal him as the real author? Is it possible that you could dig it up? I mean, you've got another day or two over there, haven't you?

Now, for your information, here are the names of just a few of the famous people who doubt that the Stratford man

is the author of Shakespeare's works:
Charles Dickens, Mark Twain, Walt
Whitman (who said, "I am firm against
Shaksper—I mean the Avon man, the
actor"), John Greenleaf Whittier, Ralph
Waldo Emerson, Henry James (who said,
"I am 'sort of' haunted by the
conviction that the divine William is
the biggest and most successful fraud
ever practiced on a patient world"),
James Joyce, John Galsworthy, Sigmund
Freud, and actors Sir John Gielgud,
Leslie Howard, Orson Welles, Charlie
Chaplin, and Sir Derek Jacobi. And
there are a lot more. Check out the
Shakespeare-Oxford sites on the
Internet!

Here's an idea for you and then
I'll sign off: Why don't you copy "The
Merchant of Venice" off the Internet
and read it on your flight home? There
could never be a better time, with the
city still fresh in your mind.
James Wood

```
Dear Dr. Wood,
Message received. Interesting about
the choirboy. I'll try to do as you
suggest.
Blue
```

The telephone rang just as Blue had finished sending the message. Vixen jumped off of Tina's lap and wobbled unsteadily over to Drusie, and Tina stood up to answer the phone. *"Pronto,"* she said, and then, holding her hand over the receiver, called out, "Franco! *Telefono!*"

Mr. Agostino opened the door and poked his head out. "Who is it?" he asked in English.

"Ennio."

Mr. Agostino shook his head and waved his hands in front of him, signaling that he didn't wish to speak to this Ennio person right now. This time he shut the door with a little bang.

"I guess we're all finished up here for now," Blue said. "Want to get going?"

Tina looked really disappointed when Drusie explained they had to take Vixen away now.

"Can he come back again?" Tina asked.

"Sure," answered Drusie. "We're baby-sitting him until Saturday morning."

Tina's eyes widened. "He is not your dog?"

"Oh, no. We're just taking care of him for a couple of days."

Tina gave him a little goodbye hug. "He is very—how do you say—*dolce*?"

"Sweet!" Drusie said, remembering the word from the dessert menu the night before.

"Yes," Tina repeated. "He is very sweet."

As soon as they were outside, Blue told her what he'd seen and *thought* he had heard from the back room. "I'd sure like to see what they were looking at in there."

"Me, too! Remember I told you yesterday I heard them quoting parts from *Romeo and Juliet*? Jeez! Do you think they really have some old Oxford papers back there? Because I'm just thinking, if they *do*, it might be hard evidence that Oxford really was Shakespeare!"

"Why would it be evidence?"

"Okay, if Oxford was here—when was it? What year?"

"Uh, let's see. Dr. Wood just mentioned it in his e-mail—1575, I think. Oxford heard a choirboy sing in a church in Campo Santa Maria Formosa and took him back to England with him."

"Well, that was before *Romeo and Juliet* was written! I read a little bit about all that—like when it was first performed and stuff—when we did the play, and I'm sure it wasn't until around at least 1595. So, if that was Oxford's notebook back there, and he was writing—"

"Yes! I see what you mean! Maybe he was beginning to think about the story, beginning to take notes. After all, Verona is really close to here. He probably even went there!"

"Vixen! No!" Drusie said sharply, as the dog made a sudden lunge for a nearby pigeon.

"Looks like the old boy's starting to perk up again."

"Okay. Let's take him to see more of Venice."

By the time they reached the Bridge of Sighs, Blue had completed his slow descent back down to earth. It was just too much—just too much of a coincidence that he should overhear a conversation about a notebook that actually belonged to Edward de Vere, a notebook that was not more than three yards away from where he was sitting. Even to Blue Avenger, that sounded too much like the storyline of a comic book.

EIGHTEEN

"So, here it is, Friday morning already! Where do you plan on meeting her *today*?" Drusie asked, a pitcher of coffee in one hand and milk in the other, carefully filling Louie's cup.

Louie glanced quickly at his sister. Did he detect a bit of hostility in her voice, or was it his imagination? He decided to let it pass. "Do you know where the Bridge of Sighs is?"

"Oh, sure. It's by the Doge's Palace. It's that famous one you see in all the pictures. Blue and I were there yesterday. You can see it best from the Ponte della Paglia, or Straw Bridge. It connects the Doge's Palace to the old prison. We read all about it in the guidebook." She paused, holding the pitchers over Blue's cup. "More?"

"No, thanks."

"So is that where you meet today? At the Bridge of Sighs?"

"No. Not really. But near there. In front of a souvenir booth there."

"Listen, Louie," Drusie said, setting the pitchers down. "I'm really curious. Are you two great lovers planning on keeping in touch with each other after we go home, or is this just a four-day fling?"

"No, sister dear, I wouldn't call it just a four-day fling—"

"So what would you call it, then?"

Blue shifted around uncomfortably in his chair. He certainly didn't want to be caught in the middle of a sibling argument, but he wasn't sure how to forestall it. However, Louie's reaction surprised him. Instead of a sarcastic retort, Louie turned thoughtful.

"I'm not sure what I would call it. I'm not sure what *she* would call it. Anyway, it's probably not what you think. She's not just some kind of—oh, some kind of pickup, because I know that's what you think, Drusie. And you're wrong." He was tempted to add that he couldn't even get up the courage to kiss her, but that was just too embarrassing for him to admit.

His words of denial didn't seem to register on Drusie. She only continued with her interrogation. "So what's her last name? Where does she live?"

"I don't know."

"Doesn't that sound kind of weird to you? Doesn't that sound kind of *weird*, Louie?"

"She's hinted it won't always be that way," he said softly.

"Well, today is Friday, and our plane leaves tomorrow afternoon at four o'clock. That doesn't give her a whole lot of time, does it?"

"No, it sure doesn't."

Blue lightly slapped the table with his open palms. "Okay, then. You guys ready? Let's get moving. I'm going straight to Agostino's. So, Drusie, are you coming with me?"

"Okay. But first I have to take Vixen for his morning walk, if you know what I mean. Oh, and he finished the last of his BesPet Dog Food this morning, so you're getting another bag today, right?"

"Right. Thanks for reminding me. I almost forgot about that."

"Go stand over there," Drusie said. "You and Vixen, go stand right there by the door, so we can see the name of the hotel."

Blue did as he was told, and Drusie snapped the picture.

"Okay, that's good," she said, checking how many pictures she had left and readjusting the neck strap of her camera.

"Shall we go the same old way today, or do you want to take a different route?" asked Blue, handing her the leash.

"Oh, let's go the same way. We want to get there this morning, don't we?" They started walking down the narrow alleyway toward Campo San Bartolomeo.

"This *week*, you mean," said Blue, expanding on her little joke. "I'm really starting to love this place, though. It's like one giant maze, isn't it? Remember yesterday when we found that Il Bovolo—"

"Oh, yeah! That beautiful spiral staircase with white arches twisting around! The Ca' Contarino del Bovolo, isn't that the name? That's where we met those Italian kids, remember? Wasn't their English good? They couldn't believe we were actually from California. Oh, wait!" she said suddenly. "Here's that place where I got my glass duck. I might want to buy some of these little glass candies, too. Don't you think they're pretty? They'd make nice souvenirs to give to my friends."

Blue's mother had told him she didn't want a souvenir, although if he had time to send her a postcard, that would be nice. He did want to get something for Omaha, but he wasn't sure what she'd like. The glass objects were okay, they were pretty enough, but— He wandered around to the other side of the stand, and then he saw it! It was so—what's the word?—oh, yeah, so *kitsch*! With her peculiar sense of humor, she'd really love it! But how would he get it home? And then he realized he was looking at the display model. The ones for sale came safely packed in boxes. He looked at the price tag. Expensive, but maybe he had enough. He took out his wallet and counted out the bills, putting aside the dog-food money. But then he had to count it over again because he remembered he wanted to download *The Merchant of Venice* at Agostino's and he would owe him for the printing. It was close, but he had enough.

Drusie walked up to him as he was completing the transaction. "My God!" she said. "Are you really *buying* that ugly thing?"

"Well, just look at it," he said. "What could be more gorgeous than this genuine eighteen-inch black plastic model of a wedding gondola, complete with red-cushioned seats, carved gilded trim, a traditionally dressed gondolier, a wedding couple, little plastic flowers, and a row of tiny colored lights that really light up? What could be more gorgeous than that!"

As soon as they opened the door to Agostino's, Vixen pulled the leash right out of Drusie's hand and ran straight over to Tina, sniffing around for the treats.

"Ooh, *buon giorno, bambino!*" she said, scooping him up in her arms. Mr. Agostino was talking on the phone, but at the same time he managed to smile at her like a benevolent potentate from a far-off land.

Blue put the plastic bag with the gondola on the little table next to the computer and sat down at the keyboard.

"Listen, Blue," said Drusie. "You're going to be here for a while, aren't you? Didn't you say you wanted to print out some Shakespeare stuff?"

Blue nodded. "Yeah—I was planning on doing that."

"Well, then, maybe I'll go wander around a bit by myself. I wanted to look at that costume store we passed yesterday. I think I can find it. And I want to buy a really nice porcelain mask, and I wanted to look at a bookstore, too. So do you know how long you'll be here? Maybe we could meet at McDonald's or something."

Blue looked at his watch. "It's a little after ten now. Do you want to meet at that San Marco McDonald's—say, around two?"

"Okay. That'll be good. What about Vixen?"

Blue glanced at Tina and the dog, who were now playing some new version of doggie hide-and-seek. "He'll be okay. So I'll see you around two. Are you sure you can find it?"

"I'll just follow the signs to *Per San Marco*. But listen, don't wait for me past two-thirty. If I'm not there, it just means I got lost. Anyway, I'll see you at the hotel tonight, for sure."

"Okay. Same goes for me."

Vixen was having so much fun with Tina he didn't even notice when Drusie left.

Blue wasted no time before signing on and checking his mail.

Dear Blue:

Ready for some good news? Remember
Councilwoman Peters? Well, she's
beginning to fight back! An article in
today's paper says she's spearheading a
referendum campaign to put your bullet-
ban proposal on the ballot! She says
they're going to bring this issue to the
people, where it belongs. It's a pretty
long article. I'll save it for you. AND
I'll save another one for you, too. It
has my name and picture! But, boy, I sure
embarrassed myself!

What happened was that my friend Andrea
(you don't know her; she was in my
Spanish class last semester and lives in
that big apartment building you pass on
the way to my house)—anyway, Andrea and I
went over to Fenton's yesterday and on

the way over we were stopped by "The Quiz Man" from the Star! Andrea didn't want to answer the question because they take your picture and she had this big pimple and didn't want her picture taken, but I said I didn't mind.

Anyway, the question was, "What is a moveable feast?" Well, I happened to know what it was (at least I thought I did!) because I read this book my mother had from her college days called ERNEST HEMINGWAY'S A MOVEABLE FEAST. (I asked her how come it wasn't called A MOVEABLE FEAST BY ERNEST HEMINGWAY, and she says it was published after he died, and that's how they usually phrase titles that are published posthumously.) Anyway, the book is all about his experiences over in Paris during the 1920s with Gertrude Stein and James Joyce and all those writer-types. It's really interesting. Anyway, at the beginning of it there's this nice quote of Hemingway's that says something like if you're lucky enough to live in Paris when you're a

young man you never forget it and it
always stays with you wherever you go
because Paris is a moveable feast. So I
told "The Quiz Man" a moveable feast was
Paris, and that's what he printed!
   I found out that it really means those
kinds of holidays that move around. Like
Easter. It always comes on the first
Sunday after the first full moon after the
vernal equinox. Well, next Sunday is
Easter, because the first full moon after
the vernal equinox happens to be on
Friday. (I'm sending this on Thursday
night, but it'll be Friday in Venice
when you get it.)
Adieu, adieu, adieu! Remember me.
Omaha

The next message was from Josh, and it was pretty
amazing:

Dear Wierdo-
You will never guess what happened this
afternoon so I will tell you. This big
truck stopped infront of our house and

the driver rang the bell and asked where
we wanted the cartins. Mom came to the
door and said what cartins? And he said I
just deliver them I don't explane them.
So now there are 54 huge boxes bigger
then the one the computer came in pilled
on our front porch and lawn and down the
walk. They are full of corn starch!!!! I
invited Trevor over and we made a really
neat fort out of them even tho they wayed
a ton but then it started to rain and mom
went a little crazy when all those
cartins started to get soggy and this
white stuff started leeking out all over
until Mr. Lawson came over and covered
them with a big blue tarp. Mom says YOU
can take care of them when you get home.
Oh, and she also wants to know if you can
explane why a loryar from a salsa company
keeps calling and asking for you but wont
tell her why. Oh and then we got a little
package from fed Xwith coopons good for
free jars of salsa. Mom added them up and
says they are worth over 500 dollars! Mom
says thats alot of salsa. She says she

has a feeling you would know something
about that too. Having a wonderful time.
Glad your not here.
Signed, Wierdo's brother.

It was a few minutes before Blue could stop smiling over Josh's note. Obviously, his letter-writing campaign had started to get results!

He decided to get the Shakespeare stuff downloaded and printing before answering his mail. While searching around the Shakespeare site for *The Merchant of Venice*, he noticed that *Shake-Speares Sonnets* were available, too, and he finally made the connection between the word SONNETS in Tuesday's cipher and the sonnets of Shakespeare, so he decided to print them, also. Maybe they would somehow hold the key to decipher-ing her original message. In a few minutes the printer was churning out his copy, but when he tried to get on-line, he discovered that the computer didn't have enough memory to do two things at once, so he just had to sit there and wait.

The store seemed busier today, mostly with browsers, but once in a while Tina would ring up a sale. Mr. Agostino seemed to be spending a lot of time on the phone, but shortly after the printer started he hung up and walked over to Blue, scowling slightly.

"I know, I know," said Blue. "The printing is extra." And then, in a sudden burst of boldness—for his name *was* Blue Avenger—he asked Mr. Agostino this question: "I was just wondering," he started, "if you happened to sell that handwritten notebook you had there in your back room. Did that British fellow—"

The expression on Mr. Agostino's face stopped him cold, and when their eyes met, Blue thought, Whoa-boy! If looks could kill, I'm a goner!

After a long, frigid moment, Mr. Agostino spoke. "I do not know what you are talking about," he said, dismissing him with a careless wave of his hand.

Talk about a brush-off! At first Mr. Agostino had made Blue feel like some kind of crawling bug to be carelessly flicked off a sleeve, but after a moment or two he was able to look at the incident more objectively. It was merely the older man's way of telling him to mind his own beeswax.

When the printing was finally done, Blue brought the pages over to Tina and asked her how much he owed. He paid her and then slid the printed pages into the bag with Omaha's gondola and was about to begin answering her e-mail when, the next thing he knew, there was Louie at his side, panting heavily and clutching a crumpled piece of pink notepaper in his fist.

"My God!" Louie exclaimed. "I thought I'd never find this place! Listen, where's Drusie? Isn't she here? I need some money, quick! I have to catch a train for Padua! If I'm not there by one o'clock this afternoon I'll never see Angela again!" He held the wrinkled sheet of pink notepaper in front of Blue's face and began to wave it back and forth in a nonverbal invitation for Blue to take it and read for himself.

Things were to happen so fast in the next few minutes that later, when it was all over, Blue would have a difficult time recalling the details. But the one inescapable fact was that Louie needed some money, and he needed it fast.

"Oh, Jeez, Louie! I don't *have* any money!" said Blue, glancing at the note without really reading it and then stuffing it in his jacket pocket. Obviously, the few small bills he had stashed away for dog food wouldn't be enough to cover *this* emergency.

Those seven—no, wait a minute, those *eight* words sent Louie swirling down into a maelstrom of uncontrolled panic. It might have been funny if it weren't so serious—if it weren't for the fact there was a distinct possibility that Louie DeSoto could lose forever the first and only girl he'd ever loved! But, then, what would be so terrible about that? Wasn't he bound to lose her anyway, somewhere down the road? Because, sooner or later, wouldn't she surely grow weary of him, sick of his clingy ways and tired of his aloofness, sick of his messiness and fed up with his neatness, sick of his stupidity and bored with his cleverness? Oh, 'twould be so much wiser for Louie to lose the real-life girl now, but hold fast in his heart the impossible dream of a perfect love, a love forever young, a love forever true, a love forever—uh—well, strong.

But philosophizing at a time like this will get us nowhere, and Louie has to get to the train station.

"Where's Drusie?" he shouted, swiveling his head from east to south and back again. "Did she go to the money machine yet? *Drusie!*" he shouted, more loudly than ever.

"Hey, man! Calm down, now, will you, please," Blue Avenger said, gripping his friend's shoulders with the superhuman strength he seemed to acquire in critical moments such as this. "Drusie's not here, but I will get you some money," he said, enunciating each word slowly and clearly. "We will go to the money machine and get you the money."

"I don't have time!" Louie screamed, jabbing at his wristwatch. "I've got to get to Padua before one o'clock!

I don't have *time* for the money machine! My life is hanging by a thread!"

A cliché, at a time like this! Blue laughed out loud in spite of himself, then quickly pulled himself together and asked, "How much does the train ticket cost, Louie?"

"I don't know!"

"What time does the train leave, Louie?"

"I don't *know!*"

Mr. Agostino, hearing the disturbance, had emerged from the back room now, and Tina had slid off her stool, and both of them were standing at opposite ends of the little office portion of the shop, fascinated by the drama unfolding before them. There were also three customers in the adjacent book-and-sheet-music room, and they, too, had come forth to witness the scene. (Vixen, however, who was now cuddled up in Tina's arms, was suffering from a slight ache in his tum-tum and couldn't have cared less.)

Blue turned to Mr. Agostino, his only hope. "Mr. Agostino, sir," he said, "would it be possible for me to borrow some money from you?" He patted himself on his wallet pocket. "I have my ATM card right here. I can repay you today." He paused, then added plaintively, "Pretty please, Mr. Agostino? As you can see, my friend Louie is truly desperate."

Mr. Agostino walked forward slowly, like a king about to ascend the throne. His usual dour expression was diluted with a hint of puzzlement, for he had never before heard the term "pretty please" and was not sure of its meaning. But one thing was sure: He was *not* reaching for his wallet.

"Ah!" Blue said, lightly hitting himself on the forehead. "I understand. You would like some collateral! Of course! You can't just lend money willy-nilly, without collateral, can you?"

"Hurry up! Oh, can't you hurry it up!" Louie implored.

Blue held up his hand. "Louie! Please. I understand, but you must be patient." Even though Blue did not underestimate Louie's frantic need, he still was enjoying his part in this little drama immensely. He imagined he was wearing his kaffiyeh and blue fishing vest, and he *knew* he would emerge victorious, because that's what always happened in his comic strips. It was only a matter of time.

But first he must produce the collateral. His eyes darted around the room in desperation, until they finally alighted on the plastic bag from the souvenir shop.

"Ah!" he said. "This will do just fine!" He pulled the box out of the bag, quickly snapped it open at one end, and removed its contents with a flourish—the black plastic gondola with its red-cushioned seats and carved gilded trim, its traditionally garbed gondolier and tiny little colored lights. Holding it aloft, he proclaimed, "And here, Mr. Agostino, is your collateral!"

For a moment, all was still in the little bookshop. And then the laughter began. It started with Tina—just a hint of a snicker. Now it spread to the customers, still standing in the doorway of the adjacent room. A hearty sailor's laugh burst forth from the sailor, soon joined by the high-pitched trill of the music teacher and, lastly, the silly muffled snorting of Mr. Michael Palin, who happened to be in Venice at the time, traveling incognito. Even Mr. Agostino himself could not hold back his sorry version of a watery-eyed grin at the sight of that tacky gondola. Blue, taking the hint, sheepishly returned Omaha's present to its box.

"Oh, *God*!" Louie cried, his words floating up to the ceiling as if they were enclosed in a cartoon-strip balloon. "Now for *sure* I'm going to miss the *#%! train!"

"How about the little dog?" a hesitant voice asked, a haunting sound that seemed to be coming out of the mist of a Venice past, but which really belonged to Tina.

Blue quickly turned to face her. "What?" he asked. "What did you say?"

"The little dog?" she repeated, holding a contented Vixen up close to her bosom and looking directly at Mr.

Agostino with wide and pleading eyes.

Franco Agostino, underneath his cold and conniving heart, was also a man—a man of a certain age, too easily swayed by a woman's soulful look and pouting lips. He walked over to her and cupped her face in his hands. Then he said something in Italian baby-talk that only she could hear and the onlookers could only imagine. Tina smiled and nodded, and he patted her cheek like a proud papa, even though he was only twenty years older than she.

(Unfortunately, since he was not attuned to the subtle, changing moods of dogs, he didn't notice Vixen's slightly bared teeth and the hint of a growl that emanated from deep within his little throat.)

Now Mr. Agostino strode back to where Blue and Louie were standing and opened his wallet, exposing a big fat wad of bills. With a slight shrug and a devil-may-care toss of his head, a deft movement of his thumb produced a fine specimen—to the tune of one hundred thousand lire.

Because Louie was not himself, because Louie was half crazy with love, he made a desperate and impolite grab for the money.

But Mr. Agostino was ready for that and skillfully thwarted the attempt. He looked at Blue. "I will be happy to lend you the money with the little dog as collateral," he said, jutting his nose in the air. "But first you must sign."

"Sign?"

"That is correct." He walked back to the counter and started scribbling on a piece of notepaper. "I shall write the terms and your young friend will be on his way."

"Hurry up! Hurry up! Hurry *up*!" Louie cried, burying his head in his hands.

Blue was momentarily stunned. He looked down at the floor and ran his fingers through his hair. Be calm, now. Think this through. What could go wrong? All I have to do is withdraw the money and return for the dog. Simple enough. "All right," he said, glancing at Louie in his anguish. "It will be as you say. I will sign."

"Here is the contract," said Mr. Agostino, beckoning to Blue and holding out a pen.

Blue bent to read the scribbled words. "Wait," he said. "Wait just one darned minute here! It says that if I don't repay the hundred thousand lire before one-thirty this afternoon, the dog will be yours!" Blue quickly checked his watch. "That's less than two hours from now! And it'll take me at least twenty minutes to get to the ATM and back. What if—what if I fall down or slip into a canal, or worse! What if I can't make it back in time?"

Mr. Agostino—bluffing, of course—shrugged and

started to tear the paper in half.

Louie stifled a sob.

"No! Wait!" Blue said. "Not so fast! Let me think this over—"

Louie collapsed on a chair in utter despair. "No, Blue," he said, his voice fraught with emotion. "You can't do that. You can't put your grandmother's dog in jeopardy for me. It's just not right." And poor Louie started to weep in earnest. He started to weep for his beautiful lost love, his beautiful and superintelligent Angela. He started to weep for Vixen, the innocent little dog who never bit anybody. (Well, how could Louie have known about that little incident with the UPS man that Grammy had never mentioned to anyone? Besides, it was just a little nip, and it didn't even count, since the driver was good enough not to report it.) But, most of all, Louie started to weep for himself—for his sacrifice, for his basic goodness, for his willingness to do the right thing when push came to shove.

"No, Louie!" Blue said. "It's all settled! I've made up my mind! You're going!"

Louie stood up. "Okay," he said. He took the money from Mr. Agostino's outstretched hand and rushed out the door.

■ ■ ■

In his moving poem "Rushing! Rushing!" ex–football great Sam E. "Killer" Haaswipe all too painfully describes some of the hazards of that action.

Rushing! Rushing! That's been my game!
Rushing! Rushing! My ticket to fame!
Guys coming at me, aiming to maim,
Hit 'em back hard, give 'em the same!
One day he caught me, Steam-Engine Joe,
Broke my back, three ribs, and a toe.
In bed now I'm laying, healin' slow.
Ain't doing no rushing any mo'.

"Rushing! Rushing!"
by Sam E. "Killer" Haaswipe (1965–),
in *Outstanding Poems from Football's Has-Beens*
Collected, printed, and sold ($6.50 postpaid) by the
Staff and Friends of St. Mary's Hospital to Benefit
The Pink Ladies Arts and Crafts Fund

nineteen

Blue was well on his way to the money machine in Campo San Bartolomeo when he happened upon a display of BesPet Dog Food (puppy-kibble size) in the window of a grocery-and-variety store along the route. The handwritten sign propped up next to the display said *Chiuso a Venerdì Santo 12:30*.

Even though Blue had been in Venice for three days now, he was still not able to discern any recognizable pattern in the business hours of its commercial establishments. He just accepted them on their terms. He estimated that he had at least an hour and forty-five minutes to spare before his one-thirty deadline, so he decided to just get the dog food now, while he had the chance, especially since all of the other stores in the area appeared to be closed. Obeying this sudden impulse, he pushed open the door and walked into the store. The narrow aisles were crowded with shoppers, but he finally located the pet-food department and made his selection. Then, choosing the shortest checkout line, he patiently waited his turn while enduring the jostling of strangers, and in less than three minutes he was handing over his money to the seated cashier. She gave him a few coins in change with a *Grazie!* and a friendly smile, and he headed for the exit door.

The careful reader will guess what happened next. He set off the alarm, of course.

A grim-looking, heavyset gentleman took his arm, led him to an alcove hidden behind a curtain in back of the canned-fruit section, and told him, in Italian, to please sit down.

Blue was confused, embarrassed, and infuriated, and he did not sit down. He reached into the grocery bag containing the dog food and pulled out his receipt. "Look!" he said. "See? Here's my receipt!" He held up the bag of BesPet Dog Food. "Here is my dog food." He turned the plastic bag inside out. "See!" he said. "Empty!"

His captor only shook his head and again indicated he should sit. "No!" Blue said. "I will not sit down! I'm— I'm in a very big hurry! I have to— Oh, nuts! You'd never get it. It's too hard to explain."

Blue looked at his watch. "Look," he said, "how long am I supposed to wait here? I'm in a very big hurry. Understand? Comprendo? Big hurry!"

"Un momento," said the Italian, moving his hands up and down in a calming motion. *"Un momento, per favore."*

After they had repeated that conversation with slight variations for what seemed to be an eternity, a short, middle-aged woman with dark, piercing eyes and no-nonsense written all over her suddenly appeared in front of the curtain.

"Good morning," she said. "May I see your passport, please?"

Blue panicked. "I don't have it," he said. "It's in my room at the hotel."

The woman's eyes suddenly turned soft. After years of experience in dealing with scofflaws of every age and creed, she immediately recognized that the fine young man standing before her was not of that ilk. "I am sorry," she said. "No doubt there has been a mistake. So, if you will kindly empty your jacket pockets for me, I think we will find the reason for the alarm."

Out came the pink, crumpled note from one pocket and, from the other one, a red metal lapel pin in the shape of a heart with the words *Kiss me! I'm Italian!* printed in white lettering. The woman took the pin from him. "I am so sorry," she said. "We are having a problem with a certain group of children." She turned to Blue's guard and said some angry words, but he only shrugged, flipped the curtain to one side, and disappeared into the canned-fruit section.

The woman glanced up at Blue for a moment and then back down at the object in her hand. "Again, I apologize for your inconvenience." With a sudden smile, she quickly peeled off the code sticker on the lapel pin and handed it back to him. "Here is a little souvenir of this occasion." She clasped his hand with both of hers. "It will make a nice story to tell when you get back home, no?"

The whole episode took only twenty-two minutes, and it was now ten minutes after twelve. Blue still had plenty of time, but his nerves were shot to bits.

Blue was aghast when he first caught sight of the line of people waiting for their turn at the ATM in Campo San Bartolomeo, for what a line it was—not straight and orderly, as in some parts of America, but a recognizable line just the same, and numbering fourteen people in all. What else could he do but take his place at the end of the queue?

He looked at his watch and timed the person who had just stepped up to the machine. It took her two minutes and thirty-five seconds to complete her transaction. A quick calculation told him that at that rate he would be up at bat in thirty-two minutes. Okay, he figured, let's say thirty-five minutes until he had the money in hand. He could make it back to Campo San Polo in ten minutes, max. That'd be forty-five minutes, total. He checked his watch again. It was now twelve-fifteen. He should be able to make it back to Agostino's by one o'clock, with a half-hour to spare. Just to be sure, he figured it again.

Ah! The next person only took one minute and fifty-five seconds! Great! He wondered if he could squeeze the little bag of dog food into his jacket pocket, and while he was putting it in there he felt the little *Kiss me! I'm Italian!* pin and took it out to have another look at it. What an unnerving experience *that* had been, but the Italian lady was very nice. He reached into his other pocket and withdrew the crumpled pink note from Angela. He pressed it against his thigh and smoothed it out as best he could, but after he'd read the salutation and the complementary close, Blue's innate respect for the privacy of others prevented him from reading the message in between. It seemed so personal, somehow—written on pink paper, with its "My Dearest Louie" and "Love Always, Angela"—that he just folded it up carefully and put it back in his jacket pocket along with the little pin.

He looked to see how the line was progressing. Uh-oh,

so *now* what's the delay? Only five people still ahead of him, but this guy seems to be taking more than his allotted time. Come on, hurry it up! I've got a little dog to bail out, for God's sake. Okay, there he goes. Next? All right, lady! Get that card in the *right* way! That's right—just keep staring at it like that. Maybe it'll jump in all by itself. Oh, brother! Poke it in again! Come on, you block, you stone, you worse than senseless thing!

Blue suddenly laughed out loud. Ah, Oxford, he thought—as if the earl were still alive and standing right beside him—you sure know how to turn a phrase.

He leaned to one side now so he could get a better view, and watched in alarm as the little gray door of the ATM slowly descended down in front of the window like a curtain signaling the end of the play.

The woman turned to the man standing in back of her and threw her hands in the air. Blue heard her say the now familiar word, *Chiuso!* Blue was dismayed to see two of the people who were standing in front of him in the line expressing themselves in no uncertain Italian terms and actually walking away! But the woman at the window was not giving up so easily. She again inserted her card, and the curtain obediently raised! *All right!* She carefully punched in her code. So far so good. That's right, that's right. Tell the machine how much you want.

Good. Oh, *no!* The window banged closed again! Blue turned to look at the young woman in the green-and-white sweater who had just gotten in line in back of him a few moments before and was now also turning to leave. "What's *wrong?*" he asked, not even stopping to think if she spoke English. By now everyone in the line had given up and walked away.

"The machine is out of money," she said. "Today is Venerdì Santo."

"Venerdì Santo? What's that?"

The woman smiled. "Good Friday. A holiday in Italy. The banks are closed." She shrugged. "Too many people come to the machine and the money runs out." His informant must have noticed his look of absolute panic, because she added sympathetically, "You can maybe try the machine in Campo Manin." She pointed to the west. "You go that way, just follow the busy streets. You will see it." She smiled. "Good luck."

Blue looked at his watch. It was a quarter to one. Forty-five minutes to go. He still had a fighting chance.

In the roughly thirteen-hundred-year-long history of the Republic of Venice, there have been some truly frightening and horrific events about which we need not elaborate here, only to say that, in comparison with these, the travails of Blue Avenger would be as a pinprick is to a gouging with the business end of a pickax. Nevertheless, his anxiety over the fate of Vixen the dog—well, to state the problem more accurately, his anxiety over his grammy's *reaction* to the fate of Vixen the dog—should not be underestimated. In other words, he was pretty darn worried!

After running nonstop all the way from Campo San Bartolomeo west to Campo Manin, he was greeted by a totally uncooperative ATM—a machine that refused to entertain his proffered card long enough even to identify the owner, let alone raise its drab gray curtain.

But Blue pressed on. Campo Sant' Angelo—no luck there, but he thought he saw what might be a bank down one of the side streets. And he was correct. It was a bank. But in place of an ATM, it had only a locked vault for making night deposits. With sagging spirits he retraced his steps back to Campo Sant' Angelo. Following the signs to the Accademia and crossing a bridge over the Rio Sant' Angelo, he arrived at Campo Santo Stefano next. Alas, he saw no ATM when he got there.

He had been following the streets—some as wide as the sidewalks in downtown Oakland and others almost as narrow as the hallway leading to his own bed-room—until, eventually, another spacious and sunny *campo* would suddenly materialize before his eyes. But now, after passing through Campo San Vidal, with its large church on the right and a flower stand on the left, there were no more *campi*. What Blue saw in front of him now was the beautiful wooden Ponte dell' Accademia, the third of the great bridges crossing over the Grand Canal.

He knew he could never make it back to the bookstore by Mr. Agostino's deadline, even if he *were* able to procure the money. He crossed over the bridge and waited for a *vaporetto* headed north up the Grand Canal, in the direction of the Piazzale Roma. When it arrived, he used the ticket Ahmed had given him and rode until he came to the Rialto stop. From there he crossed the Rialto Bridge and again made his way on foot to Campo San Polo and Agostino's bookstore, where he intended to throw himself on the mercy of Mr. Franco Agostino and, he hoped against hope, regain possession of Vixen in return for a new promissory note of a hundred thousand lire plus a generous bonus to be negotiated in good faith by the two concerned parties.

But Blue's plan would prove to be impossible to implement, for when he arrived at his destination he was advised by a sign on the door of the special half-day hours in observance of the occasion.

There was absolutely nothing Blue could do about Grammy's dog until nine o'clock the following morning. And then there was the unspoken question he dared not ask—was there really anything he could do after nine o'clock the following morning?

Even though it was past two-thirty when Blue finally dragged himself into McDonald's, Drusie was still there, drinking a soda and improving the English of two very cool high-school-age Italian boys who were sitting across from her in a booth next to the counter.

"Blue!" she called out. "Over here!"

Blue's head was pounding and he felt weak from hunger. He fell into the booth and suspiciously eyed the two Italian youths. "Hello, Drusie," he muttered. "What's new?"

"This is my friend Blue!" she said brightly. And then, to Blue, "And this is Antonio and Elvis."

Blue looked up. "Elvis?"

"His mother was a fan."

Blue just nodded halfheartedly and glared at them. He was in no mood for small talk with Italian high-school boys.

Antonio and Elvis took the hint. They stood up and collected their empty French-fry bags and hamburger wrappers. Then they each took one last swig from their milkshake containers and stuffed them full with the paper trash.

"Pleasantly we must went," Antonio said, very slowly and politely.

"It is mostly nice to greet you, Drusie," Elvis said formally. And with a slight nod in Blue's direction, they quickly made their exit.

Ordinarily, Blue would have smiled at their fractured English, but at the moment he was too depressed. "Sorry I scared away your new boyfriends," he said, not sounding sorry at all.

Drusie laughed. "Those guys? Don't be silly." She paused, a little smile playing around her lips. "But, actually, I do have a date tonight, with a *real* Italian Romeo."

Blue looked up quickly. "Oh?"

Drusie blushed slightly and bent her head low, as if confiding in a girlfriend. "Remember on Tuesday when we were on that *vaporetto* from the airport? Well, I took another ride today and guess what? You know that guy who opens the gate and throws that rope around that pole? Well, the same cute Italian dude who was working that afternoon was on duty again this morning, and he recognized me! We're meeting tonight at the Rialto Bridge at nine o'clock. He's going to take me for a ride on a gondola!" She took a sip of her drink. "So what have you been doing?"

"Listen. I'm starving and out of money. Could you please go buy me a cheeseburger and a drink? And then I'll tell you all about it."

Blue needed a minute alone to figure out his plan of action. He certainly couldn't tell her not to meet her Romeo! That would go over like a lead balloon. Now, if Louie got home before then, the two of them could just follow her, maybe hire their own gondola—they could handle it, somehow. But if Louie doesn't get home, he thought, it's up to me. The Rialto Bridge at nine, and Blue Avenger will be there!

"So let's see the note!" Drusie exclaimed, as soon as Blue had finished telling her how Louie had burst into Agostino's in such a frantic state, waving the note from Angela and demanding money.

Blue took another bite of the cheeseburger Drusie had bought for him and wiped his hands on the small paper napkin. Then he reached into his jacket pocket and placed the red-heart pin on the table and handed her the note.

Drusie smoothed it out on the table and bent her head low to read it. A lock of her long, dark hair happened to fall on Blue's hand, and his arm jerked away in a reflex action so sudden that he almost spilled his drink.

Drusie looked up. "What was that?" she asked.

"I almost spilled my drink."

"Oh." When she had finished reading the note, she looked at Blue as if it had been written in Sanskrit and she had been unable to understand a word of what it said. "Did you read this?" she asked, turning it over to see if perhaps there was more on the other side.

Blue shook his head. "No."

"Well, listen to this: *My dearest Louie: I left this note with the lady at the souvenir booth very early this morning and she assured me she would give it to you. When I got home last night my father asked me why have I been going to Venice for three days in a row, so I told him about you— and how we met on Tuesday evening and then spent all of Wednesday and Thursday together. I guess he could tell that I thought you were the boy of my dreams, because he said if I wanted to see you again there was only one way I could do it—and that was to invite you to our house and we would all have lunch together. I'm sorry I have been so mysterious. I just thought it would be more fun that way. Anyway, I was planning to tell you my full name and address today so we could stay in touch after you went back to America, but my father said you have to pass this little test first. I live in Padua, and my father and I will wait for you in the train station there until one o'clock this afternoon. He says he doesn't think you will be there, but I know you will. Love always, Angela."*

Drusie kept staring at the note even after she had finished reading it. And then she said to Blue, "What *is* this? It sounds like something from another century, for God's sake!" Then she noticed the red heart-shaped pin on the table. She picked it up and almost smiled. "Cute," she said. "Can I have it?"

Blue shrugged. "Sure."

Luckily, Drusie had managed to get to an ATM machine early enough to make a withdrawal, and now she repaid Blue the money she and Louie owed, less the cost of his lunch. And then the two of them wandered around Venice for the rest of the afternoon, discussing every possible way imaginable to get Vixen back— which ultimately amounted to only two basic plans: Talk Mr. Agostino into handing him back peaceably, and offering him more money if need be—or simply grab the dog and run.

"But what if they don't even bring him to the shop tomorrow?" Blue asked. "That's possible, too! You know, we shouldn't underestimate that Agostino guy. You should've seen the wad of bills in his wallet! I don't think tempting him with more money is going to have any effect at all."

It was after five when they got back to the hotel. Drusie went up to Blue's room with him and they each stretched out on one of the narrow beds. Things were looking very hopeless indeed.

The phone rang at a quarter to six. Blue answered. It was Louie.

"I'm still at Angela's," he said. "I'm invited for dinner." Someone else was talking in the background. Blue heard Louie say, "Just a minute." And then, talking into the phone again, he asked, "So did you get the money all right? Did Agostino give back the dog?"

Blue sighed. "No. I had some trouble. I couldn't get the money, and when I got back there the place was closed."

"So where's the dog?"

"Louie, I don't know. I don't *know* where the dog is."

Blue waited while Louie relayed this bit of information to Angela.

"God, that's terrible!" Louie was saying now. "What are you going to do? Are they open tomorrow? What time is your grandmother coming back?"

"The sign in their window said they'll open tomorrow

at nine, and I don't have an exact time for my grand-mother. She just said in the morning sometime."

"Listen, I won't be back there until pretty late. But we can talk about it when I get there, okay?"

"Right," said Blue. "We'll talk about it then." He started to hang up the phone.

"Wait!" Louie said. "Are you still there?"

"Yeah."

"Angela says to tell you she's really, *really* sorry. She's saying it's all her fault. She's— Listen, I've got to hang up. I'll see you later. We'll think of something."

Meanwhile—yes, that's right—in another part of the city, Vixen was quickly learning how to bark in Italian. So far he could say, "Ouch! Tina, *please*! My stitches! Don't squeeze me so hard!" and "Could you please toss me another little piece of that delicious pepperoni pizza?"

But what he enjoyed the very most was the chance to show what he was really made of whenever that cigar-smoking human came anywhere near his sweet, lovely Tina.

Blue began standing on guard by the door to his room at a quarter to nine that evening, listening for Drusie. At ten minutes before the hour he heard her come out into the hallway and close and lock her door. He followed her into Campo San Bartolomeo, which was crowded with people standing together in small groups, talking and laughing and smoking as if they were at a neighborhood cocktail party. Drusie snaked her way through the crowd and headed directly for the Rialto.

The starless night was chilly and slightly windy, and the sky was filled with huge black clouds. As Blue followed Drusie across the *campo*, the clouds parted and suddenly the faces in the square seemed to glow in reflected moonlight for one brief moment, until once again the moon disappeared behind a curtain of black.

Blue devised his plan of action as soon as he became aware of the row of telephone kiosks standing adjacent to the gondola dock alongside the Grand Canal. He quickly ducked into one and watched with pounding heart as Drusie rendezvoused with her date at the top of the bridge. Her suitor was agile and quick, and before they had reached the bottom step, one of his arms had already encircled her waist and his free hand was stroking her hair. Even though they passed several feet away from Blue's hiding place, he was still able to see the look of growing panic on Drusie's face. He watched intently as her suitor and the gondolier exchanged a quick handshake that implied a certain camaraderie, and in another moment there was Drusie, seated on a red velvet cushion beside none other than Niccolò "Nicky" Casanova, a direct descendant of Venetian-born Giovanni Giacomo Casanova de Seingalt (1725–98), the most infamous seducer in the history of the world.

Blue immediately sprang into action. Three giant strides and a highly controlled low-powered vault landed him smack in the center of the would-be seducer's lair. "Well, hello, Drusie," he said with a wonderful nonchalant air. "Fancy meeting you here."

"Oh, *Blue*!" she exclaimed, clasping his hands and pulling him down beside her, while the young Casanova nimbly jumped off the gondola and onto the dock, wondering if this might be a good night to go home and work on his memoirs.

"Are we ready now?" asked the slightly confused gondolier, as he swiveled his head from the quickly departing Italian to the newly arrived American.

"Oh, yes!" said Drusie. "Yes!"

"Very good! My name is Lorenzo, and I will be your gondolier."

Oh, my God! thought Blue, seated beside the beautiful Drusie DeSoto in a gondola, remembering what he had felt at the *Gobbo* and looking up at the dark and still-moonless sky, all the while imagining Omaha's sweet voice saying, *Adieu, adieu, adieu! Remember me.* Oh, my God. What do I do now?

After a hard night's work, the *gondolieri* like to gather together in the bar and talk about Venice, their families, and the tourists. Tonight they are listening to the words of Lorenzo, and if you understood Italian, this is what you would hear:

"So this redheaded kid jumps into my gondola, and Nicky, he takes off—whoosh, like that. Well, first of all, this wuss won't put his arm around the girl. I motion to him—Go ahead! Go ahead! But still he sits there, stiff like a board. The girl is beautiful, right? But neither does she make any moves. What the heck, I say. Are they brother and sister? So I ask them, Are you brother and sister? No, no, they say. So I shrug and take them down the *rio*, and the boy is fidgety looking this way and that, very, very strange. And then, suddenly, he stands up! I say, No, no! You must sit! But the moon is out now and I can see his face, and his eyes look wild and scared. A big cloud comes, the sky gets dark, and the boy sits down. Pretty soon, the same thing! The moon comes out, the boy pops up! Now the girl says, Sit down, sit down! We'll tip over! The wind blows, the moon goes away, the boy sits down. Now I'm getting very nervous, you see? I mean, you know how difficult it is to row with people standing and moving about! Now I watch the sky, I watch the clouds begin to separate, out comes the moon, and I swear, there he goes standing up again! This time I threaten him. I threaten him with my oar. I hold it over his head and say, Sit! He won't sit. It's crazy! The girl begins to pull him down. They struggle. I say, Okay, that's it! You sit down or the ride, she is ended! The moon goes away, the boy sits down. Pretty soon I circle around and take them back. So what was that all about? the girl asks. The boy steps off my boat. He is sweating like a pig. He lets her pay, and then he says, Just remember this, he says, I never took you on a gondola ride—you took me. And I never sat next to you in a gondola in the moonlight! Is that true, or no? The girl makes a big sigh and shakes her head at him. This is about Omaha, she says, isn't it? (I remember she says Omaha, because I know the states of the United States.) Why didn't you *tell* me? she says. I would have understood!"

Lorenzo finishes his glass of beer. He shakes his head. "Americans," he says. "They are crazy as loons." And the other *gondolieri* nod and shrug and order another round.

twenty

Blue Avenger was having trouble sleeping. It became almost impossible after around midnight, when things livened up in the bar across the alley and the sounds of Friday-night Venetian merry-making came wafting in through his open window. He quietly slipped on his pants so as not to disturb Louie and went downstairs, thinking perhaps he might have a chat with Ahmed.

"Ah, Blue!" Ahmed said, flicking the ashes from his cigarette and putting aside his crossword puzzle. "Tomorrow you will say goodbye to *la bella Venezia*. What will you remember most about *la Serenissima*?"

"Not what you'd expect," said Blue, sitting down on the brown couch and putting his head in his hands.

Ahmed listened most somberly to Blue's story, leaning back in his chair and taking long, thoughtful drags on his cigarette. And though he didn't promise a solution, he sent Blue back upstairs with a hearty pat on the back and the well-meaning but still the most useless and infuriating bit of advice that can ever be dispensed in this sometimes heartless and unfathomable world: *Just try not to think about it.*

"I'd better stay here in the lobby in case she comes in, don't you think?" Drusie asked. "But I'm not going to tell her what's happened. And whatever you do, *please*, don't get yourselves arrested, okay? Remember, we have a four o'clock plane to catch this afternoon."

Venezia in late March is a particularly enchanting time—as, of course, are the other eleven months of the year, in their own individual ways. But in March the temperature is refreshingly cool, and the sky can be cloudy one moment and ever so blue the next, except at sunset, when, if one is looking westward from the Ponte Rialto, the scattering of slender clouds above the Canal Grande take on the unique and lovely shades of pinks and grays and soft tangerines that can be seen from nowhere else on this earth.

But Blue and Louie had other things on their minds besides sunsets in Venice as they stood together in a far corner of Campo San Polo in view of the still-closed door of Agostino's bookstore a few minutes before nine on this Saturday morning in March.

"Look!" Blue exclaimed softly. "The door is opening!

They were in there all the time. And, Louie, look! See that guy coming out? That guy in the suit! It's that English guy—the one who was looking at those old books!"

"Yeah! And see that bundle under his arm? It looks like he bought something!"

A hand, visible through the glass portion of the door, could now be seen flipping the cardboard sign from CHIUSO to APERTO. Agostino's was now open for business.

"Listen, Louie," Blue said urgently. "I'm going to follow that guy! You go in the store and see if the dog is there. I'll be back in a minute!"

The Englishman was walking along at a very brisk pace, but Blue almost caught up to him a short distance past a small fruit-and-vegetable stand.

"Excuse me! Sir, excuse me!" Blue called out.

The man turned his head briefly but neither acknowledged Blue nor slowed his pace.

Only a few short sprints more, however, and Blue was at his side. "I just wanted to ask you about that note-book—that notebook you were looking at in—"

"Who *are* you?" the man asked, momentarily stealing a sideways glance in Blue's direction and adjusting his grip on the twine-wrapped bundle. "What do you want?"

The man suddenly turned a corner into a narrow

alleyway. "I thought I heard you mention the name of Edward de Vere," Blue said, squeezing himself past an old woman with a mesh bag filled with vegetables and then double-stepping his way back to the man's side. "And I'm *really* interested in any information I can get my hands on—"

They were now approaching a small docking area under a bridge spanning a nameless canal. The man stood at the edge of the canal and whistled sharply. A nearby water taxi seemed to be waiting for him. The driver maneuvered his small craft over to where the Englishman was standing, and in a moment they were speeding off down the canal, leaving behind only a sudden splash of water on a lurching rowboat covered with blue canvas and tied to the dock.

Blue's first and immediate response was a sickening sense of loss, a feeling that a rare opportunity had just slipped out of his reach. Yet, from somewhere deep down in his heart or mind, he could hear a soft, comforting whisper of hope. He listened to it for only a moment, just long enough to know it was real, and then he fashioned a special bin of gold to keep it safe and let it grow until the time was ripe for him to hear its message.

Though Blue would think of that notebook often in the coming months and years, he would never get a chance to examine it for himself. But who was that Englishman, he would wonder, and what will be the ultimate fate of that mysterious notebook? Might the man be a professor from Oxford or Cambridge who was not the least bit interested in Edward de Vere but was attracted to the notebook for other scholarly reasons? Or perhaps a museum curator specializing in sixteenth-century ephemera making a purchase to round out a particular display? Ah! But wait! Could he possibly be an emissary sent by certain vested monied interests, dependent on the continued prosperity of a certain multi-billion-dollar tourist industry and bent on destroying any damning evidence which could— No! Even the most psychotic of hallucinating mental patients hopelessly addicted to conspiracy theories could not *conceive* of a scenario so outlandishly sinister as that! That is *beyond* comic books! *That* is pure Hollywood!

Blue hurried back to Agostino's and swung open the door, not knowing what to expect. Louie was standing next to Tina's vacant stool with his hands in his pockets as if he were waiting for a bus, while Mr. Agostino was at the counter discussing the price, piece by piece, of a six-inch stack of old sheet music with a man who looked like Luciano Pavarotti.

"The dog's here!" Louie said in a loud whisper. "Agostino was getting mad because the dog wouldn't stop barking at him, so Tina took him to the back room."

"What did Agostino say when he saw you?"

"Nothing. He's just been ignoring me." Louie paused. "Hey, that guy sure looks like Pavarotti, doesn't he?"

Blue grunted. Keeping one eye on Mr. Agostino, he opened his wallet and took out the hundred-thousand-lire note he'd gotten from Drusie. She'd broken the other one at McDonald's buying his lunch, so he had a bunch of smaller bills besides. Should he offer more? Was Agostino going to be hard-nosed about that little contract? Would money make any difference?

"Do you think it's really him?"

Blue looked up from his wallet. "What?"

"That guy at the counter. Do you think it's really Pavarotti?"

"Louie, I'm trying to figure something out here, for God's sake! So shut up about Pavarotti, will you? Stick to the subject, okay?"

"Sorry."

Now the Pavarotti look-alike was bending down studying the music with a small magnifying glass while Mr. Agostino idly tapped the top of the counter with the eraser side of his pencil.

Tina cautiously emerged from the back room holding Vixen, who suddenly jumped out of her arms and ran over to Mr. Agostino and starting barking at his ankles and dancing around like a boxer in the ring. Tina quickly snatched him up again before he came to any harm and slunk back to her stool, with her hand over Vixen's mouth.

"Well, it's now or never!" Blue said. And, with that, he strode up to the counter, once again imagining that he was wearing his Blue Avenger outfit—the blue fishing vest and home-styled kaffiyeh that had made him famous just two short months before.

He gripped the hundred-thousand-lire note with two hands and held it up as if it were a check for two million dollars from the Publishers Clearing House. "Here is the money I borrowed from you, Mr. Agostino, and in view of the fact that all the ATMs were out of cash because of Good Friday and it was impossible for me to be here before the appointed time, I trust you will be a true gentleman and not hold me to the letter of the law—that is, to the letter of the *words* that were agreed to—or, uh, that is, contained in our original agreement." Blue cringed at the way that sentence came out. Why didn't I rehearse it first? Mr. Agostino must think I'm a complete idiot!

The fat man with the heavy beard looked up from the sheet music and peered at Blue and the hundred-thousand-lire note from over his black-rimmed reading glasses.

Mr. Agostino didn't answer at first, and for a second there, Blue thought he might just be considering his offer.

But then Tina said something to him in Italian, and he looked at her for a long time, as if he were having trouble making up his mind. Tina said something else, and this time it seemed to make an impression on him, because now he laughed an evil ha-ha and waved Blue and the money away with a careless flick of his wrist. "A deal is a deal," he said, looking at Tina again just to make sure she was listening. "It is *finito*."

Just then the door of the shop swung open and a most imposing woman dressed in an official-looking blue uniform strode in and quickly took stock of her surroundings. She was wearing large dark glasses, and her bobbed hair was a nondescript salt-and-pepper gray, and Blue noticed that the large black wart on her chin was sprouting several short black hairs. And there was something very odd about her figure. Her hips seemed to bulge out in a most unusual way, making her legs appear to be much too thin to support that extra weight.

Now she extended her arm and pointed directly at little Vixen, and, suddenly turning toward Blue, she said something in Italian—a question, obviously, judging by the tone and inflection of it.

Blue, taken aback by this sudden turn of events, quickly glanced at Louie and then back at the woman. He had no idea what she was asking, but even so, she seemed encouraged by his nonreply.

She reached into her shoulder bag and withdrew a small, thin wallet which she flipped open to reveal some sort of identification, and this she quickly presented to Mr. Agostino for just a fraction of a second before flipping it closed again. That done, she withdrew a little booklet about the size of a *TV Guide* from her shoulder bag and started reading from it quite rapidly, alternately pointing at Vixen and then Blue, and then straight at Mr. Agostino, who seemed to be watching her with a strange, puzzled look, as if he didn't quite know what to make of her. Blue thought he caught the words "Stati Uniti," "passaporto," and "Washington, D.C.," more than once during her tirade.

Blue finally caught on. "Ahmed must have called someone," he said in Louie's ear. "I think we're home free!"

"Hey, it's a good thing you had *him* up your sleeve," Louie whispered back.

Now Mr. Agostino, looking extremely sad and crestfallen, beckoned for Tina to come over to the counter. As soon as Vixen got within range, he suddenly made a lunge for Mr. Agostino's wrist, and for one awful second

Blue feared he might actually strike the little dog. Instead, he just swore at it in Italian. Then he asked the woman official a question and she again produced her information booklet. He started to thumb through the pages, nodding and looking quite worried. He pointed to one of the pages and shook his head sadly and again said something to Tina in Italian. What he said was this: "I'm afraid we're going to have to give him back, my dear. The woman is from the United States Passport Office, and she informs me that the little dog there has a valid United States passport, and we must give him back or the law will be after us!"

That's what Mr. Agostino said, but he didn't believe a word of it. Truth to tell, he didn't know *who* that strange woman was, although he suspected the American boys had a hand in it. But he had just had it up to here with that mutt, and now he had an easy out. "It's the law, sweetheart," he added, still speaking in his native tongue. "I'm afraid our hands are tied."

Oddly enough, the strange-looking woman from the Passport Office looked more surprised than anyone. But now she just gave a little shrug and looked at Louie and said something to *him* in Italian.

"What?" asked Louie, obviously flustered. *"Non parle italiano."*

"*Non par*lo," the woman corrected, and then she sighed and shook her head as if to say, How come I have to do everything? Then she went over to Tina and very gently lifted the dog out of her arms and presented him to Louie. Tina seemed sad, but resigned. Mr. Agostino, without being asked, walked to the back room and fetched Vixen's leash, all the while shaking his head and looking at the floor.

Then the woman said something to Blue. "*Non parlo italiano,*" said Blue, who was a quick study. Again the woman sighed and took matters into her own hands. She delicately lifted the hundred-thousand-lire note from Blue's hand and held it in front of Mr. Agostino, saying, "*Contratto, per favore?*" After a slight pause, Mr. Agostino obligingly rummaged around in a drawer and finally found the scribbled note with Blue's signature at the bottom. Before handing it over, he again looked at Tina with big, sorrowful eyes and a hopeless shrug.

With a stiff little nod, the woman headed for the door. As Blue held it open for her, he happened to notice that the box with Omaha's gondola and the plastic bag containing the Shakespeare pages were still where he had left them on the little table next to the computer. Mr. Agostino—actually looking rather jolly now, in a subdued way, of course—didn't stop him from making a quick dash to the back of the little office and snatching them up.

"So long, Mr. Agostino," he said as he strode past him. He glanced at Tina. "Nice meeting you, Tina. Sorry about the dog." And then, just for fun and because he was feeling so relieved, he smiled at the customer buying sheet music and said, "And goodbye to you, Mr. Pavarotti!" The fat man with the beard looked up and smiled broadly. He had the toothiest, scariest smile Blue had ever seen.

When Blue came out of the store, Louie was busy attaching the leash to Vixen's collar while the woman was petting the dog and speaking to him in Italian.

"Thank you *very much* for your help!" Blue said to her, even though he wasn't sure she could understand. *"Grazie! Grazie!"*

"Yeah," Louie added. "Thanks a lot—"

She stood up and put her hand up to her face in a gesture of modesty, partially covering the large black mole on her chin. And then she reeled off several sentences in Italian, not one word of which made any sense to either Louie or Blue. Trying to read her expression was no help either, since her outsized dark glasses covered most of her upper face. All of a sudden she stopped speaking and reached out her hand to touch the box with the gondola. *"Ohh, bella, molto bella!"* she exclaimed. *"Bella gondola!"*

To Blue's surprise, she actually took the box from him, opened it, and pulled out the gaudy black plastic gondola. She appeared to swoon with delight, gently touching the tiny gondolier and caressing the red velvet seats.

"Why don't you just give it to her?" Louie whispered. "She sure pulled our chestnuts out of the fire."

Blue was taken aback, not by the cliché, but by the suggestion. "But it's for Omaha—" he started to say.

But what was this now? By her gestures and pleading tone, she was actually *asking* for the gondola! Blue had no choice. "Okay, you may have it," he said slowly, as if speaking to a child. "Yes, yes. Take it. It is yours—"

"It's the least we can do," Louie remarked.

The woman quickly put the gondola back in the box and readjusted her shoulder bag. *"Arrivederci,"* she said gaily. And off she went, in the same direction the Englishman had taken—except that she was headed for the public restroom around the corner and out of their sight, where she had left a change of clothes with the attendant, and where she couldn't wait to shed her wig and her mole and the five pairs of baggy shorts she was wearing under her slacks.

"You got him! You got him back!" Drusie exclaimed, jumping up from the couch in the lobby of the hotel and scooping Vixen up in her arms. "Oh, Vixen! What an adventure you had!"

"Grammy's not here yet?" asked Blue, glancing at the clock on the wall over the couch.

"Nope. And I haven't left this room. So come on. Sit down and tell me what happened at Agostino's. Did he give you a bad time?"

The boys sat down on the couch while Drusie sprawled on the rug at their feet and began grooming Vixen's coat with her own personal comb, being extra careful around his stitches. Both Blue and Louie told their own versions of the strange Italian woman—no doubt sent by Ahmed—and how she single-handedly took control and saved the day.

"Did you hear her mention Washington, D.C.?" Louie asked. "What do you suppose she was saying?"

"I heard *passaporto*, too." Blue smiled and shook his head. "Whatever it was, it worked. It looked like Agostino got pretty worried—"

"Louie, look!" Drusie said suddenly, pointing to the swinging glass doors of the hotel. "Isn't that Angela?"

"Yeah!" Louie jumped up and opened the door, and in walked Angela, holding an overflowing shopping bag in one hand and, behind her back, what appeared to be some sort of long, skinny box.

Blue stood up, too, and so did Drusie. They looked at Louie, waiting for him to make the introductions, but he was too flustered at the moment to speak. Angela didn't say anything, either. She just stood there—as Louie would say later—looking like the cat who swallowed the canary. She set the shopping bag down beside her and handed the box containing the gondola to Blue, smiling first at him, then at Louie, and back again at Blue. A little surreptitious nudge with her foot sent the shopping bag tipping over on its side, and out tumbled the *pièce de résistance*—a wig of salt-and-pepper gray.

Before the boys could even begin to express their incredulity over this totally surprising turn of events, Grammy burst in the door, with Byron following close behind.

"*There* he is—Mommy's widdle darling Vixie-poo!" Grammy bent down and hugged the dog to her chest. "Were you a good boy while Mommy was away?" She glanced up at Drusie for confirmation.

"Oh, yes!" Drusie stammered. "He was a good little boy the whole time! Yes! Yes, he was!"

Meanwhile, Byron was totally confused by the behavior of Blue and Louie and that blond girl he had not yet had the privilege of meeting. How silly these kids are today! What could be so funny that would cause them to act like that—the two boys hitting themselves on the forehead and shaking their heads as if they'd just seen a miracle, and the girl speaking in little bursts of Italian and then bending over in laughter. Ah, well. We'll be whisking them off to the airport in a few hours, so might as well let them have their fun.

Louie was getting very nervous. Checkout time at the hotel was two o'clock—only about fifteen minutes away, but that wasn't the cause of his nervousness. What was really worrying him was that he wouldn't be able to get up the nerve to kiss Angela goodbye. Grammy and Byron had taken them all out to lunch, and that was all he could think about the whole time. He thought she probably wouldn't, but what if she pushed him away? What would he do then?

One good thing, though, he was happy that Drusie and Angela had hit it off so well. He wondered what they were talking about so seriously during the walk back from the restaurant. Maybe Angela was telling her how she was a late bloomer, too. Just like him. Two peas in a pod. But one major problem with late bloomers is that, even if they've known a girl for three whole days, they're still afraid to kiss her.

"So—what's the deal with Angela," Blue asked, as he

folded his Shakespeare printouts and slid them into a side pocket of his backpack. "Are you guys going to keep in touch, or what? You live thousands of miles apart, and—"

"Yeah, I know. But she's planning to go to college in the States. That's only a year from now—God, listen to me. *Only* a year! And I can probably arrange to come back here at least once this summer. Anyway, sure, we're going to keep in touch! We'll probably be e-mailing each other a couple of times a day."

"Well, that's good. Is she coming with us to the airport?"

"Yeah. Byron asked her if she wanted to come. It was sure nice of him to offer to take us in a water taxi. Those things don't come cheap, you know."

"Well, yes, but remember, we *did* take extra-good care of Vixen, right?"

Louie laughed. "That was a close one. Barely made it by the skin of our teeth, didn't we?"

"You ain't just whistlin' 'Dixie,' " Blue said, trying not to smile. He looked around the room. "Well, I guess I've got all my stuff. Except for this." He picked up the box with the gondola and stood there holding it for a moment. Of course, it reminded him of those heart-churning events of the previous evening—that one perilous moment of indecision, and his final victory—but, somehow, the model gondola in his hand had suddenly lost its charm.

"Listen, Louie," he said suddenly, "I've got to run down to the souvenir stand for a minute. I'll leave my stuff in the lobby and meet you guys there at two o'clock." He paused a moment. "By the way, don't you think Angela would get a kick out of a special little remembrance of the occasion—something like this tacky plastic gondola with little lights that really work?"

On the first leg of their flight back home—from Venice to Rome—Drusie had a window seat, with Louie in the middle and Blue on the aisle. Drusie was thumbing through Blue's Venice guidebook and wondering when she would be able to return to see all the sights she had missed, while Blue was reading everything pertaining to both Venice and *The Merchant of Venice* in the book Dr. Wood had given him back in the States.

Louie, however, was thinking about Angela. He leaned back his head and closed his eyes and relived those final moments with her, as they stood together in a secluded spot outdoors in back of the small terminal. She had certainly made it easy for him, starting with the moment when she and Drusie had emerged from the women's restroom there in the airport. He'd never forget the shy little smile on her face and that wonderful red heart-shaped pin on her blouse—which, after it had served its purpose, she unpinned and pressed into his hand, saying she wouldn't be needing it anymore.

Now he sat up and reached into his jacket pocket for the small paperback book she had given to him. It was a well-worn copy of *The Merchant of Venice*, in English. She told him it was the one she had used in the special "Shakespeare in English" class she had taken the summer before. Louie opened the book and read her inscription. *My Dearest Louie: I don't know what will happen to us in the years to come, but whatever it is, we'll always have Venice, and this book will always belong to us in a very special way. All my love, Angela.*

Of course, Louie wondered why she would say the book would always belong to them in a very special way, and he couldn't wait to find out. So he opened it right there and then and began reading the most famous play Shakespeare ever wrote about the city and citizens of Venice.

The flight to Rome was a short one, but long enough for Louie to finish reading the first act. He couldn't believe it. He kept jabbing Blue's arm and saying things like, "You won't *believe* what this play is about! See, this guy wants to borrow money—for his *friend*—I mean, you won't believe this! God! I can't wait to see how it ends!"

Blue, who had not yet read the play, didn't understand what all the excitement was about, and had no way of knowing that Louie was already changing his tune—the old lyrics of which were *Shakespeare's just not relevant, and until somebody can prove that his plays actually have something to do with my life—with our lives today—I mean, just look at his plots, for God's sake!*

Meanwhile, back at Agostino's, one final e-mail message addressed to Blue had arrived through cyberspace. It was from Josh.

```
Hi! Boy am I MAD!! moms getting a
BABYSITTER FOR ME. Mrs. Lawson is coming
over tonight because mom is going out.
She says its not a date but i know its IS
A DATE!! She is going somewhere witha
vetinarion that put the Lawsons old dog
to sleep. Did I tell you Rex died
yesterday? Mom went over to hold Mrs.
Lawsons hand while Res got his shot and
she knew the vet from when they went to
school. She got mad when I called him
doctor DEATH but that is what he is and
besides I DONT WANT A BABYSITTER!!! See
you later.
Josh
```

twenty-one

After their twenty-minute stopover in Rome, our three travelers were soon in a very crowded charter flight taking off on its long journey across the Atlantic. Drusie was seated by the window again and Louie was beside her, but this time Blue was assigned a seat several rows in back of them. Drusie offered to switch places with him so he could talk with Louie, but Blue said it was okay, because he had some stuff he wanted to do before they arrived back home.

First of all, he wanted to finally get to work on decoding Tuesday's message. And after that he planned to read *The Merchant of Venice*. And if he was still awake after all that, he might even make another entry in his Shakespeare Mystery Notebook.

So, following his schedule, he opened his wallet and took out the printout of the original message Tuesday had sent on the sixth of March. Then he removed the Shakespeare printout pages from his backpack. Because

Tuesday had hidden the word SONNETS in her Baconian cipher sentence, he returned the printout of *The Merchant of Venice* to his backpack for later reading and started to look at the sonnets.

He immediately noted that there were 154 sonnets in all, and that each sonnet consisted of fourteen lines. He took another look at Tuesday's first coded message—

55K10C81D28F135G36C138F24M76L147G127A

—and remembered what he had observed about it before—that the numbers ranged from 10 to 147, and there were no letters in the code past M. Since the numerical value of M is 13, and since there were 14 lines in a sonnet, the letters in the code (given numerical values) *could* refer to specific lines in the sonnets.

Well, he decided, may as well begin with the obvious. He looked up sonnet number 55 and began to read it:

Not marble, nor the gilded monuments
Of princes, shall outlive this powerful rhyme;
But you shall shine more bright in these contents
Than unswept stone, besmear'd with sluttish time.

He stopped there, in mid-sonnet, and thought, Hey, that

is really cool. Especially that last line. He read it again out loud, just to see how it would sound. No one heard him, of course, over the cabin noise, but still it filled him with a strange new kind of pleasure.

Well, back to business. Since K is the eleventh letter of the alphabet, he highlighted line 11.

Even in the eyes of all posterity

Because this code was not a life-and-death matter involving secret weapons or world security, Blue imagined that Tuesday would probably use the most simple and direct method—which would be to take the first letter of the first word in the line to spell out her message. Blue wrote down the letter E. Then, using the same system, he checked the third line in the tenth sonnet—

Grant, if thy wilt, thou art beloved of many,

—and wrote down the letter G. After doing the same with sonnets 81, 28, and 135, his heart suddenly skipped a beat. He had formed the word EGADS.

After deciphering the entire message, he was almost positive he would soon be able to accomplish a feat that would make Louie *very* happy indeed. But first he wanted to contact Tuesday, just to be sure he had it right. He would call her as soon as they arrived at the airport in New York.

After basking for several minutes in the wonderful possibilities ahead for Louie, and deciding that he would keep this knowledge from him until the cat was safely in the bag, he exchanged the sonnet pages for those of *The Merchant of Venice*. The first page had the heading DRAMATIS PERSONAE, and the word GOBBO practically jumped off the page. There it was, listed twice: LAUNCELOT GOBBO, the clown, servant to Shylock; and OLD GOBBO, father to Launcelot.

It took Blue over three hours to finish reading the play. Of course, with no footnotes or other aids to guide him, he missed a great deal, but he understood enough to make him smile and shake his head in wonder. Now he understood Louie's excitement and wanted to share it with him, but when he made his way up the aisle to where Louie and Drusie were sitting, he saw that they were both asleep. When he got back to his own seat, he made another entry in his Shakespeare notebook:

SHAKESPEARE MYSTERY NOTEBOOK
(ENTRY #3)
    I've just read The Merchant of Venice and

here are three interesting items that link
Edward de Vere to that play. (The first two I
noticed myself, and the last one I read in the
book Dr. Wood gave me.)

(1) Two minor characters in <u>The Merchant
of Venice</u> have the surname "Gobbo." They
are Launcelot Gobbo, a servant first to
Shylock and later to Bassanio, and his father,
"Old Gobbo." Just north of the Rialto Bridge in
Venice is a crouching stone figure sculpted in
1541 and known as the <u>Gobbo of the Rialto</u>.
Edward de Vere no doubt became familiar
with this figure when he was in Venice in the
year 1575, but it is hardly likely that some
"traveler" could have mentioned this obscure
fact to William Shakspere, and that he would
subsequently use it in this play.

(2) I noticed that, when Launcelot Gobbo
gave directions to Shylock's house in the
Ghetto, he said: "Turn up on your right hand
at the next turning, but at the next turning
of all, on your left; marry, at the very next
turning, turn of no hand, but turn down
indirectly to the Jew's house." I can't see
how anyone who hasn't actually been to

Venice and walked through the streets could have gotten that description (with all its confusing turnings) so right!

(3) Stratfordian scholars have been unable to determine the origin of the name Shylock. However, Oxfordians tell us that Edward de Vere is known to have invested three thousand British pounds in the purchase of shares in the third of Martin Frobisher's voyages (seeking a northwest passage to Asia and/or gold ore) from a London merchant named Michael Lok—sometimes spelled Lock. The prefix shy can mean distrustful or wary, thus Shylock. Also, in that same play, the amount of money for which Antonio posts bond is three thousand ducats, the same number as Oxford's investment. More coincidences? Maybe. And, then again, maybe not.

"Hello, Tuesday?"

"Yes?"

"Hi. This is Blue. Listen—uh, I finally decoded your message—"

"Oh? Both of them? But, hey, where are you, anyway? Are you guys still in Venice?"

"No. We're in New York. I have to talk fast. Our plane's about to board. But I have to find out something. Do you *really* still have those puppets?"

"They've been living in a shoe box all this time! Oh, I know, I'm just a big ol' sentimental fool—"

"Oh, man! That's *great*! Do me a big favor, okay? Take extra-good care of them until I get home. I might want to borrow those little guys—"

"Really? What for?"

"Tell you later. Gotta go now. Thanks, Tuesday! I'll call you when I get home!"

Blue was seated between the twins in the middle section of the plane on the last leg of their flight, from New York to San Francisco. He had no idea what time it was, but it was dark and most of the people around him were asleep, including Louie and Drusie. Just a few more hours and they'd be home.

Blue rubbed his stiff neck and tried to get more comfortable in his seat. It would be too late to call Omaha, of course, but he knew she'd love the little glass snail he got at the souvenir stand. Maybe I could even write a sonnet to go with it, he thought. None of those guys on the swim team would ever think of doing that! Some of those sonnets Shakespeare wrote were so *good*—the ones I could understand, at least. Like that number 81—how did it go? *Your name from hence immortal life shall have, / Though I, once gone, to all the world must die.* God, that gives me a chill. Hey, maybe I really *could* write one for Omaha. I know each line has like ten beats—da-dah, da-dah, da-dah, da-dah, da-dah—and there are fourteen lines and the last two of them rhyme. All I have to do is check and see the rhyming scheme of the other lines. Oh, jeez. I'd probably wake these guys up if I tried to get those sonnet pages out of my backpack now.

Listen to Louie, snoring away there. I don't know how he can sleep all scrunched up like that. My letter to Seratt is going to be really great. Let's see: *Dear Mr. Seratt: A group of four very interesting objects has recently surfaced that may persuade you to reconsider your cavalier treatment of my friend Louie DeSoto*—yeah, something like that'll work. Probably should check with Mr. DeSoto first, though, in case he wants to talk with a lawyer before we send any letters. But how great it'll be to finally see Louie get the credit he deserves for *Chimera*.

So how about Oxford? Will he ever get the credit *he* deserves? Okay, okay, I'll admit that just because *I* think he is the true author doesn't mean that he *really* is. But the Stratfordians certainly have had their chance—all those thousands of scholars searching and searching throughout the years, trying to find something, *any*thing, that *unmistakably* connects Shakspere the Stratford man to Shakespeare the writer—and still they've found nothing. If they could prove conclusively that their man was the true author, we wouldn't be in this fix! We wouldn't have all those doubters Dr. Wood mentioned in his e-mail.

So, if somewhere—somehow—real, hard evidence *does* exist that will prove Oxford's case, then someday someone is going to find it. Ah! That must be the reason I wasn't completely depressed when that English guy and the mysterious notebook just slipped out of my hands. Oh, who am I kidding? I never even got close. And it's not likely I'll ever get an opportunity like that again. But, still, I can't forget that look in Oxford's eyes. There must be something I can do— Uh-oh, what's this? I think Drusie's waking up.

"Ooh! My arm's all numb. Are we there yet? What time is it, anyway?" Drusie started to uncoil and come to life.

"I don't know. I'd have to turn on my light to see," Blue said, leaning over and speaking close to her ear. "And I don't want to wake up Louie."

"Did you sleep?"

"No. I've just been sitting here thinking."

Drusie yawned. "What about?" she asked.

"Lots of stuff. The big three mostly—Shakspere,

Oxford, Shakespeare—"

Drusie quickly ran her fingers through her hair and then sat up straight and leaned toward Blue. "That's funny," she said. "I was thinking about that earlier, too—all that stuff you told me about Shakspere—those six signatures, all different, and the fact that his own daughters couldn't even read or write. That's pretty hard to believe. Do you really think it's *possible* that we've had the wrong guy all this time? It just seems so—I don't know—so weird." She paused. "And if it weren't for you, I wouldn't know anything about it."

"Yeah. And if it weren't for Dr. Wood, *I* wouldn't know anything about it. Listen, if you want to know even more, I'll lend you that book he gave me—as soon as I finish reading it. I'm finding out so much about Oxford's life and how it shows up in so many ways in Shakespeare's works. It's like Anthony Trollope said, *The man of letters is, in truth, ever writing his own biography.*"

"Hey! Like Louie and the puppets!" Drusie said with a smile. "Do you think there's an Omo, Bomo, Nomo, and Egads in Oxford's childhood?" She unbuckled her seat belt and started to stand up. "I'm going to take a little walk around the cabin," she said. "Be back in a minute."

Blue leaned back and closed his eyes. *If it weren't for you,*

Drusie had said, *I wouldn't know anything about it*. Well, maybe that's the answer! Maybe that's what I can do!

Suddenly Blue began to feel that almost surreal surge of power, that feeling that Blue Avenger was somehow larger than life and capable of accomplishing the most daunting of challenges. Someday, someone is going to solve this mystery, he thought, and how cool it would be if they first heard about it from me! So, starting now, my new mission is to *spread the word* until the day when the truth is finally uncovered and the whole world will come to acknowledge the genius and unrivaled achievements of Edward de Vere—and proclaim at last, Goodbye, William Shakespeare; hello, Edward de Vere!

Blue felt a hand on his arm. "Blue, wake up. I'm back. They're coming around with some juice. You must have been having a pleasant dream—you were smiling."

"No, I wasn't dreaming. I was just wondering how I, personally, could begin to get more people thinking about this whole Shakespeare mystery."

Drusie adjusted her seat belt and rearranged the blanket on her lap. "You know something, Blue?" she said with a strange, mysterious smile. "I'm sure you'll find a way."

auThor's Final noTe

A Tribute to Charlton Ogburn

I first became acquainted with the Shakespeare author-ship question in April 1996, when I saw a rerun of a public television *Frontline* program called "The Shakespeare Mystery." I was deeply affected by Charlton Ogburn's sincere and moving demeanor as he pleaded the case for Edward de Vere, the seventeenth Earl of Oxford, as the true author of the works attributed to William Shakespeare. Soon after, I obtained a copy of *The Mysterious William Shakespeare: The Myth and the Reality* (EPM Publications, 1984), Mr. Ogburn's book on the subject. I was immediately impressed, not only with the sheer volume of his research, but also with his writing style—eminently fair, honest, and down-to-earth, with a generous sprinkling of humor and wit. I also learned that he was the author of several other well-received books, among them *The Marauders*, *The Winter Beach*, and *The Adventure of Birds*. I would love to have met Charlton Ogburn. He died in October 1998 at the age of eighty-seven and was truly mourned by Oxfordians everywhere—many of whom, like me, were first made aware of the life of Edward de Vere by his writings and appearances.

I don't know who really wrote the plays and poems attributed to William Shakespeare; still, the Shakespeare mystery remains an intriguing one—fraught with both seemingly meaningless minutiae and convoluted stories and events from long ago. One thing is certain: until some definitive proof is found, the Stratfordians and Oxfordians will continue to do battle.

Charlton Ogburn's greatest wish was that Edward de Vere, the seventeenth Earl of Oxford, would finally receive the recognition he deserves. Someday, perhaps, Mr. Ogburn's wish will come true. You may be the one to make it happen.